# Terry Pratchett

## Mort

### A Novel of Discworld®

# HARPER

*An Imprint of HarperCollinsPublishers*

Originally published in Great Britain by Victor Gollancz Ltd in association with Colin Smythe Ltd

## HARPER

*An Imprint of* HarperCollins*Publishers*
10 East 53rd Street
New York, New York 10022-5299

Copyright © 1987 by Terry Pratchett
ISBN 978-0-06-102068-1

First Harper paperback printing: March 2008
First HarperTorch paperback printing: February 2001

HarperCollins® and Harper® are registered trademarks of HarperCollins Publishers.

Printed in the United States of America

Visit Harper paperbacks on the World Wide Web
at www.harpercollins.com

30  29  28  27  26  25  24  23

*To Rhianna*

This is the bright candlelit room where the life-timers are stored—shelf upon shelf of them, squat hourglasses, one for every living person, pouring their fine sand from the future into the past. The accumulated hiss of the falling grains makes the room roar like the sea.

This is the owner of the room, stalking through it with a preoccupied air. His name is Death.

But not any Death. This is the Death whose particular sphere of operations is, well, not a sphere at all, but the Disc-world, which is flat and rides on the back of four giant elephants who stand on the shell of the enormous star turtle Great A'Tuin, and which is bounded by a waterfall that cascades endlessly into space.

Scientists have calculated that the chance of anything so patently absurd actually existing are millions to one.

But magicians have calculated that million-to-one chances crop up nine times out of ten.

Death clicks across the black and white tiled floor on toes of bone, muttering inside his cowl as his skeletal fingers count along the rows of busy hourglasses.

Finally he finds one that seems to satisfy him, lifts it carefully from its shelf and carries it across to the nearest candle. He holds it so that the light glints off it, and stares at the little point of reflected brilliance.

The steady gaze from those twinkling eye sockets encompasses the world turtle, sculling through the deeps of space,

1

carapace scarred by comets and pitted by meteors. One day even Great A'Tuin will die, Death knows; now, that would be a challenge.

But the focus of his gaze dives onwards towards the blue-green magnificence of the Disc itself, turning slowly under its tiny orbiting sun.

Now it curves away towards the great mountain range called the Ramtops. The Ramtops are full of deep valleys and unexpected crags and considerably more geography than they know what to do with. They have their own peculiar weather, full of shrapnel rain and whiplash winds and permanent thunderstorms. Some people say it's all because the Ramtops are the home of old, wild magic. Mind you, some people will say anything.

Death blinks, adjusts for depth of vision. Now he sees the grassy country on the turnwise slopes of the mountains.

Now he sees a particular hillside.

Now he sees a field.

Now he sees a boy, running.

Now he watches.

Now, in a voice like lead slabs being dropped on granite, he says: YES.

There was no doubt that there was something magical in the soil of that hilly, broken area which—because of the strange tint that it gave to the local flora—was known as the octarine grass country. For example, it was one of the few places on the Disc where plants produced reannual varieties.

Reannuals are plants that grow backwards in time. You sow the seed this year and they grow last year.

Mort's family specialized in distilling the wine from reannual grapes. These were very powerful and much sought after by fortune-tellers, since of course they enabled them to see the future. The only snag was that you got the hangover the morning *before*, and had to drink a lot to get over it.

Reannual growers tended to be big, serious men, much

given to introspection and close examination of the calendar. A farmer who neglects to sow ordinary seeds only loses the crop, whereas anyone who forgets to sow seeds of a crop that has already been harvested twelve months before risks disturbing the entire fabric of causality, not to mention acute embarrassment.

It was also acutely embarrassing to Mort's family that the youngest son was not at all serious and had about the same talent for horticulture that you would find in a dead starfish. It wasn't that he was unhelpful, but he had the kind of vague, cheerful helpfulness that serious men soon learn to dread. There was something infectious, possibly even fatal, about it. He was tall, red-haired and freckled, with the sort of body that seems to be only marginally under its owner's control; it appeared to have been built out of knees.

On this particular day it was hurtling across the high fields, waving its hands and yelling.

Mort's father and uncle watched it disconsolately from the stone wall.

"What I don't understand," said father Lezek, "is that the birds don't even fly away. I'd fly away, if I saw it coming towards me."

"Ah. The human body's a wonderful thing. I mean, his legs go all over the place but there's a fair turn of speed there."

Mort reached the end of a furrow. An overfull wood-pigeon lurched slowly out of his way.

"His heart's in the right place, mind," said Lezek, carefully.

"Ah. 'Course, 'tis the rest of him that isn't."

"He's clean about the house. Doesn't eat much," said Lezek.

"No, I can see that."

Lezek looked sideways at his brother, who was staring fixedly at the sky.

"I did hear you'd got a place going up at your farm, Hamesh," he said.

"Ah. Got an apprentice in, didn't I?"

"Ah," said Lezek gloomily, "when was that, then?"

"Yesterday," said his brother, lying with rattlesnake speed. "All signed and sealed. Sorry. Look, I got nothing against young Mort, see, he's as nice a boy as you could wish to meet, it's just that—"

"I know, I know," said Lezek. "He couldn't find his arse with both hands."

They stared at the distant figure. It had fallen over. Some pigeons had waddled over to inspect it.

"He's not stupid, mind," said Hamesh. "Not what you'd call stupid."

"There's a brain there all right," Lezek conceded. "Sometimes he starts thinking so hard you has to hit him round the head to get his attention. His granny taught him to read, see. I reckon it overheated his mind."

Mort had got up and tripped over his robe.

"You ought to set him to a trade," said Hamesh, reflectively. "The priesthood, maybe. Or wizardry. They do a lot of reading, wizards."

They looked at each other. Into both their minds stole an inkling of what Mort might be capable of if he got his well-meaning hands on a book of magic.

"All right," said Hamesh hurriedly. "Something else, then. There must be lots of things he could turn his hand to."

"He starts thinking too much, that's the trouble," said Lezek. "Look at him now. You don't think about how to scare birds, you just does it. A normal boy, I mean."

Hamesh scratched his chin thoughtfully.

"It could be someone else's problem," he said.

Lezek's expression did not alter, but there was a subtle change around his eyes.

"How do you mean?" he said.

"There's the hiring fair at Sheepridge next week. You set him as a prentice, see, and his new master'll have the job of knocking him into shape. 'Tis the law. Get him indentured, and 'tis binding."

Lezek looked across the field at his son, who was examining a rock.

"I wouldn't want anything to happen to him, mind," he said doubtfully. "We're quite fond of him, his mother and me. You get used to people."

"It'd be for his own good, you'll see. Make a man of him."

"Ah. Well. There's certainly plenty of raw material," sighed Lezek.

Mort was getting interested in the rock. It had curly shells in it, relics of the early days of the world when the Creator had made creatures out of stone, no one knew why.

Mort was interested in lots of things. Why people's teeth fitted together so neatly, for example. He'd given that one a lot of thought. Then there was the puzzle of why the sun came out during the day, instead of at night when the light would come in useful. He knew the standard explanation, which somehow didn't seem satisfying.

In short, Mort was one of those people who are more dangerous than a bag full of rattlesnakes. He was determined to discover the underlying logic behind the universe.

Which was going to be hard, because there wasn't one. The Creator had a lot of remarkably good ideas when he put the world together, but making it understandable hadn't been one of them.

Tragic heroes always moan when the gods take an interest in them, but it's the people the gods ignore who get the really tough deals.

His father was yelling at him, as usual. Mort threw the rock at a pigeon, which was almost too full to lurch out of the way, and wandered back across the field.

And that was why Mort and his father walked down through the mountains into Sheepridge on Hogswatch Eve, with Mort's rather sparse possessions in a sack on the back of a donkey. The town wasn't much more than four sides to a cobbled square, lined with shops that provided all the service industry of the farming community.

After five minutes Mort came out of the tailor's wearing a loose fitting brown garment of imprecise function, which had been understandably unclaimed by a previous owner and had plenty of room for him to grow, on the assumption that he would grow into a nineteen-legged elephant.

His father regarded him critically.

"Very nice," he said, "for the money."

"It itches," said Mort. "I think there's *things* in here with me."

"There's thousands of lads in the world'd be very thankful for a nice warm—" Lezek paused, and gave up—"garment like that, my lad."

"I could share it with them?" Mort said hopefully.

"You've got to look smart," said Lezek severely. "You've got to make an impression, stand out in the crowd."

There was no doubt about it. He would. They set out among the throng crowding the square, each listening to his own thoughts. Usually Mort enjoyed visiting the town, with its cosmopolitan atmosphere and strange dialects from villages as far away as five, even ten miles, but this time he felt unpleasantly apprehensive, as if he could remember something that hadn't happened yet.

The fair seemed to work like this: men looking for work stood in ragged lines in the center of the square. Many of them sported little symbols in their hats to tell the world the kind of work they were trained in—shepherds wore a wisp of wool, carters a hank of horsehair, interior decorators a strip of rather interesting hessian wallcovering, and so on.

The boys seeking apprenticeships were clustered on the Hub side of the square.

"You just go and stand there, and someone comes and offers you an apprenticeship," said Lezek, his voice trimmed with uncertainty. "If they like the look of you, that is."

"How do they do that?" said Mort.

"Well," said Lezek, and paused. Hamesh hadn't explained about this bit. He drew on his limited knowledge of the marketplace, which was restricted to livestock sales, and ventured, "I suppose they count your teeth and that. And make sure you don't wheeze and your feet are all right. I shouldn't let on about the reading, it unsettles people."

"And then what?" said Mort.

"Then you go and learn a trade," said Lezek.

"What trade in particular?"

"Well . . . carpentry is a good one," Lezek hazarded. "Or thievery. Someone's got to do it."

Mort looked at his feet. He was a dutiful son, when he remembered, and if being an apprentice was what was expected of him then he was determined to be a good one. Carpentry didn't sound very promising, though—wood had a stubborn life of its own, and a tendency to split. And official thieves were rare in the Ramtops, where people weren't rich enough to afford them.

"All right," he said eventually, "I'll go and give it a try. But what happens if I don't get prenticed?"

Lezek scratched his head.

"I don't know," he said. "I expect you just wait until the end of the fair. At midnight. I suppose."

And now midnight approached.

A light frost began to crisp the cobblestones. In the ornamental clock tower that overlooked the square a couple of delicately-carved little automatons whirred out of trapdoors in the clockface and struck the quarter hour.

Fifteen minutes to midnight. Mort shivered, but the crimson fires of shame and stubbornness flared up inside him, hotter than the slopes of Hell. He blew on his fingers for something to do and stared up at the freezing sky, trying to avoid the stares of the few stragglers among what remained of the fair.

Most of the stallkeepers had packed up and gone. Even the hot meat pie man had stopped crying his wares and, with no regard for personal safety, was eating one.

The last of Mort's fellow hopefuls had vanished hours ago. He was a wall-eyed young man with a stoop and a running nose, and Sheepridge's one licensed beggar had pronounced him to be ideal material. The lad on the other side of Mort had gone off to be a toymaker. One by one they had trooped off—the masons, the farriers, the assassins, the mercers, coopers, hoodwinkers and ploughmen. In a few minutes it would be the new year and a hundred boys would be starting out hopefully on their careers, new worthwhile lives of useful service rolling out in front of them.

Mort wondered miserably why he hadn't been picked. He'd tried to look respectable, and had looked all prospective masters squarely in the eye to impress them with his excellent nature and extremely likeable qualities. This didn't seem to have the right effect.

"Would you like a hot meat pie?" said his father.

"No."

"He's selling them cheap."

"No. Thank you."

"Oh."

Lezek hesitated.

"I could ask the man if he wants an apprentice," he said, helpfully. "Very reliable, the catering trade."

"I don't think he does," said Mort.

"No, probably not," said Lezek. "Bit of a one-man business, I expect. He's gone now, anyway. Tell you what, I'll save you a bit of mine."

"I don't actually feel very hungry, Dad."

"There's hardly any gristle."

"No. But thanks all the same."

"Oh." Lezek deflated a little. He danced about a bit to stamp some life back into his feet, and whistled a few tuneless bars between his teeth. He felt he ought to say something, to offer some kind of advice, to point out that life had its ups and downs, to put his arm around his son's shoulder and talk expansively about the problems of growing up, to indicate—in short—that the world is a funny old place where one should never, metaphorically speaking, be so proud as to turn down the offer of a perfectly good hot meat pie.

They were alone now. The frost, the last one of the year, tightened its grip on the stones.

High in the tower above them a cogged wheel went *clonk*, tripped a lever, released a ratchet and let a heavy lead weight drop down. There was a dreadful metallic wheezing noise and the trapdoors in the clock face slid open, releasing the clockwork men. Swinging their hammers jerkily, as if they were afflicted with robotic arthritis, they began to ring in the new day.

"Well, that's it," said Lezek, hopefully. They'd have to find somewhere to sleep—Hogswatchnight was no time to be walking in the mountains. Perhaps there was a stable somewhere. . . .

"It's not midnight until the last stroke," said Mort, distantly.

Lezek shrugged. The sheer strength of Mort's obstinacy was defeating him.

"All right," he said. "We'll wait, then."

And then they heard the clip-clop of hooves, which boomed rather more loudly around the chilly square than common acoustics should really allow. In fact clip-clop was an astonishingly inaccurate word for the kind of noise which rattled around Mort's head; clip-clop suggested a rather jolly little pony, quite possibly wearing a straw hat with holes cut out for its ears. An edge to *this* sound made it very clear that straw hats weren't an option.

The horse entered the square by the Hub road, steam curling off its huge damp white flanks and sparks striking up from the cobbles beneath it. It trotted proudly, like a war charger. It was definitely not wearing a straw hat.

The tall figure on its back was wrapped up against the

cold. When the horse reached the center of the square the rider dismounted, slowly, and fumbled with something behind the saddle. Eventually he—or she—produced a nose-bag, fastened it over the horse's ears, and gave it a friendly pat on the neck.

The air took on a thick, greasy feel, and the deep shadows around Mort became edged with blue and purple rainbows. The rider strode towards him, black cloak billowing and feet making little clicking sounds on the cobbles. They were the only noises—silence clamped down on the square like great drifts of cotton wool.

The impressive effect was rather spoilt by a patch of ice.

OH, BUGGER.

It wasn't exactly a voice. The words were there all right, but they arrived in Mort's head without bothering to pass through his ears.

He rushed forward to help the fallen figure, and found himself grabbing hold of a hand that was nothing more than polished bone, smooth and rather yellowed like an old billiard ball. The figure's hood fell back, and a naked skull turned its empty eyesockets towards him.

Not quite empty, though. Deep within them, as though they were windows looking across the gulfs of space, were two tiny blue stars.

It occurred to Mort that he ought to feel horrified, so he was slightly shocked to find that he wasn't. It was a skeleton sitting in front of him, rubbing its knees and grumbling, but it was a live one, curiously impressive but not, for some strange reason, very frightening.

THANK YOU, BOY, said the skull. WHAT IS YOUR NAME?

"Uh," said Mort, "Mortimer . . . sir. They call me Mort."

WHAT A COINCIDENCE, said the skull. HELP ME UP, PLEASE.

The figure rose unsteadily, brushing itself down. Now Mort could see there was a heavy belt around its waist, from which was slung a white-handled sword.

"I hope you are not hurt, sir," he said politely.

The skull grinned. Of course, Mort thought, it hasn't much of a choice.

NO HARM DONE, I AM SURE. The skull looked around and seemed to see Lezek, who appeared to be frozen to the spot, for the first time. Mort thought an explanation was called for.

"My father," he said, trying to move protectively in front of Exhibit A without causing any offense. "Excuse me, sir, but are you Death?"

CORRECT. FULL MARKS FOR OBSERVATION, THAT BOY.

Mort swallowed.

"My father is a good man," he said. He thought for a while, and added, "Quite good. I'd rather you left him alone, if it's all the same to you. I don't know what you have done to him, but I'd like you to stop it. No offense meant."

Death stepped back, his skull on one side.

I HAVE MERELY PUT US OUTSIDE TIME FOR A MOMENT, he said. HE WILL SEE AND HEAR NOTHING THAT DISTURBS HIM. NO, BOY, IT WAS YOU I CAME FOR.

"Me?"

YOU ARE HERE SEEKING EMPLOYMENT?

Light dawned on Mort. "You are looking for an *apprentice*?" he said.

The eyesockets turned towards him, their actinic pinpoints flaring.

OF COURSE.

Death waved a bony hand. There was a wash of purple light, a sort of visible "pop," and Lezek unfroze. Above his head the clockwork automatons got on with the job of proclaiming midnight, as Time was allowed to come creeping back.

Lezek blinked.

"Didn't see you there for a minute," he said. "Sorry—mind must have been elsewhere."

I WAS OFFERING YOUR BOY A POSITION, said Death. I TRUST THAT MEETS WITH YOUR APPROVAL?

"What was your job again?" said Lezek, talking to a black-robed skeleton without showing even a flicker of surprise.

I USHER SOULS INTO THE NEXT WORLD, said Death.

"Ah," said Lezek, "of course, sorry, should have guessed from the clothes. Very necessary work, very steady. Established business?"

I HAVE BEEN GOING FOR SOME TIME, YES, said Death.

"Good. Good. Never really thought of it as a job for Mort, you know, but it's good work, good work, always very reliable. What's your name?"

DEATH.

"Dad—" said Mort urgently.

"Can't say I recognize the firm," said Lezek. "Where are you based exactly?"

FROM THE UTTERMOST DEPTHS OF THE SEA TO THE HEIGHTS WHERE EVEN THE EAGLE MAY NOT GO, said Death.

"That's fair enough," nodded Lezek. "Well, I—"

"Dad—" said Mort, pulling at his father's coat.

Death laid a hand on Mort's shoulder.

WHAT YOUR FATHER SEES AND HEARS IS NOT WHAT YOU SEE AND HEAR, he said. DO NOT WORRY HIM. DO YOU THINK HE WOULD WANT TO SEE ME—IN THE FLESH, AS IT WERE?

"But you're Death," said Mort. "You go around killing people!"

I? KILL? said Death, obviously offended. CERTAINLY NOT. PEOPLE GET KILLED, BUT THAT'S THEIR BUSINESS. I JUST TAKE OVER FROM THEN ON. AFTER ALL, IT'D BE A BLOODY STUPID WORLD IF PEOPLE GOT KILLED WITHOUT DYING, WOULDN'T IT?

"Well, yes—" said Mort, doubtfully.

Mort had never heard the word "intrigued." It was not in regular use in the family vocabulary. But a spark in his soul told him that here was something weird and fascinating and not entirely horrible, and that if he let this moment go he'd spend the rest of his life regretting it. And he remembered the humiliations of the day, and the long walk back home. . . .

"Er," he began, "I don't have to die to get the job, do I?"

BEING DEAD IS NOT COMPULSORY.

"And . . . the bones . . . ?"

NOT IF YOU DON'T WANT TO.

Mort breathed out again. It had been starting to prey on his mind.

"If Father says it's all right," he said.

They looked at Lezek, who was scratching his beard.

"How do you feel about this, Mort?" he said, with the brittle brightness of a fever victim. "It's not everyone's idea of an occupation. It's not what I had in mind, I admit. But they do say that undertaking is an honored profession. It's your choice."

"Undertaking?" said Mort. Death nodded, and raised his finger to his lips in a conspiratorial gesture.

"It's interesting," said Mort slowly. "I think I'd like to try it."

"Where did you say your business was?" said Lezek. "Is it far?"

NO FURTHER THAN THE THICKNESS OF A SHADOW, said Death. WHERE THE FIRST PRIMAL CELL WAS, THERE WAS I ALSO. WHERE MAN IS, THERE AM I. WHEN THE LAST LIFE CRAWLS UNDER FREEZING STARS, THERE WILL I BE.

"Ah," said Lezek, "you get about a bit, then." He looked puzzled, like a man struggling to remember something important, and then obviously gave up.

Death patted him on the shoulder in a friendly fashion and turned to Mort.

HAVE YOU ANY POSSESSIONS, BOY?

"Yes," said Mort, and then remembered. "Only I think I left them in the shop. Dad, we left the sack in the clothes shop!"

"It'll be shut," said Lezek. "Shops don't open on Hogswatch Day. You'll have to go back the day after tomorrow—well, tomorrow now."

IT IS OF LITTLE ACCOUNT, said Death. WE WILL LEAVE NOW. NO DOUBT I WILL HAVE BUSINESS HERE SOON ENOUGH.

"I hope you'll be able to drop in and see us soon," said Lezek. He seemed to be struggling with his thoughts.

"I'm not sure that will be a good idea," said Mort.

"Well, goodbye, lad," said Lezek. "You're to do what you're told, you understand? And—excuse me, sir, do you have a son?"

Death looked rather taken aback.

No, he said, I HAVE NO SONS.

"I'll just have a last word with my boy, if you've no objection."

THEN I WILL GO AND SEE TO THE HORSE, said Death, with more than normal tact.

Lezek put his arm around his son's shoulders, with some difficulty in view of their difference in height, and gently propelled him across the square.

"Mort, you know your uncle Hemesh told me about this prenticing business?" he whispered.

"Yes?"

"Well, he told me something else," the old man confided. "He said it's not unknown for an apprentice to inherit his master's business. What do you think of that, then?"

"Uh. I'm not sure," said Mort.

"It's worth thinking about," said Lezek.

"I *am* thinking about it, Father."

"Many a young lad has started out that way," Hemesh said. "He makes himself useful, earns his master's confidence, and, well, if there's any daughters in the house . . . did Mr. er, Mr. say anything about daughters?"

"Mr. who?" said Mort.

"Mr . . . your new master."

"Oh. Him. No. No, I don't think so," said Mort slowly. "I don't think he's the marrying type."

"Many a keen young man owes his advancement to his nuptials," said Lezek.

"He does?"

"Mort, I don't think you're really listening."

"What?"

Lezek came to a halt on the frosty cobbles and spun the boy around to face him.

"You're really going to have to do better than this," he said. "Don't you understand, boy? If you're going to amount to anything in this world then you've got to listen. I'm your father telling you these things."

Mort looked down at his father's face. He wanted to say a lot of things: he wanted to say how much he loved him, how worried he was; he wanted to ask what his father really thought he'd just seen and heard. He wanted to say that he felt as though he stepped on a molehill and found that it was really a volcano. He wanted to ask what "nuptials" meant.

What he actually said was, "Yes. Thank you. I'd better be going. I'll try and write you a letter."

"There's bound to be someone passing who can read it to us," said Lezek. "Goodbye, Mort." He blew his nose.

"Goodbye, Dad. I'll come back to visit," said Mort. Death coughed tactfully, although it sounded like the pistol-crack of an ancient beam full of death-watch beetle.

WE HAD BETTER BE GOING, he said. HOP UP, MORT.

As Mort scrambled behind the ornate silver saddle Death leaned down and shook Lezek's hand.

THANK YOU, he said.

"He's a good lad at heart," said Lezek. "A bit dreamy, that's all. I suppose we were all young once."

Death considered this.

NO, he said, I DON'T THINK SO.

He gathered up the reins and turned the horse towards the Rim road. From his perch behind the black-robed figure Mort waved desperately.

Lezek waved back. Then, as the horse and its two riders disappeared from view, he lowered his hand and looked at it. The handshake . . . it had felt strange. But, somehow, he couldn't remember exactly why.

* * *

Mort listened to the clatter of stone under the horse's hooves. Then there was the soft thud of packed earth as they reached the road, and then there was nothing at all.

He looked down and saw the landscape spread out below him, the night etched with moonlight silver. If he fell off, the only thing he'd hit was air.

He redoubled his grip on the saddle.

Then Death said, ARE YOU HUNGRY, BOY?

"Yes, sir." The words came straight from his stomach without the intervention of his brain.

Death nodded, and reined in the horse. It stood on the air, the great circular panorama of the Disc glittering below it. Here and there a city was an orange glow; in the warm seas nearer the Rim there was a hint of phosphorescence. In some of the deep valleys the trapped daylight of the Disc, which is slow and slightly heavy\*, was evaporating like silver steam.

But it was outshone by the glow that rose towards the stars from the Rim itself. Vast streamers of light shimmered and glittered across the night. Great golden walls surrounded the world.

"It's beautiful," said Mort softly. "What is it?"

THE SUN IS UNDER THE DISC, said Death.

"Is it like this every night?"

EVERY NIGHT, said Death. NATURE'S LIKE THAT.

"Doesn't anyone know?"

---

\*Practically anything can go faster than Disc light, which is lazy and tame, unlike ordinary light. The only thing known to go faster than ordinary light is monarchy, according to the philosopher Ly Tin Wheedle. He reasoned like this: you can't have more than one king, and tradition demands that there is no gap between kings, so when a king dies the succession must therefore pass to the heir *instantaneously*. Presumably, he said, there must be some elementary particles—kingons, or possibly queons—that do this job, but of course succession sometimes fails if, in mid-flight, they strike an anti-particle, or republicon. His ambitious plans to use his discovery to send messages, involving the careful torturing of a small king in order to modulate the signal, were never fully expounded because, at that point, the bar closed.

ME. YOU. THE GODS. GOOD, IS IT?

"Gosh!"

Death leaned over the saddle and looked down at the kingdoms of the world.

I DON'T KNOW ABOUT YOU, he said, BUT I COULD MURDER A CURRY.

Although it was well after midnight the twin city of Ankh-Morpork was roaring with life. Mort had thought Sheep-ridge looked busy, but compared to the turmoil of the street around him the town was, well, a morgue.

Poets have tried to describe Ankh-Morpork. They have failed. Perhaps it's the sheer zestful vitality of the place, or maybe it's just that a city with a million inhabitants and no sewers is rather robust for poets, who prefer daffodils and no wonder. So let's just say that Ankh-Morpork is as full of life as an old cheese on a hot day, as loud as a curse in a cathedral, as bright as an oil slick, as colorful as a bruise and as full of activity, industry, bustle and sheer exuberant busyness as a dead dog on a termite mound.

There were temples, their doors wide open, filling the streets with the sounds of gongs, cymbals and, in the case of some of the more conservative fundamentalist religions, the brief screams of the victims. There were shops whose strange wares spilled out on to the pavement. There seemed to be rather a lot of friendly young ladies who couldn't afford many clothes. There were flares, and jugglers, and assorted sellers of instant transcendence.

And Death stalked through it all. Mort had half expected him to pass through the crowds like smoke, but it wasn't like that at all. The simple truth was that wherever Death walked, people just drifted out of the way.

It didn't work like that for Mort. The crowds that gently parted for his new master closed again just in time to get in his way. His toes got trodden on, his ribs were bruised, people kept trying to sell him unpleasant spices and suggestively-shaped vegetables, and a rather elderly lady said, against all the evidence, that he looked a well set-up young lad who would like a nice time.

He thanked her very much, and said that he hoped he was having a nice time already.

Death reached the street corner, the light from the flares raising brilliant highlights on the polished dome of his skull, and sniffed the air. A drunk staggered up, and without quite realizing why made a slight detour in his erratic passage for no visible reason.

THIS IS THE CITY, BOY, said Death. WHAT DO YOU THINK?

"It's very big," said Mort, uncertainly. "I mean, why does everyone want to live all squeezed together like this?"

Death shrugged.

I LIKE IT, he said. IT'S FULL OF LIFE.

"Sir?"

YES?

"What's a curry?"

The blue fires flared deep in the eyes of Death.

HAVE YOU EVER BITTEN A RED-HOT ICE CUBE?

"No, sir," said Mort.

CURRY'S LIKE THAT.

"Sir?"

YES?

Mort swallowed hard. "Excuse me, sir, but my dad said, if I don't understand, I was to ask questions, sir?"

VERY COMMENDABLE, said Death. He set off down a side street, the crowds parting in front of him like random molecules.

"Well, sir, I can't help noticing, the point is, well, the plain fact of it, sir, is—"

OUT WITH IT, BOY.

"How can you eat things, sir?"

Death pulled up short, so that Mort walked into him. When the boy started to speak he waved him into silence. He appeared to be listening to something.

THERE ARE TIMES, YOU KNOW, he said, half to himself, WHEN I GET REALLY UPSET.

He turned on one heel and set off down an alleyway at high speed, his cloak flying out behind him. The alley wound between dark walls and sleeping buildings, not so much a thoroughfare as a meandering gap.

Death stopped by a decrepit water butt and plunged his arm in at full length, bringing out a small sack with a brick tied to it. He drew his sword, a line of flickering blue fire in the darkness, and sliced through the string.

I GET VERY ANGRY INDEED, he said. He upended the sack and Mort watched the pathetic scraps of sodden fur slide out, to lie in their spreading puddle on the cobbles. Death reached out with his white fingers and stroked them gently.

After a while something like gray smoke curled up from the kittens and formed three small cat-shaped clouds in the air. They billowed occasionally, unsure of their shape, and blinked at Mort with puzzled gray eyes. When he tried to touch one his hand went straight through it, and tingled.

YOU DON'T SEE PEOPLE AT THEIR BEST IN THIS JOB, said Death. He blew on a kitten, sending it gently tumbling. Its miaow of complaint sounded as though it had come from a long way away via a tin tube.

"They're souls, aren't they?" said Mort. "What do people look like?"

PEOPLE SHAPED, said Death. IT'S BASICALLY ALL DOWN TO THE CHARACTERISTIC MORPHOGENETIC FIELD.

He sighed like the swish of a shroud, picked the kittens out of the air, and carefully stowed them away somewhere in the dark recesses of his robe. He stood up.

CURRY TIME, he said.

It was crowded in the *Curry Gardens* on the corner of God Street and Blood Alley, but only with the cream of society— at least, with those people who are found floating on the top and who, therefore, it's wisest to call the cream. Fragrant

bushes planted among the tables nearly concealed the basic
smell of the city itself, which has been likened to the nasal
equivalent of a foghorn.

Mort ate ravenously, but curbed his curiosity and didn't
watch to see how Death could possibly eat anything. The
food was there to start with and wasn't there later, so presumably something must have happened in between. Mort
got the feeling that Death wasn't really used to all this but
was doing it to put him at his ease, like an elderly bachelor
uncle who has been landed with his nephew for a holiday
and is terrified of getting it wrong.

The other diners didn't take much notice, even when
Death leaned back and lit a rather fine pipe. Someone with
smoke curling out of their eye sockets takes some ignoring,
but everyone managed it.

"Is it magic?" said Mort.

WHAT DO YOU THINK? said Death. AM I REALLY HERE, BOY?

"Yes," said Mort slowly. "I . . . I've watched people. They
look at you but they don't see you, I think. You do something
to their minds."

Death shook his head.

THEY DO IT ALL THEMSELVES, he said. THERE'S NO MAGIC.
PEOPLE CAN'T SEE ME, THEY SIMPLY WON'T ALLOW THEM-
SELVES TO DO IT. UNTIL IT'S TIME, OF COURSE. WIZARDS CAN
SEE ME, AND CATS. BUT YOUR AVERAGE HUMAN . . . NO, NEVER.
He blew a smoke ring at the sky, and added, STRANGE BUT
TRUE.

Mort watched the smoke ring wobble into the sky and
drift away towards the river.

"I can see you," he said.

THAT'S DIFFERENT.

The Klatchian waiter arrived with the bill, and placed it in
front of Death. The man was squat and brown, with a hair-
style like a coconut gone nova, and his round face creased
into a puzzled frown when Death nodded politely to him. He

shook his head like someone trying to dislodge soap from his ears, and walked away.

Death reached into the depths of his robe and brought out a large leather bag full of assorted copper coinage, most of it blue and green with age. He inspected the bill carefully. Then he counted out a dozen coins.

COME, he said, standing up. WE MUST GO.

Mort trotted along behind him as he stalked out of the garden and into the street, which was still fairly busy even though there were the first suggestions of dawn on the horizon.

"What are we going to do now?"

BUY YOU SOME NEW CLOTHES.

"These were new today—yesterday, I mean."

REALLY?

"Father said the shop was famous for its budget clothing," said Mort, running to keep up.

IT CERTAINLY ADDS A NEW TERROR TO POVERTY.

They turned into a wider street leading into a more affluent part of the city (the torches were closer together and the middens further apart). There were no stalls and alley corner traders here, but proper buildings with signs hanging outside. They weren't mere shops, they were emporia; they had purveyors in them, and chairs, and spittoons. Most of them were open even at this time of night, because the average Ankhian trader can't sleep for thinking of the money he's not making.

"Doesn't anyone ever go to bed around here?" said Mort.

THIS IS A CITY, said Death, and pushed open the door of a clothing store. When they came out twenty minutes later Mort was wearing a neatly-fitting black robe with faint silver embroidery, and the shopkeeper was looking at a handful of antique copper coins and wondering precisely how he came to have them.

"How do you get all those coins?" asked Mort.

IN PAIRS.

An all-night barber sheared Mort's hair into the latest fashion among the city's young bloods while Death relaxed in the next chair, humming to himself. Much to his surprise, he felt in a good humor.

In fact after a while he pushed his hood back and glanced up at the barber's apprentice, who tied a towel around his neck in that unseeing, hypnotized way that Mort was coming to recognize, and said, A SPLASH OF TOILET WATER AND A POLISH, MY GOOD MAN.

An elderly wizard having a beard-trim on the other side stiffened when he heard those somber, leaden tones and swung around. He blanched and muttered a few protective incantations after Death turned, very slowly for maximum effect, and treated him to a grin.

A few minutes later, feeling rather self-conscious and chilly around the ears, Mort was heading back towards the stables where Death had lodged his horse. He tried an experimental swagger; he felt his new suit and haircut rather demanded it. It didn't quite work.

Mort awoke.

He lay looking at the ceiling while his memory did a fast-rewind and the events of the previous day crystallized in his mind like little ice cubes.

He couldn't have met Death. He couldn't have eaten a meal with a skeleton with glowing blue eyes. It had to be a weird dream. He couldn't have ridden pillion on a great white horse that had cantered up into the sky and then went . . .

. . . where?

The answer flowed into his mind with all the inevitability of a tax demand.

*Here.*

His searching hands reached up to his cropped hair, and

down to sheets of some smooth slippery material. It was much finer than the wool he was used to at home, which was coarse and always smelled of sheep; it felt like warm, dry ice.

He swung out of the bed hastily and stared around the room.

First of all it was large, larger than the entire house back home, and dry, dry as old tombs under ancient deserts. The air tasted as though it had been cooked for hours and then allowed to cool. The carpet under his feet was deep enough to hide a tribe of pygmies and crackled electrically as he padded through it. And everything had been designed in shades of purple and black.

He looked down at his own body, which was wearing a long white nightshirt. His clothes had been neatly folded on a chair by the bed; the chair, he couldn't help noticing, was delicately carved with a skull-and-bones motif.

Mort sat down on the edge of the bed and began to dress, his mind racing.

He eased open the heavy oak door, and felt oddly disappointed when it failed to creak ominously.

There was a bare wooden corridor outside, with big yellow candles set in holders on the far wall. Mort crept out and sidled along the boards until he reached a staircase. He negotiated that successfully without anything ghastly happening, arriving in what looked like an entrance hall full of doors. There were a lot of funereal drapes here, and a grandfather clock with a tick like the heartbeat of a mountain. There was an umbrella stand beside it.

It had a scythe in it.

Mort looked around at the doors. They looked important. Their arches were carved in the now-familiar bones motif. He went to try the nearest one, and a voice behind him said:

"You mustn't go in there, boy."

It took him a moment to realize that this wasn't a voice in his head, but real human words that had been formed by a mouth and transferred to his ears by a convenient system of air compression, as nature intended. Nature had gone to a lot of trouble for six words with a slightly petulant tone to them.

He turned around. There was a girl there, about his own height and perhaps a few years older than him. She had silver hair, and eyes with a pearly sheen to them, and the kind of interesting but impractical long dress that tends to be worn by tragic heroines who clasp single roses to their bosom while gazing soulfully at the moon. Mort had never heard the phrase "Pre-Raphaelite," which was a pity because it would have been almost the right description. However, such girls tend to be on the translucent, consumptive side, whereas this one had a slight suggestion of too many chocolates.

She stared at him with her head on one side, and one foot tapping irritably on the floor. Then she reached out quickly and pinched him sharply on the arm.

"Ow!"

"Hmm. So you're really real," she said. "What's your name, boy?"

"Mortimer. They call me Mort," he said, rubbing his elbow. "What did you do that for?"

"I shall call you Boy," she said. "And I don't really have to explain myself, you understand, but if you must know I thought you were dead. You *look* dead."

Mort said nothing.

"Lost your tongue?"

Mort was, in fact, counting to ten.

"I'm not dead," he said eventually. "At least, I don't think so. It's a little hard to tell. Who are you?"

"You may call me Miss Ysabell," she said haughtily. "Father told me you must have something to eat. Follow me."

She swept away towards one of the other doors. Mort trailed behind her at just the right distance to have it swing back and hit his other elbow.

There was a kitchen on the other side of the door—long,

low and warm, with copper pans hanging from the ceiling and a vast black iron stove occupying the whole of one long wall. An old man was standing in front of it, frying eggs and bacon and whistling between his teeth.

The smell attracted Mort's taste buds from across the room, hinting that if they got together they could really enjoy themselves. He found himself moving forward without even consulting his legs.

"Albert," snapped Ysabell, "another one for breakfast."

The man turned his head slowly, and nodded at her without saying a word. She turned back to Mort.

"I must say," she said, "that with the whole Disc to choose from, I should think Father could have done rather better than you. I suppose you'll just have to do."

She swept out of the room, slamming the door behind her.

"Have to do what?" said Mort, to no one in particular.

The room was silent, except for the sizzle of the frying pan and the crumbling of coals in the molten heart of the stove. Mort saw that it had the words "The Little Moloch (Ptntd)" embossed on its oven door.

The cook didn't seem to notice him, so Mort pulled up a chair and sat down at the white scrubbed table.

"Mushrooms?" said the old man, without looking around.

"Hmm? What?"

"I said, do you want mushrooms?"

"Oh. Sorry. No, thank you," said Mort.

"Right you are, young sir."

He turned around and set out for the table.

Even after he got used to it, Mort always held his breath when he watched Albert walking. Death's manservant was one of those stick-thin, raw-nosed old men who always look as though they are wearing gloves with the fingers cut out— even when they're not—and his walking involved a complicated sequence of movements. Albert leaned forward and his left arm started to swing, slowly at first but soon evolving into a wild jerking movement that finally and suddenly, at about the time when a watcher would have expected the arm to fly off at the elbow, transferred itself down the length of his body to his legs and propelled him forward like a high-speed stilt walker. The frying pan followed a series of intricate curves in the air and was brought to a halt just over Mort's plate.

Albert did indeed have exactly the right type of half-moon spectacles to peer over the top of.

"There could be some porridge to follow," he said, and winked, apparently to include Mort in the world porridge conspiracy.

"Excuse me," said Mort, "but where am I, exactly?"

"Don't you know? This is the house of Death, lad. He brought you here last night."

"I—sort of remember. Only". . . .

"Hmm?"

"Well. The bacon and eggs," said Mort, vaguely. "It doesn't seem, well, appropriate."

"I've got some black pudding somewhere," said Albert.

"No, I mean . . ." Mort hesitated. "It's just that I can't see *him* sitting down to a couple of rashers and a fried slice."

Albert grinned. "Oh, he doesn't, lad. Not as a regular thing, no. Very easy to cater for, the master. I just cook for me and—" he paused—"the young lady, of course."

Mort nodded. "Your daughter," he said.

"Mine? Ha," said Albert. "You're wrong there. She's his."

Mort stared down at his fried eggs. They stared back from their lake of fat. Albert had heard of nutritional values, and didn't hold with them.

"Are we talking about the same person?" he said at last. "Tall, wears black, he's a bit . . . skinny. . . ."

"Adopted," said Albert, kindly. "It's rather a long story—"

A bell jangled by his head.

"—which will have to wait. He wants to see you in his study. I should run along if I were you. He doesn't like to be kept waiting. Understandable, really. Up the steps and first door on the left. You can't miss it—"

"It's got skulls and bones around the door?" said Mort, pushing back his chair.

"They all have, most of them," sighed Albert. "It's only his fancy. He doesn't mean anything by it."

Leaving his breakfast to congeal, Mort hurried up the steps, along the corridor and paused in front of the first door. He raised his hand to knock.

ENTER.

The handle turned of its own accord. The door swung inward.

Death was seated behind a desk, peering intently into a vast leather book almost bigger than the desk itself. He looked up as Mort came in, keeping one calcareous finger marking his place, and grinned. There wasn't much of an alternative.

AH, he said, and then paused. Then he scratched his chin, with a noise like a fingernail being pulled across a comb.

WHO ARE YOU, BOY?

"Mort, sir," said Mort. "Your apprentice. You remember?"

Death stared at him for some time. Then the pinpoint blue eyes turned back to the book.

OH YES, he said, MORT. WELL, BOY, DO YOU SINCERELY WISH TO LEARN THE UTTERMOST SECRETS OF TIME AND SPACE?

"Yes, sir. I think so, sir."

GOOD. THE STABLES ARE AROUND THE BACK. THE SHOVEL HANGS JUST INSIDE THE DOOR.

He looked down. He looked up. Mort hadn't moved.

IS IT BY ANY CHANCE POSSIBLE THAT YOU FAIL TO UNDER-STAND ME?

"Not fully, sir," said Mort.

DUNG, BOY. DUNG. ALBERT HAS A COMPOST HEAP IN THE GARDEN. I IMAGINE THERE'S A WHEELBARROW SOMEWHERE ON THE PREMISES. GET ON WITH IT.

Mort nodded mournfully. "Yes, sir. I see, sir. Sir?"

YES?

"Sir, I don't see what this has to do with the secrets of time and space."

Death did not look up from his book.

THAT, he said, IS BECAUSE YOU ARE HERE TO LEARN.

It is a fact that although the Death of the Discworld is, in his own words, an ANTHROPOMORPHIC PERSONIFICATION, he long ago gave up using the traditional skeletal horses, because of the bother of having to stop all the time to wire bits back on. Now his horses were always flesh-and-blood beasts, from the finest stock.

And, Mort learned, very well fed.

Some jobs offer increments. This one offered—well, quite the reverse, but at least it was in the warm and fairly easy to get the hang of. After a while he got into the rhythm of it, and started playing the private little quantity-surveying game that everyone plays in these circumstances. Let's see, he thought, I've done nearly a quarter, let's call it a third, so when I've done *that* corner by the hayrack it'll be more than half, call it five-eighths, which means three more wheelbarrow loads. . . . It doesn't prove anything very much except that the awesome splendor of the universe is much easier to deal with if you think of it as a series of small chunks.

The horse watched him from its stall, occasionally trying to eat his hair in a friendly sort of way.

After a while he became aware that someone else was watching him. The girl Ysabell was leaning on the half-door, her chin in her hands.

"Are you a servant?" she said.

Mort straightened up.

"No," he said, "I'm an apprentice."

"That's silly. Albert said you can't be an apprentice."

Mort concentrated on hefting a shovelful into the wheelbarrow. Two more shovelfuls, call it three if it's well pressed down, and that means four more barrows, all right, call it five, before I've done halfway to the . . .

"He says," said Ysabell in a louder voice, "that apprentices become masters, and you can't have more than one Death. So you're just a servant and you have to do what I say."

. . . and then eight more barrows means it's all done all the way to the door, which is nearly two-thirds of the whole thing, which means. . . .

"Did you hear what I said, boy?"

Mort nodded. And then it'll be fourteen more barrows, only call it fifteen because I haven't swept up properly in the corner, and. . . .

"Have you lost your tongue?"

"Mort," said Mort mildly.

She looked at him furiously. "What?"

"My name is Mort," said Mort. "Or Mortimer. Most people call me Mort. Did you want to talk to me about something?"

She was speechless for a moment, staring from his face to the shovel and back again.

"Only I've been told to get on with this," said Mort.

She exploded.

"Why are you here? Why did Father bring you here?"

"He hired me at the hiring fair," said Mort. "All the boys got hired. And me."

"And you wanted to be hired?" she snapped. "He's Death, you know. The Grim Reaper. He's very important. He's not something you *become*, he's something you *are*."

Mort gestured vaguely at the wheelbarrow.

"I expect it'll turn out for the best," he said. "My father always says things generally do."

He picked up the shovel and turned away, and grinned at the horse's backside as he heard Ysabell snort and walk away.

Mort worked steadily through the sixteenths, eighths,

quarters and thirds, wheeling the barrow out through the yard to the heap by the apple tree.

Death's garden was big, neat and well-tended. It was also very, very black. The grass was black. The flowers were black. Black apples gleamed among the black leaves of a black apple tree. Even the air looked inky.

After a while Mort thought he could see—no, he couldn't possibly imagine he could see . . . different colors of black.

That's to say, not simply very dark tones of red and green and whatever, but real shades of black. A whole spectrum of colors, all different and all—well, black. He tipped out the last load, put the barrow away, and went back to the house.

ENTER.

Death was standing behind a lectern, poring over a map. He looked at Mort as if he wasn't entirely there.

YOU HAVEN'T HEARD OF THE BAY OF MANTE, HAVE YOU? he said.

"No, sir," said Mort.

FAMOUS SHIPWRECK THERE.

"Was there?"

THERE WILL BE, said Death, IF I CAN FIND THE DAMN PLACE.

Mort walked around the lectern and peered at the map.

"You're going to sink the ship?" he said.

Death looked horrified.

CERTAINLY NOT. THERE WILL BE A COMBINATION OF BAD SEAMANSHIP, SHALLOW WATER AND A CONTRARY WIND.

"That's horrible," said Mort. "Will there be many drowned?"

THAT'S UP TO FATE, said Death, turning to the bookcase behind him and pulling out a heavy gazetteer. THERE'S NOTHING I CAN DO ABOUT IT. WHAT IS THAT SMELL?

"Me," said Mort, simply.

AH. THE STABLES. Death paused, his hand on the spine of the book. AND WHY DO YOU THINK I DIRECTED YOU TO THE STABLES? THINK CAREFULLY, NOW.

Mort hesitated. He *had* been thinking carefully, in between counting wheelbarrows. He'd wondered if it had been to coordinate his hand and eye, or teach him the habit of obedience, or bring home to him the importance, on the human scale, of small tasks, or make him realize that even great men must start at the bottom. None of these explanations seemed exactly right.

"I think . . ." he began.

YES?

"Well, I think it was because you were up to your knees in horseshit, to tell you the truth."

Death looked at him for a long time. Mort shifted uneasily from one foot to the other.

ABSOLUTELY CORRECT, snapped Death. CLARITY OF THOUGHT. REALISTIC APPROACH. VERY IMPORTANT IN A JOB LIKE OURS.

"Yes, sir. Sir?"

HMM? Death was struggling with the index.

"People die all the time, sir, don't they? Millions. You must be very busy. But—"

Death gave Mort the look he was coming to be familiar with. It started off as blank surprise, flickered briefly towards annoyance, called in for a drink at recognition and settled finally on vague forbearance.

BUT?

"I'd have thought you'd have been, well, out and about a bit more. You know. Stalking the streets. My granny's almanack's got a picture of you with a scythe and stuff."

I SEE. I AM AFRAID IT IS HARD TO EXPLAIN UNLESS YOU KNOW ABOUT POINT INCARNATION AND NODE FOCUSING. I DON'T EXPECT YOU DO?

"I don't think so."

GENERALLY I'M ONLY EXPECTED TO MAKE AN ACTUAL APPEARANCE ON SPECIAL OCCASIONS.

"Like a king, I suppose," said Mort. "I mean, a king is reigning even when he's doing something else or asleep, even. Is that it, sir?"

IT'LL DO, said Death, rolling up the maps. AND NOW, BOY, IF YOU'VE FINISHED THE STABLE YOU CAN GO AND SEE IF ALBERT HAS ANY JOBS HE WANTS DOING. IF YOU LIKE, YOU CAN COME OUT ON THE ROUND WITH ME THIS EVENING.

Mort nodded. Death went back to his big leather book, took up a pen, stared at it for a moment, and then looked up at Mort with his skull on one side.

HAVE YOU MET MY DAUGHTER? he said.

"Er. Yes, sir," said Mort, his hand on the doorknob.

SHE IS A VERY PLEASANT GIRL, said Death, BUT I THINK SHE QUITE LIKES HAVING SOMEONE OF HER OWN AGE AROUND TO TALK TO.

"Sir?"

AND, OF COURSE, ONE DAY ALL THIS WILL BELONG TO HER.

Something like a small blue supernova flared for a moment in the depths of his eyesockets. It dawned on Mort that, with some embarrassment and complete lack of expertise, Death was trying to wink.

In a landscape that owed nothing to time and space, which appeared on no map, which existed only in those far reaches of the multiplexed cosmos known to the few astrophysicists who have taken really bad acid, Mort spent the afternoon helping Albert plant out broccoli. It was black, tinted with purple.

"He tries, see," said Albert, flourishing the dibber. "It's just that when it comes to color, he hasn't got much imagination."

"I'm not sure I understand all this," said Mort. "Did you say he *made* all this?"

Beyond the garden wall the ground dropped towards a deep valley and then rose into dark moorland that marched all the way to distant mountains, jagged as cats' teeth.

"Yeah," said Albert. "Mind what you're doing with that watering can."

"What was here before?"

"I dunno," said Albert, starting a fresh row. "Firmament, I

suppose. That's the fancy name for raw nothing. It's not a very good job of work, to tell the truth. I mean, the garden's okay, but the mountains are downright shoddy. They're all fuzzy when you get up close. I went and had a look once."

Mort squinted hard at the trees nearest him. They seemed commendably solid.

"What'd he do it all for?" he said.

Albert grunted. "Do you know what happens to lads who ask too many questions?"

Mort thought for a moment.

"No," he said eventually, "what?"

There was silence.

Then Albert straightened up and said, "Damned if I know. Probably they get answers, and serve 'em right."

"He said I could go out with him tonight," said Mort.

"You're a lucky boy then, aren't you," said Albert vaguely, heading back for the cottage.

"Did he *really* make all this?" said Mort, tagging along after him.

"Yes."

"Why?"

"I suppose he wanted somewhere where he could feel at home."

"Are you dead, Albert?"

"Me? Do I look dead?" The old man snorted when Mort started to give him a slow, critical look. "And you can stop that. I'm as alive as you are. Probably more."

"Sorry."

"Right." Albert pushed open the back door, and turned to regard Mort as kindly as he could manage.

"It's best not to ask all these questions," he said, "it upsets people. Now, how about a nice fry-up?"

The bell rang while they were playing dominoes. Mort sat to attention.

"He'll want the horse made ready," said Albert. "Come on."

They went out to the stable in the gathering dusk, and Mort watched the old man saddle up Death's horse.

"His name's Binky," said Albert, fastening the girth. "It just goes to show, you never can tell."

Binky tried to eat his scarf in an affectionate way.

Mort remembered the woodcut in his grandmother's almanack, between the page on planting times and the phases of the moon section, showing Dethe thee Great Levyller Comes To Alle Menne. He'd stared at it hundreds of times when learning his letters. It wouldn't have been half so impressive if it had been generally known that the flame-breathing horse the specter rode was called Binky.

"I would have thought something like Fang or Sabre or Ebony," Albert continued, "but the master will have his little fancies, you know. Looking forward to it, are you?"

"I think so," said Mort uncertainly. "I've never seen Death actually at work."

"Not many have," said Albert. "Not twice, at any rate."

Mort took a deep breath.

"About this daughter of his—" he began.

AH. GOOD EVENING, ALBERT. BOY.

"Mort," said Mort automatically.

Death strode into the stable, stooping a little to clear the ceiling. Albert nodded, not in any subservient way, Mort noticed, but simply out of form. Mort had met one or two servants, on the rare occasions he'd been taken into town, and Albert wasn't like any of them. He seemed to act as though the house really belonged to him and its owner was just a passing guest, something to be tolerated like peeling paintwork or spiders in the lavatory. Death put up with it too, as though he and Albert had said everything that needed to be said a long time ago and were simply content, now, to get on with their jobs with the minimum of inconvenience all round. To Mort it was rather like going for a walk after a really bad thunderstorm—everything was quite fresh, nothing was particularly unpleasant, but there was the sense of vast energies just expended.

Finding out about Albert tagged itself on to the end of his list of things to do.

HOLD THIS, said Death, and pushed a scythe into his hand while he swung himself up on to Binky. The scythe looked normal enough, except for the blade: it was so thin that Mort could see through it, a pale blue shimmer in the air that could slice flame and chop sound. He held it very carefully.

RIGHT, BOY, said Death. COME ON UP. ALBERT. DON'T WAIT UP.

The horse trotted out of the courtyard and into the sky.

There should have been a flash or rush of stars. The air should have spiralled and turned into speeding sparks such as normally happens in the common, everyday transdimensional hyper-jumps. But this was Death, who has mastered the art of going everywhere without ostentation and could slide between dimensions as easily as he could slip through a locked door, and they moved at an easy gallop through cloud canyons, past great billowing mountains of cumulus, until the wisps parted in front of them and the Disc lay below, basking in sunlight.

THAT'S BECAUSE TIME IS ADJUSTABLE, said Death, when Mort pointed this out. IT'S NOT REALLY IMPORTANT.

"I always thought it was."

PEOPLE THINK IT'S IMPORTANT ONLY BECAUSE THEY INVENTED IT, said Death somberly. Mort considered this rather trite, but decided not to argue.

"What are we going to do now?" he said.

THERE'S A PROMISING WAR IN KLATCHISTAN, said Death. SEVERAL PLAGUE OUTBREAKS. ONE RATHER IMPORTANT ASSASSINATION, IF YOU'D PREFER.

"What, a murder?"

AYE, A KING.

"Oh, kings," said Mort dismissively. He knew about

kings. Once a year a band of strolling players, or at any rate ambling ones, came to Sheepridge and the plays they performed were invariably about kings. Kings were always killing one another, or being killed. The plots were quite complicated, involving mistaken identity, poisons, battles, long-lost sons, ghosts, witches and, usually, lots of daggers. Since it was clear that being a king was no picnic it was amazing that half the cast were apparently trying to become one. Mort's idea of palace life was a little hazy, but he imagined that no one got much sleep.

"I'd quite like to see a real king," he said. "They wear crowns all the time, my granny said. Even when they go to the lavatory."

Death considered this carefully.

THERE'S NO TECHNICAL REASON WHY NOT, he conceded. IN MY EXPERIENCE, HOWEVER, IT IS GENERALLY NOT THE CASE.

The horse wheeled, and the vast flat checkerboard of the Sto plain sped underneath them at lightning speed. This was rich country, full of silt and rolling cabbage fields and neat little kingdoms whose boundaries wriggled like snakes as small, formal wars, marriage pacts, complex alliances and the occasional bit of sloppy cartography changed the political shape of the land.

"This king," said Mort, as a forest zipped beneath them, "is he good or bad?"

I NEVER CONCERN MYSELF WITH SUCH THINGS, said Death. HE'S NO WORSE THAN ANY OTHER KING, I IMAGINE.

"Does he have people put to death?" said Mort, and remembering who he was talking to added, "Saving y'honor's presence, of course."

SOMETIMES. THERE ARE SOME THINGS YOU HAVE TO DO, WHEN YOU'RE A KING.

A city slid below them, clustered around a castle built on a rock outcrop that poked up out of the plain like a geological pimple. It was one huge rock from the distant Ramtops,

Death said, left there by the retreating ice in the legendary days when the Ice Giants waged war on the gods and rode their glaciers across the land in an attempt to freeze the whole world. They'd given up in the end, however, and driven their great glittering flocks back to their hidden lands among the razor-backed mountains near the Hub. No one on the plains knew why they had done this; it was generally considered by the younger generation in the city of Sto Lat, the city around the rock, that it was because the place was dead boring.

Binky trotted down over nothingness and touched down on the flagstones of the castle's topmost tower. Death dismounted and told Mort to sort out the nosebag.

"Won't people notice there's a horse up here?" he said, as they strolled to a stairwell.

Death shook his head.

WOULD YOU BELIEVE THERE COULD BE A HORSE AT THE TOP OF THIS TOWER? he said.

"No. You couldn't get one up these stairs," said Mort.

WELL, THEN?

"Oh. I see. People don't want to see what can't possibly exist."

WELL DONE.

Now they were walking along a wide corridor hung with tapestries. Death reached into his robe and pulled out an hourglass, peering closely at it in the dim light.

It was a particularly fine one, its glass cut into intricate facets and imprisoned in an ornate framework of wood and brass. The words "King Olerve the Bastard" were engraved deeply into it.

The sand inside sparkled oddly. There wasn't a lot left.

Death hummed to himself and stowed the glass away in whatever mysterious recess it had occupied.

They turned a corner and hit a wall of sound. There was a hall full of people there, under a cloud of smoke and chatter that rose all the way up into the banner-haunted shadows in the roof. Up in a gallery a trio of minstrels were doing their best to be heard and not succeeding.

The appearance of Death didn't cause much of a stir. A footman by the door turned to him, opened his mouth and then frowned in a distracted way and thought of something else. A few courtiers glanced in their direction, their eyes instantly unfocusing as common sense overruled the other five.

WE'VE GOT A FEW MINUTES, said Death, taking a drink from a passing tray. LET'S MINGLE.

"They can't see me either!" said Mort. "But I'm real!"

REALITY IS NOT ALWAYS WHAT IT SEEMS, said Death. ANYWAY, IF THEY DON'T WANT TO SEE ME, THEY CERTAINLY DON'T WANT TO SEE YOU. THESE ARE ARISTOCRATS, BOY. THEY'RE GOOD AT NOT SEEING THINGS. WHY IS THERE A CHERRY ON A STICK IN THIS DRINK?

"Mort," said Mort automatically.

IT'S NOT AS IF IT DOES ANYTHING FOR THE FLAVOR. WHY DOES ANYONE TAKE A PERFECTLY GOOD DRINK AND THEN PUT IN A CHERRY ON A POLE?

"What's going to happen next?" said Mort. An elderly earl bumped into his elbow, looked everywhere but directly at him, shrugged and walked away.

TAKE THESE THINGS, NOW, said Death, fingering a passing canape. I MEAN, MUSHROOMS YES, CHICKEN YES, CREAM YES, I'VE NOTHING AGAINST ANY OF THEM, BUT WHY IN THE NAME OF SANITY MINCE THEM ALL UP AND PUT THEM IN LITTLE PASTRY CASES?

"Pardon?" said Mort.

THAT'S MORTALS FOR YOU, Death continued. THEY'VE ONLY GOT A FEW YEARS IN THIS WORLD AND THEY SPEND THEM ALL IN MAKING THINGS COMPLICATED FOR THEMSELVES. FASCINATING. HAVE A GHERKIN.

"Where's the king?" said Mort, craning to look over the heads of the court.

CHAP WITH THE GOLDEN BEARD, said Death. He tapped a flunky on the shoulder, and as the man turned and looked around in puzzlement deftly piloted another drink from his tray.

Mort cast around until he saw the figure standing in a little group in the center of the crowd, leaning over slightly the better to hear what a rather short courtier was saying to him. He was a tall, heavily-built man with the kind of stolid, patient face that one would confidently buy a used horse from.

"He doesn't look a *bad* king," said Mort. "Why would anyone want to kill him?"

SEE THE MAN NEXT TO HIM? WITH THE LITTLE MOUSTACHE AND THE GRIN LIKE A LIZARD? Death pointed with his scythe.

"Yes?"

HIS COUSIN, THE DUKE OF STO HELIT. NOT THE NICEST OF PEOPLE, said Death. A HANDY MAN WITH A BOTTLE OF POISON. FIFTH IN LINE TO THE THRONE LAST YEAR, NOW SECOND IN LINE. BIT OF A SOCIAL CLIMBER, YOU MIGHT SAY. He fumbled inside his robe and produced an hourglass in which black sand coursed between a spiked iron latticework. He gave it an experimental shake. AND DUE TO LIVE ANOTHER THIRTY, THIRTY-FIVE YEARS, he said, with a sigh.

"And he goes around killing people?" said Mort. He shook his head. "There's no justice."

Death sighed. NO, he said, handing his drink to a page who was surprised to find he was suddenly holding an empty glass, THERE'S JUST ME.

He drew his sword, which had the same ice blue, shadow-thin blade as the scythe of office, and stepped forward.

"I thought you used the scythe," whispered Mort.

KINGS GET THE SWORD, said Death. IT'S A ROYAL WHATS-NAME, PREROGATIVE.

His free hand thrust its bony digits beneath his robe again and brought out King Olerve's glass. In the top half the last few grains of sand were huddling together.

PAY CAREFUL ATTENTION, said Death, YOU MAY BE ASKED
QUESTIONS AFTERWARDS.

"Wait," said Mort, wretchedly. "It's not fair. Can't you
stop it?"

FAIR? said Death. WHO SAID ANYTHING ABOUT FAIR?

"Well, if the other man is such a—"

LISTEN, said Death, FAIR DOESN'T COME INTO IT. YOU
CAN'T TAKE SIDES. GOOD GRIEF. WHEN IT'S TIME, IT'S TIME.
THAT'S ALL THERE IS TO IT, BOY.

"Mort," moaned Mort, staring at the crowd.

And then he saw her. A random movement in the people
opened up a channel between Mort and a slim, red-haired
girl seated among a group of older women behind the king.
She wasn't exactly beautiful, being over-endowed in the
freckle department and, frankly, rather on the skinny side.
But the sight of her caused a shock that hot-wired Mort's
hindbrain and drove it all the way to the pit of his stomach,
laughing nastily.

IT'S TIME, said Death, giving Mort a nudge with a sharp
elbow. FOLLOW ME.

Death walked toward the king, weighing his sword in his
hand. Mort blinked, and started to follow. The girl's eyes
met his for a second and immediately looked away—then
swiveled back, dragging her head around, her mouth starting
to open in an "o" of horror.

Mort's backbone melted. He started to run towards the
king.

"Look out!" he screamed. "You're in great danger!"

And the world turned into treacle. It began to fill up with
blue and purple shadows, like a heatstroke dream, and sound
faded away until the roar of the court became distant and
scritchy, like the music in someone else's headphones. Mort
saw Death standing companionably by the king, his eyes
turned up towards—

—the minstrel gallery.

Mort saw the bowman, saw the bow, saw the bolt now

winging through the air at the speed of a sick snail. Slow as it was, he couldn't outrun it. It seemed like hours before he could bring his leaden legs under control, but finally he managed to get both feet to touch the floor at the same time and kicked away with all the apparent acceleration of continental drift.

As he twisted slowly through the air Death said, without rancor, IT WON'T WORK, YOU KNOW. IT'S ONLY NATURAL THAT YOU SHOULD WANT TO TRY, BUT IT WON'T WORK.

Dream-like, Mort drifted through a silent world. . . .

The bolt struck. Death brought his sword around in a double-handed swing that passed gently through the king's neck without leaving a mark. To Mort, spiraling gently through the twilight world, it looked as though a ghostly shape had dropped away.

It couldn't be the king, because he was manifestly still standing there, looking directly at Death with an expression of extreme surprise. There was a shadowy *something* around his feet, and a long way away people were reacting with shouts and screams.

A GOOD CLEAN JOB, said Death. ROYALTY ARE ALWAYS A PROBLEM. THEY TEND TO WANT TO HANG ON. YOUR AVERAGE PEASANT, NOW, HE CAN'T WAIT.

"Who the hell are you?" said the king. "What are you doing here? Eh? Guards! I deman—"

The insistent message from his eyes finally battered through to his brain. Mort was impressed. King Olerve had held on to his throne for many years and, even when dead, knew how to behave.

"Oh," he said, "I see. I didn't expect to see you so soon."

YOUR MAJESTY, said Death, bowing, FEW DO.

The king looked around. It was quiet and dim in this shadow world, but outside there seemed to be a lot of excitement.

"That's me down there, is it?"

I AM AFRAID SO, SIRE.

"Clean job. Crossbow, was it?"

YES. AND NOW, SIRE, IF YOU WOULD—

"Who did it?" said the king. Death hesitated.

A HIRED ASSASSIN FROM ANKH-MORPORK, he said.

"Hmm. Clever. I congratulate Sto Helit. And here's me filling myself with antidotes. No antidote to cold steel, eh? Eh?"

INDEED NOT, SIRE.

"The old rope ladder and fast horse by the drawbridge trick, eh?"

SO IT WOULD APPEAR, SIRE, said Death, taking the king's shade gently by the arm. IF IT'S ANY CONSOLATION, THOUGH, THE HORSE *NEEDS* TO BE FAST.

"Eh?"

Death allowed his fixed grin to widen a little.

I HAVE AN APPOINTMENT WITH ITS RIDER TOMORROW IN ANKH, said Death. YOU SEE, HE ALLOWED THE DUKE TO PROVIDE HIM WITH A PACKED LUNCH.

The king, whose eminent suitability for his job meant that he was not automatically quick on the uptake, considered this for a moment and then gave a short laugh. He noticed Mort for the first time.

"Who's this?" he said, "He dead too?"

MY APPRENTICE, said Death. WHO WILL BE GETTING A GOOD TALKING-TO BEFORE HE'S MUCH OLDER, THE SCALLYWAG.

"Mort," said Mort automatically. The sound of their talking washed around him, but he couldn't take his eyes off the scene around them. He felt real. Death looked solid. The king looked surprisingly fit and well for someone who was dead. But the rest of the world was a mass of sliding shadows. Figures were bent over the slumped body, moving through Mort as if they were no more substantial than a mist.

The girl was kneeling down, weeping.

"That's my daughter," said the king. "I ought to feel sad. Why don't I?"

EMOTIONS GET LEFT BEHIND. IT'S ALL A MATTER OF GLANDS.

"Ah. That would be it, I suppose. She can't see us, can she?"

No.

"I suppose there's no chance that I could—?"

NONE, said Death.

"Only she's going to be queen, and if I could only let her—"

SORRY.

The girl looked up and through Mort. He watched the duke walk up behind her and lay a comforting hand on her shoulder. A faint smile hovered around the man's lips. It was the sort of smile that lies on sandbanks waiting for incautious swimmers.

I can't make you hear me, Mort said. Don't trust him!

She peered at Mort, screwing up her eyes. He reached out, and watched his hand pass straight through hers.

COME ALONG, BOY. NO LALLYGAGGING.

Mort felt Death's hand tighten on his shoulder, not in an unfriendly fashion. He turned away reluctantly, following Death and the king.

They walked out through the wall. He was halfway after them before he realized that walking through walls was impossible.

The suicidal logic of this nearly killed him. He felt the chill of the stone around his limbs before a voice in his ear said:

LOOK AT IT THIS WAY. THE WALL CAN'T BE THERE. OTHERWISE YOU WOULDN'T BE WALKING THROUGH IT. WOULD YOU, BOY?

"Mort," said Mort.

WHAT?

"My name is Mort. Or Mortimer," said Mort angrily, pushing forward. The chill fell behind him.

THERE. THAT WASN'T SO HARD, WAS IT?

Mort looked up and down the length of the corridor, and slapped the wall experimentally. He must have walked through it, but it felt solid enough now. Little specks of mica glittered at him.

"How do you do that stuff?" he said. "How do *I* do it? Is it magic?"

MAGIC IS THE ONE THING IT ISN'T, BOY. WHEN YOU CAN DO IT BY YOURSELF, THERE WILL BE NOTHING MORE THAT I CAN TEACH YOU.

The king, who was considerably more diffuse now, said, "It's impressive, I'll grant you. By the way, I seem to be fading."

IT'S THE MORPHOGENETIC FIELD WEAKENING, said Death.

The king's voice was no louder than a whisper. "Is that what it is?"

IT HAPPENS TO EVERYONE. TRY TO ENJOY IT.

"How?" Now the voice was no more than a shape in the air. JUST BE YOURSELF.

At that moment the king collapsed, growing smaller and smaller in the air as the field finally collapsed into a tiny, brilliant pinpoint. It happened so quickly that Mort almost missed it. From ghost to mote in half a second, with a faint sigh.

Death gently caught the glittering thing and stowed it away somewhere under his robe.

"What's happened to him?" said Mort.

ONLY HE KNOWS, said Death. COME.

"My granny says that dying is like going to sleep," Mort added, a shade hopefully.

I WOULDN'T KNOW. I HAVE DONE NEITHER.

Mort took a last look along the corridor. The big doors had been flung back and the court was spilling out. Two older women were endeavoring to comfort the princess, but she was striding ahead of them so that they bounced along behind her like a couple of fussy balloons. They disappeared up another corridor.

ALREADY A QUEEN, said Death, approvingly. Death liked style.

They were on the roof before he spoke again.

YOU TRIED TO WARN HIM, he said, removing Binky's nose-bag.

"Yes, sir. Sorry."

YOU CANNOT INTERFERE WITH FATE. WHO ARE YOU TO JUDGE WHO SHOULD LIVE AND WHO SHOULD DIE?

Death watched Mort's expression carefully.

ONLY THE GODS ARE ALLOWED TO DO THAT, he added. TO TINKER WITH THE FATE OF EVEN ONE INDIVIDUAL COULD DESTROY THE WHOLE WORLD. DO YOU UNDERSTAND?

Mort nodded miserably.

"Are you going to send me home?" he said.

Death reached down and swung him up behind the saddle.

BECAUSE YOU SHOWED COMPASSION? NO. I MIGHT HAVE DONE IF YOU HAD SHOWN PLEASURE. BUT YOU MUST LEARN THE COMPASSION PROPER TO YOUR TRADE.

"What's that?"

A *SHARP* EDGE.

Days passed, although Mort wasn't certain how many. The gloomy sun of Death's world rolled regularly across the sky, but the visits to mortal space seemed to adhere to no particular system. Nor did Death visit only kings and important battles; most of the personal visits were to quite ordinary people.

Meals were served up by Albert, who smiled to himself a lot and didn't say anything much. Ysabell kept to her room most of the time, or rode her own pony on the black moors above the cottage. The sight of her with her hair streaming in the wind would have been more impressive if she was a better horse-woman, or if the pony had been rather larger, or if her hair was the sort that streams naturally. Some hair has got it, and some hasn't. Hers hadn't.

When he wasn't out on what Death referred to as THE DUTY Mort assisted Albert, or found jobs in the garden or stable, or browsed through Death's extensive library, reading with the speed and omnivorousness common to those who discover the magic of the written word for the first time.

Most of the books in the library were biographies, of course.

They were unusual in one respect. They were writing themselves. People who had already died, obviously, filled their books from cover to cover, and those who hadn't been born yet had to put up with blank pages. Those in between . . . Mort took note, marking the place and counting the extra lines, and estimated that some books were adding paragraphs at the rate of four or five every day. He didn't recognize the handwriting.

And finally he plucked up his courage.

A WHAT? said Death in astonishment, sitting behind his ornate desk and turning his scythe-shaped paperknife over and over in his hands.

"An afternoon off," repeated Mort. The room suddenly seemed to be oppressively big, with himself very exposed in the middle of a carpet about the size of a field.

BUT WHY? said Death. IT CAN'T BE TO ATTEND YOUR GRANDMOTHER'S FUNERAL, he added. I WOULD KNOW.

"I just want to, you know, get out and meet people," said Mort, trying to outstare that unflinching blue gaze.

BUT YOU MEET PEOPLE EVERY DAY, protested Death.

"Yes, I know, only, well, not for very long," said Mort. "I mean, it'd be nice to meet someone with a life expectancy of more than a few minutes. Sir," he added.

Death drummed his fingers on the desk, making a sound not unlike a mouse tap-dancing, and gave Mort another few seconds of stare. He noticed that the boy seemed rather less elbows than he remembered, stood a little more upright and, bluntly, could use a word like "expectancy." It was all that library.

ALLRIGHT, he said grudgingly. BUT IT SEEMS TO ME YOU HAVE EVERYTHING YOU NEED RIGHT HERE. THE DUTY IS NOT ONEROUS, IS IT?

"No, sir."

AND YOU HAVE GOOD FOOD AND A WARM BED AND RECREATION AND PEOPLE YOUR OWN AGE.

"Pardon, sir?" said Mort.

MY DAUGHTER, said Death. YOU HAVE MET HER, I BELIEVE.

"Oh. Yes, sir."

SHE HAS A VERY WARM PERSONALITY WHEN YOU GET TO KNOW HER.

"I am sure she has, sir."

NEVERTHELESS, YOU WISH—Death launched the words with a spin of distaste—AN AFTERNOON OFF?

"Yes, sir. If you please, sir."

VERY WELL. SO BE IT. YOU MAY HAVE UNTIL SUNSET.

Death opened his great ledger, picked up a pen, and began to write. Occasionally he'd reach out and flick the beads of an abacus.

After a minute he looked up.

YOU'RE STILL HERE, he said. AND IN YOUR OWN TIME, TOO, he added sourly.

"Um," said Mort, "will people be able to see me, sir?"

I IMAGINE SO, I'M SURE, said Death. IS THERE ANYTHING ELSE I MIGHT BE ABLE TO ASSIST YOU WITH BEFORE YOU LEAVE FOR THIS DEBAUCH?

"Well, sir, there is one thing, sir, I don't know how to get to the mortal world, sir," said Mort desperately.

Death sighed loudly, and pulled open a desk drawer.

JUST WALK THERE.

Mort nodded miserably, and took the long walk to the study door. As he pulled it open Death coughed.

BOY! he called, and tossed something across the room.

Mort caught it automatically as the door creaked open.

The doorway vanished. The deep carpet underfoot became muddy cobbles. Broad daylight poured over him like quicksilver.

"Mort," said Mort, to the universe at large.

"What?" said a stallholder beside him. Mort stared

around. He was in a crowded marketplace, packed with people and animals. Every kind of thing was being sold from needles to (via a few itinerant prophets) visions of salvation. It was impossible to hold any conversation quieter than a shout.

Mort tapped the stallholder in the small of the back.

"Can you see me?" he demanded.

The stallholder squinted critically at him.

"I reckon so," he said, "or someone very much like you."

"Thank you," said Mort, immensely relieved.

"Don't mention it. I see lots of people every day, no charge. Want to buy any bootlaces?"

"I don't think so," said Mort. "What place is this?"

"You don't know?"

A couple of people at the next stall were looking at Mort thoughtfully. His mind went into overdrive.

"My master travels a lot," he said, truthfully. "We arrived last night, and I was asleep on the cart. Now I've got the afternoon off."

"Ah," said the stallholder. He leaned forward conspiratorially. "Looking for a good time, are you? I could fix you up."

"I'd quite enjoy knowing where I am," Mort conceded.

The man was taken aback.

"This is Ankh-Morpork," he said. "Anyone ought to be able to see that. Smell it, too."

Mort sniffed. There was a certain something about the air in the city. You got the feeling that it was air that had seen life. You couldn't help noting with every breath that thousands of other people were very close to you and nearly all of them had armpits.

The stallholder regarded Mort critically, noting the pale face, well-cut clothes and strange presence, a sort of coiled spring effect.

"Look, I'll be frank," he said. "I could point you in the direction of a great brothel."

"I've already had lunch," said Mort, vaguely. "But you can tell me if we're anywhere near, I think it's called Sto Lat?"

"About twenty miles Hubwards, but there's nothing there for a young man of your kidney," said the trader hurriedly. "I know, you're out by yourself, you want new experiences, you want excitement, romance—"

Mort, meanwhile, had opened the bag Death had given him. It was full of small gold coins, about the size of sequins.

An image formed again in his mind, of a pale young face under a head of red hair who had somehow known he was there. The unfocused feelings that had haunted his mind for the last few days suddenly sharpened to a point.

"I want," he said firmly, "a very fast horse."

Five minutes later, Mort was lost.

This part of Ankh-Morpork was known as The Shades, an inner-city area sorely in need either of governmental help or, for preference, a flamethrower. It couldn't be called squalid because that would be stretching the word to breaking point. It was beyond squalor and out the other side, where by a sort of Einsteinian reversal it achieved a magnificent horribleness that it wore like an architectural award. It was noisy and sultry and smelled like a cowshed floor.

It didn't so much have a neighborhood as an ecology, like a great land-based coral reef. There were the humans, all right, humanoid equivalents of lobsters, squid, shrimps and so on. And sharks.

Mort wandered hopelessly along the winding streets. Anyone hovering at rooftop height would have noticed a certain pattern in the crowds behind him, suggesting a number of men converging nonchalantly on a target, and would rightly have concluded that Mort and his gold had about the same life expectancy as a three-legged hedgehog on a six-lane motorway.

It is probably already apparent that The Shades was not

the sort of place to have inhabitants. It had denizens. Periodically Mort would try to engage one in conversation, to find the way to a good horse dealer. The denizen would usually mutter something and hurry away, since anyone wishing to live in The Shades for longer than maybe three hours developed very specialized senses indeed and would no more hang around near Mort than a peasant would stand near a tall tree in thundery weather.

And so Mort came at last to the river Ankh, greatest of rivers. Even before it entered the city it was slow and heavy with the silt of the plains, and by the time it got to The Shades even an agnostic could have walked across it. It was hard to drown in the Ankh, but easy to suffocate.

Mort looked at the surface doubtfully. It seemed to be moving. There were bubbles in it. It had to be water.

He sighed, and turned away.

Three men had appeared behind him, as though extruded from the stonework. They had the heavy, stolid look of those thugs whose appearance in any narrative means that it's time for the hero to be menaced a bit, although not too much, because it's also obvious that they're going to be horribly surprised.

They were leering. They were good at it.

One of them had drawn a knife, which he waved in little circles in the air. He advanced slowly towards Mort, while the other two hung back to provide immoral support.

"Give us the money," he rasped.

Mort's hand went to the bag on his belt.

"Hang on a minute," he said. "What happens then?"

"What?"

"I mean, is it my money or my life?" said Mort. "That's the sort of thing robbers are supposed to demand. Your money or your life. I read that in a book once," he added.

"Possibly, possibly," conceded the robber. He felt he was losing the initiative, but rallied magnificently. "On the other hand, it could be your money *and* your life. Pulling off the double, you might say." The man looked sideways at his colleagues, who sniggered on cue.

"In that case—" said Mort, and hefted the bag in one hand preparatory to chucking it as far out into the Ankh as he could, even though there was a reasonable chance it would bounce.

"Hey, what are you doing," said the robber. He started to run forward, but halted when Mort gave the bag a threatening jerk.

"Well," said Mort, "I look at it like this. If you're going to kill me anyway, I might as well get rid of the money. It's entirely up to you." To illustrate his point he took one coin out of the bag and flicked it out across the water, which accepted it with an unfortunate sucking noise. The thieves shuddered.

The leading thief looked at the bag. He looked at his knife. He looked at Mort's face. He looked at his colleagues.

"Excuse me," he said, and they went into a huddle.

Mort measured the distance to the end of the alley. He wouldn't make it. Anyway, these three looked as though chasing people was another thing they were good at. It was only logic that left them feeling a little stretched.

Their leader turned back to Mort. He gave a final glance at the other two. They both nodded decisively.

"I think we kill you and take a chance on the money," he said. "We don't want this sort of thing to spread."

The other two drew their knives.

Mort swallowed. "This could be unwise," he said.

"Why?"

"Well, *I* won't like it, for one."

"You're not supposed to like it, you're supposed to—die," said the thief, advancing.

"I don't think I'm due to die," said Mort, backing away. "I'm sure I would have been told."

"Yeah," said the thief, who was getting fed up with this. "Yeah, well, you have been, haven't you? Great steaming elephant turds!"

Mort had just stepped backwards again. Through a wall.

The leading thief glared at the solid stone that had swallowed Mort, and then threw down his knife.

"Well,----me," he said. "A----ing wizard. I *hate*----ing wizards!"

"You shouldn't----them, then," muttered one of his henchmen, effortlessly pronouncing a row of dashes.

The third member of the trio, who was a little slow of thinking, said, "Here, he walked through the wall!"

"And we bin following him for ages, too," muttered the second one. "Fine one you are, Pilgarlic. I said I thought he was a wizard, only wizards'd walk round here by themselves. Dint I say he looked like a wizard? I said—"

"You're saying a good deal too much," growled the leader. *"I saw him, he walked right through the wall there—"*

"Oh, yeah?"

"Yeah!"

*"Right through it, dint you see?"*

"Think you're sharp, do you?"

"Sharp enough, come to that!"

The leader scooped his knife out of the dirt in one snaky movement.

"Sharp as this?"

The third thief lurched over to the wall and kicked it hard a few times, while behind him there were the sounds of scuffle and some damp bubbling noises.

"Yep, it's a wall okay," he said. "That's a wall if ever I saw one. How d'you think they do it, lads?"

"Lads?"

He tripped over the prone bodies.

"Oh," he said. Slow as his mind was, it was quick enough to realize something very important. He was in a back alley in The Shades, and he was alone. He ran for it, and got quite a long way.

Death walked slowly across tiles in the lifetimer room, inspecting the serried rows of busy hourglasses. Albert followed dutifully behind with the great ledger open in his arms.

The sound roared around them, a vast gray waterfall of noise.

It came from the shelves where, stretching away into the infinite distance, row upon row of hourglasses poured away the sands of mortal time. It was a heavy sound, a dull sound, a sound that poured like sullen custard over the bright roly-poly pudding of the soul.

VERY WELL, said Death at last. I MAKE IT THREE. A QUIET NIGHT.

"That'd be Goodie Hamstring, the Abbot Lobsang again, and this Princess Keli," said Albert.

Death looked at the three hourglasses in his hand.

I WAS THINKING OF SENDING THE LAD OUT, he said.

Albert consulted his ledger.

"Well, Goodie wouldn't be any trouble and the Abbot is what you might call experienced," he said. "Shame about the princess. Only fifteen. Could be tricky."

YES. IT IS A PITY.

"Master?"

Death stood with the third glass in his hand, staring thoughtfully at the play of light across its surface. He sighed.

ONE SO YOUNG . . .

"Are you feeling all right, master?" said Albert, his voice full of concern.

TIME LIKE AN EVER-ROLLING STREAM BEARS ALL ITS . . .

"Master!"

WHAT? said Death, snapping out of it.

"You've been overdoing it, master, that's what it is—"

WHAT ARE YOU BLATHERING ABOUT, MAN?

"You had a bit of a funny turn there, master."

NONSENSE. I HAVE NEVER FELT BETTER. NOW, WHAT WERE WE TALKING ABOUT?

Albert shrugged, and peered down at the entries in the book.

"Goodie's a witch," he said. "She might get a bit annoyed if you send Mort."

All practitioners of magic earned the right, once their own personal sands had run out, of being claimed by Death himself rather than his minor functionaries.

Death didn't appear to hear Albert. He was staring at Princess Keli's hourglass again.

WHAT IS THAT SENSE INSIDE YOUR HEAD OF WISTFUL REGRET THAT THINGS ARE THE WAY THEY APPARENTLY ARE?

"Sadness, master. I think. Now—"

I AM SADNESS.

Albert stood with his mouth open. Finally he got a grip on himself long enough to blurt out, "Master, we were talking about Mort!"

MORT WHO?

"Your apprentice, master," said Albert patiently. "Tall young lad."

OF COURSE. WELL, WE'LL SEND HIM.

"Is he ready to go solo, master?" said Albert doubtfully.

Death thought about it. HE CAN DO IT, he said at last. HE'S KEEN, HE'S QUICK TO LEARN AND, REALLY, he added, PEOPLE CAN'T EXPECT TO HAVE ME RUNNING AROUND AFTER THEM ALL THE TIME.

Mort stared blankly at the velvet wall hangings a few inches from his eyes.

I've walked through a wall, he thought. And that's impossible.

He gingerly moved the hangings aside to see if a door was

lurking somewhere, but there was nothing but crumbling plaster which had cracked away in places to reveal some dampish but emphatically solid brickwork.

He prodded it experimentally. It was quite clear that he wasn't going back out that way.

"Well," he said to the wall. "What now?"

A voice behind him said, "Um. Excuse please?"

He turned around slowly.

Grouped around a table in the middle of the room was a Klatchian family of father, mother and half a dozen children of dwindling size. Eight pairs of round eyes were fixed on Mort. A ninth pair belonging to an aged grandparent of indeterminate sex weren't, because their owner had taken advantage of the interruption to get some elbow room at the communal rice bowl, taking the view that a boiled fish in the hand was worth any amount of unexplained manifestations, and the silence was punctuated by the sound of determined mastication.

In one corner of the crowded room was a little shrine to Offler, the six-armed Crocodile God of Klatch. It was grinning just like Death, except of course Death didn't have a flock of holy birds that brought him news of his worshippers and also kept his teeth clean.

Klatchians prize hospitality above all other virtues. As Mort stared the woman took another plate off the shelf behind her and silently began to fill it from the big bowl, snatching a choice cut of catfish from the ancient's hands after a brief struggle. Her kohl-rimmed eyes remained steadily on Mort, however.

It was the father who had spoken. Mort bowed nervously.

"Sorry," he said. "Er, I seem to have walked through this wall." It was rather lame, he had to admit.

"Please?" said the man. The woman, her bangles jangling, carefully arranged a few slices of pepper across the plate and sprinkled it with a dark green sauce that Mort was afraid he recognized. He'd tried it a few weeks before, and although it was a complicated recipe one taste had been enough to know that it was made out of fish entrails marinated for several years in a vat of shark bile. Death had said that it was an acquired taste. Mort had decided not to make the effort.

He tried to sidle around the edge of the room towards the bead-hung doorway, all the heads turning to watch him. He tried a grin.

The woman said: "Why does the demon show his teeth, husband of my life?"

The man said: "It could be hunger, moon of my desire. Pile on more fish!"

And the ancestor grumbled: "I was eating that, wretched child. Woe unto the world when there is no respect for age!"

Now the fact is that while the words entered Mort's ear in their spoken Klatchian, with all the curlicues and subtle diphthongs of a language so ancient and sophisticated that it had fifteen words meaning "assassination" before the rest of the world had caught on to the idea of bashing one another over the head with rocks, they arrived in his brain as clear and understandable as his mother tongue.

"I'm no demon! I'm a human!" he said, and stopped in shock as his words emerged in perfect Klatch.

"You're a thief?" said the father. "A murderer? To creep in thus, are you a *tax-gatherer*?" His hand slipped under the table and came up holding a meat cleaver honed to paper thinness. His wife screamed and dropped the plate and clutched the youngest children to her.

Mort watched the blade weave through the air, and gave in.

"I bring you greetings from the uttermost circles of hell," he hazarded.

The change was remarkable. The cleaver was lowered and the family broke into broad smiles.

"There is much luck to us if a demon visits," beamed the father. "What is your wish, O foul spawn of Offler's loins?"

"Sorry?" said Mort.

"A demon brings blessing and good fortune on the man that helps it," said the man. "How may we be of assistance, O evil dogsbreath of the nether pit?"

"Well, I'm not very hungry," said Mort, "but if you know where I can get a fast horse, I could be in Sto Lat before sunset."

The man beamed and bowed. "I know the very place, noxious extrusion of the bowels, if you would be so good as to follow me."

Mort hurried out after him. The ancient ancestor watched them go with a critical expression, its jowls rhythmically chewing.

"That was what they call a demon around here?" it said. "Offler rot this country of dampness, even their demons are third-rate, not a patch on the demons we had in the Old Country."

The wife placed a small bowl of rice in the folded middle pair of hands of the Offler statue (it would be gone in the morning) and stood back.

"Husband did say that last month at the *Curry Gardens* he served a creature who was not there," she said. "He was impressed."

Ten minutes later the man returned and, in solemn silence, placed a small heap of gold coins on the table. They represented enough wealth to purchase quite a large part of the city.

"He had a bag of them," he said.

The family stared at the money for some time. The wife sighed.

"Riches bring many problems," she said. "What are we to do?"

"We return to Klatch," said the husband firmly, "where our children can grow up in a proper country, true to the glorious traditions of our ancient race and men do not need to work as waiters for wicked masters but can stand tall and proud. And we must leave right now, fragrant blossom of the date palm."

"Why so soon, O hardworking son of the desert?"

"Because," said the man, "I have just sold the Patrician's champion racehorse."

The horse wasn't as fine or as fast as Binky, but it swept the miles away under its hooves and easily outdistanced a few mounted guards who, for some reason, appeared anxious to talk to Mort. Soon the shanty suburbs of Morpork were left behind and the road ran out into rich black earth country of the Sto plain, constructed over eons by the periodic flooding of the great slow Ankh that brought to the region prosperity, security and chronic arthritis.

It was also extremely boring. As the light distilled from silver to gold Mort galloped across a flat, chilly landscape, checkered with cabbage fields from edge to edge. There are many things to be said about cabbages. One may talk at length about their high vitamin content, their vital iron contribution, the valuable roughage and commendable food value. In the mass, however, they lack a certain something; despite their claim to immense nutritional and moral superiority over, say, daffodils, they have never been a sight to inspire the poet's muse. Unless he was hungry, of course. It was only twenty miles to Sto Lat, but in terms of meaningless human experience it seemed like two thousand.

There were guards on the gates of Sto Lat, although compared to the ones that patrolled Ankh they had a sheepish, amateurish look. Mort trotted past and one of them, feeling a bit of a fool, asked him who went there.

"I'm afraid I can't stop," said Mort.

The guard was new to the job, and quite keen. Guarding wasn't what he'd been led to expect. Standing around all day in chain mail with an axe on a long pole wasn't what he'd volunteered for; he'd expected excitement and challenge and a crossbow and a uniform that didn't go rusty in the rain.

He stepped forward, ready to defend the city against people who didn't respect commands given by duly authorized civic employees. Mort considered the pike blade hovering a few inches from his face. There was getting to be too much of this.

"On the other hand," he said calmly, "how would you like it if I made you a present of this rather fine horse?"

It wasn't hard to find the entrance to the castle. There were guards there, too, and they had crossbows and a considerably more unsympathetic outlook on life and, in any case, Mort had run out of horses. He loitered a bit until they started paying him a generous amount of attention, and then wandered disconsolately away into the streets of the little city, feeling stupid.

After all this, after miles of brassicas and a backside that now felt like a block of wood, he didn't even know why he was there. So she'd seen him even when he was invisible? Did it mean anything? Of course it didn't. Only he kept seeing her face, and the flicker of hope in her eyes. He wanted to tell her that everything was going to be all right. He wanted to tell her about himself and everything he wanted to be. He wanted to find out which was her room in the castle and watch it all night until the light went out. And so on.

A little later a blacksmith, whose business was in one of the narrow streets that looked out on to the castle walls, glanced up from his work to see a tall, gangling young man, rather red in the face, who kept trying to walk through the walls.

Rather later than that a young man with a few superficial bruises on his head called in at one of the city's taverns and asked for directions to the nearest wizard.

And it was later still that Mort turned up outside a peeling plaster house which announced itself on a blackened brass plaque to be the abode of Igneous Cutwell, DM (Unseen), Marster of the Infinit, Illuminartus, Wyzard to Princes, Gardian of the Sacred Portalls, If Out leave Maile with Mrs. Nugent Next Door.

Suitably impressed despite his pounding heart, Mort lifted

the heavy knocker, which was in the shape of a repulsive gargoyle with a heavy iron ring in its mouth, and knocked twice.

There was a brief commotion from within, the series of hasty domestic sounds that might, in a less exalted house, have been made by, say, someone shoveling the lunch plates into the sink and tidying the laundry out of sight.

Eventually the door swung open, slowly and mysteriously.

"You'd fbetter pretend to be impreffed," said the door-knocker conversationally, but hampered somewhat by the ring. "He does it with pulleys and a bit of ftring. No good at opening-fpells, fee?"

Mort looked at the grinning metal face. I work for a skeleton who can walk through walls, he told himself. Who am I to be surprised at anything?

"Thank you," he said.

"You're welcome. Wipe your feet on the doormat, it's the bootfcraper's day off."

The big low room inside was dark and shadowy and smelled mainly of incense but slightly of boiled cabbage and elderly laundry and the kind of person who throws all his socks at the wall and wears the ones that don't stick. There was a large crystal ball with a crack in it, an astrolabe with several bits missing, a rather scuffed octogram on the floor, and a stuffed alligator hanging from the ceiling. A stuffed alligator is absolutely standard equipment in any properly-run magical establishment. This one looked as though it hadn't enjoyed it much.

A bead curtain on the far wall was flung aside with a dramatic gesture and a hooded figure stood revealed.

"Beneficent constellations shine on the hour of our meeting!" it boomed.

"Which ones?" said Mort.

There was a sudden worried silence.

"Pardon?"

"Which constellations would these be?" said Mort.

"Beneficent ones," said the figure, uncertainly. It rallied. "Why do you trouble Igneous Cutwell, Holder of the Eight Keys, Traveler in the Dungeon Dimensions, Supreme Mage of—"

"Excuse me," said Mort, "are you really?"

"Really what?"

"Master of the thingy, Lord High Wossname of the Sacred Dungeons?"

Cutwell pushed back his hood with an annoyed flourish. Instead of the gray-bearded mystic Mort had expected he saw a round, rather plump face, pink and white like a pork pie, which it somewhat resembled in other respects. For example, like most pork pies, it didn't have a beard and, like most pork pies, it looked basically good-humored.

"In a figurative sense," he said.

"What does that mean?"

"Well, it means no," said Cutwell.

"But you said—"

"That was advertising," said the wizard. "It's a kind of magic I've been working on. What was it you were wanting, anyway?" He leered suggestively. "A love philter, yes? Something to encourage the young ladies?"

"Is it possible to walk through walls?" said Mort desperately. Cutwell paused with his hand already halfway to a large bottle full of sticky liquid.

"Using magic?"

"Um," said Mort, "I don't think so."

"Then pick very thin walls," said Cutwell. "Better still, use the door. The one over there would be favorite, if you've just come here to waste my time."

Mort hesitated, and then put the bag of gold coins on the table. The wizard glanced at them, made a little whinnying noise in the back of his throat, and reached out. Mort's hand shot across and grabbed his wrist.

"I've walked through walls," he said, slowly and deliberately.

"Of course you have, of course you have," mumbled Cutwell, not taking his eyes off the bag. He flicked the cork out of the bottle of blue liquid and took an absent-minded swig.

"Only before I did it I didn't know that I could, and when I was doing it I didn't know I was, and now I've done it I can't remember how it was done. And I want to do it again."

"Why?"

"Because," said Mort, "if I could walk through walls I could do anything."

"Very deep," agreed Cutwell. "Philosophical. And the name of the young lady on the other side of this wall?"

"She's—" Mort swallowed. "I don't know her name. Even if there is a girl," he added haughtily, "and I'm not saying there is."

"Right," said Cutwell. He took another swig, and shuddered. "Fine. How to walk through walls. I'll do some research. It might be expensive, though."

Mort carefully picked up the bag and pulled out one small gold coin.

"A down payment," he said, putting it on the table.

Cutwell picked up the coin as if he expected it to go bang or evaporate, and examined it carefully.

"I've never seen this sort of coin before," he said accusingly. "What's all this curly writing?"

"It's gold, though, isn't it?" said Mort. "I mean, you don't have to accept it—"

"Sure, sure, it's gold," said Cutwell hurriedly. "It's gold all right. I just wondered where it had come from, that's all."

"You wouldn't believe me," said Mort. "What time's sunset around here?"

"We normally manage to fit it in between night and day," said Cutwell, still staring at the coin and taking little sips from the blue bottle. "About now."

Mort glanced out of the window. The street outside already had a twilight look to it.

"I'll be back," he muttered, and made for the door. He heard the wizard call out something, but Mort was heading down the street at a dead run.

He started to panic. Death would be waiting for him forty miles away. There would be a row. There would be a terrible—

AH, BOY.

A familiar figure stepped out from the flare around a jellied eel stall, holding a plate of winkles.

THE VINEGAR IS PARTICULARLY PIQUANT. HELP YOURSELF, I HAVE AN EXTRA PIN.

But, of course, just because he was forty miles away didn't mean he wasn't here as well. . . .

And in his untidy room Cutwell turned the gold coin over and over in his fingers, muttering "walls" to himself, and draining the bottle.

He appeared to notice what he was doing only when there was no more to drink, at which point his eyes focused on the bottle and, through a rising pink mist, read the label which said "Granny Weatherwax's Ramrub Invigoratore and Passion's Philter, Onne Spoonful Onlie before bed and that Smalle."

"By myself?" said Mort.

CERTAINLY. I HAVE EVERY FAITH IN YOU.

"Gosh!"

The suggestion put everything else out of Mort's mind, and he was rather surprised to find that he didn't feel particularly squeamish. He'd seen quite a few deaths in the last week or so, and all the horror went out of it when you knew you'd be speaking to the victim afterwards. Most of them were relieved, one or two of them were angry, but they were all glad of a few helpful words.

THINK YOU CAN DO IT?

"Well, sir. Yes. I think."

THAT'S THE SPIRIT. I'VE LEFT BINKY BY THE HORSETROUGH
ROUND THE CORNER. TAKE HIM STRAIGHT HOME WHEN YOU'VE
FINISHED.

"You're staying here, sir?"

Death looked up and down the street. His eyesockets
flared.

I THOUGHT I MIGHT STROLL AROUND A BIT, he said mysteriously. I DON'T SEEM TO FEEL QUITE RIGHT. I COULD DO WITH
THE FRESH AIR. He seemed to remember something, reached
into the mysterious shadows of his cloak, and pulled out
three hourglasses.

ALL STRAIGHTFORWARD, he said. ENJOY YOURSELF.

He turned and strode off down the street, humming.

"Um. Thank you," said Mort. He held the hourglasses up
to the light, noting the one that was on its very last few
grains of sand.

"Does this mean I'm in charge?" he called, but Death had
turned the corner.

Binky greeted him with a faint whinny of recognition.
Mort mounted up, his heart pounding with apprehension and
responsibility. His fingers worked automatically, taking the
scythe out of its sheath and adjusting and locking the blade
(which flashed steely blue in the night, slicing the starlight
like salami). He mounted carefully, wincing at the stab from
his saddlesores, but Binky was like riding a pillow. As an
afterthought, drunk with delegated authority, he pulled
Death's riding cloak out of its saddlebag and fastened it by
its silver brooch.

He took another look at the first hourglass, and nudged
Binky with his knees. The horse sniffed the chilly air, and
began to trot.

Behind them Cutwell burst out of his doorway, accelerat-
ing down the frosty street with his robes flying out behind
him.

Now the horse was cantering, widening the distance between its hooves and the cobbles. With a swish of its tail it cleared the housetops and floated up into the chilly sky.

Cutwell ignored it. He had more pressing things on his mind. He took a flying leap and landed full length in the freezing waters of the horsetrough, lying back gratefully among the bobbing ice splinters. After a while the water began to steam. Mort kept low for the sheer exhilaration of the speed. The sleeping countryside roared soundlessly underneath. Binky moved at an easy gallop, his great muscles sliding under his skin as easily as alligators off a sandbank, his mane whipping in Mort's face. The night swirled away from the speeding edge of the scythe, cut into two curling halves.

They sped under the moonlight as silent as a shadow, visible only to cats and people who dabbled in things men were not meant to wot of.

Mort couldn't remember afterwards, but very probably he laughed.

Soon the frosty plains gave way to the broken lands around the mountains, and then the marching ranks of the Ramtops themselves raced across the world towards them. Binky put his head down and opened his stride, aiming for a pass between two mountains as sharp as goblins' teeth in the silver light. Somewhere a wolf howled.

Mort took another look at the hourglass. Its frame was carved with oak leaves and mandrake roots, and the sand inside, even by moonlight, was pale gold. By turning the glass this way and that, he could just make out the name "Ammeline Hamstring" etched in the faintest of lines.

Binky slowed to a canter. Mort looked down at the roof of a forest, dusted with snow that was either early or very, very late; it could have been either, because the Ramtops hoarded their weather and doled it out with no real reference to the time of year.

A gap opened up beneath them. Binky slowed again,

wheeled around and descended towards a clearing that was white with drifted snow. It was circular, with a tiny cottage in the exact middle. If the ground around it hadn't been covered in snow, Mort would have noticed that there were no tree stumps to be seen; the trees hadn't been cut down in the circle, they'd simply been discouraged from growing there. Or had moved away.

Candlelight spilled from one downstairs window, making a pale orange pool on the snow.

Binky touched down smoothly and trotted across the freezing crust without sinking. He left no hoofprints, of course.

Mort dismounted and walked towards the door, muttering to himself and making experimental sweeps with the scythe.

The cottage roof had been built with wide eaves, to shed snow and cover the logpile. No dweller in the high Ramtops would dream of starting a winter without a logpile on three sides of the house. But there wasn't a logpile here, even though spring was still a long way off.

There was, however, a bundle of hay in a net by the door. It had a note attached, written in big, slightly shaky capitals: FOR THEE HORS.

It would have worried Mort if he'd let it. Someone was expecting him. He'd learned in recent days, though, that rather than drown in uncertainty it was best to surf right over the top of it. Anyway, Binky wasn't worried by moral scruples and bit straight in.

It did leave the problem of whether to knock. Somehow, it didn't seem appropriate. Supposing no one answered, or told him to go away?

So he lifted the thumb latch and pushed at the door. It swung inwards quite easily, without a creak.

There was a low-ceilinged kitchen, its beams at trepanning height for Mort. The light from the solitary candle glinted off crockery on a long dresser and flagstones that had been scrubbed and polished into iridescence. The fire in the

cave-like inglenook didn't add much light, because it was no
more than a heap of white ash under the remains of a log.
Mort knew, without being told, that it was the last log.

An elderly lady was sitting at the kitchen table, writing
furiously with her hooked nose only a few inches from the
paper. A gray cat curled on the table beside her blinked
calmly at Mort.

The scythe bumped off a beam. The woman looked up.

"Be with you in a minute," she said. She frowned at the
paper. "I haven't put in the bit about being of sound mind
and body yet, lot of foolishness anyway, no one sound in
mind and body would be dead. Would you like a drink?"

"Pardon?" said Mort. He recalled himself, and repeated
"PARDON?"

"If you drink, that is. It's raspberry port. On the dresser.
You might as well finish the bottle."

Mort eyed the dresser suspiciously. He felt he'd rather lost
the initiative. He pulled out the hourglass and glared at it.
There was a little heap of sand left.

"There's still a few minutes yet," said the witch, without
looking up.

"How, I mean, HOW DO YOU KNOW?"

She ignored him, and dried the ink in front of the candle,
sealed the letter with a drip of wax, and tucked it under the
candlestick. Then she picked up the cat.

"Granny Beedle will be around directly tomorrow to tidy
up and you're to go with her, understand? And see she lets
Gammer Nutley have the pink marble washstand, she's had
her eye on it for years."

The cat yawped knowingly.

"I haven't, that is, I HAVEN'T GOT ALL NIGHT, YOU KNOW,"
said Mort reproachfully.

"You have, I haven't, and there's no need to shout," said
the witch. She slid off her stall and then Mort saw how bent
she was, like a bow. With some difficulty she unhooked a tall
pointed hat from its nail on the wall, skewered it into place

on her white hair with a battery of hatpins, and grasped two walking sticks.

She tottered across the floor towards Mort, and looked up at him with eyes as small and bright as blackcurrants.

"Will I need my shawl? Shall I need a shawl, d'you think? No, I suppose not. I imagine it's quite warm where I'm going." She peered closely at Mort, and frowned.

"You're rather *younger* than I imagined," she said. Mort said nothing. Then Goodie Hamstring said, quietly, "You know, I don't think you're who I was expecting at all."

Mort cleared his throat.

"Who were you expecting, precisely?" he said.

"Death," said the witch, simply. "It's part of the arrangement, you see. One gets to know the time of one's death in advance, and one is guaranteed—personal attention."

"I'm it," said Mort.

"It?"

"The personal attention. He sent me. I work for him. No-one else would have me." Mort paused. This was all wrong. He'd be sent home again in disgrace. His first bit of responsibility, and he'd ruined it. He could already hear people laughing at him.

The wail started in the depths of his embarrassment and blared out like a foghorn. "Only this is my first real job and it's all gone wrong!"

The scythe fell to the floor with a clatter, slicing a piece off the table leg and cutting a flagstone in half.

Goodie watched him for some time, with her head on one side. Then she said, "I see. What is your name, young man?"

"Mort," sniffed Mort. "Short for Mortimer."

"Well, Mort, I expect you've got an hourglass somewhere about your person."

Mort nodded vaguely. He reached down to his belt and produced the glass. The witch inspected it critically.

"Still a minute or so," she said. "We don't have much time to lose. Just give me a moment to lock up."

"But you don't understand!" Mort wailed. "I'll mess it all up! I've never done this before!"

She patted his hand. "Neither have I," she said. "We can learn together. Now pick up the scythe and try to act your age, there's a good boy."

Against his protestations she shooed him out into the snow and followed behind him, pulling the door shut and locking it with a heavy iron key which she hung on a nail by the door.

The frost had tightened its grip on the forest, squeezing it until the roots creaked. The moon was setting, but the sky was full of hard white stars that made the winter seem colder still. Goodie Hamstring shivered.

"There's an old log over there," she said conversationally. "There's quite a good view across the valley. In the summertime, of course. I should like to sit down."

Mort helped her through the drifts and brushed as much snow as possible off the wood. They sat down with the hourglass between them. Whatever the view might have been in the summer, it now consisted of black rocks against a sky from which little flakes of snow were now tumbling.

"I can't believe all this," said Mort. "I mean you sound as if you want to die."

"There's some things I shall miss," she said. "But it gets thin, you know. Life, I'm referring to. You can't trust your own body any more, and it's time to move on. I reckon it's about time I tried something else. Did he tell you magical folk can see him all the time?"

"No," said Mort, inaccurately.

"Well, we can."

"He doesn't like wizards and witches much," Mort volunteered.

"Nobody likes a smartass," she said with some satisfaction. "We give him trouble, you see. Priests don't, so he likes priests."

"He's never said," said Mort.

"Ah. They're always telling folk how much better it's

going to be when they're dead. We tell them it could be pretty good right here if only they'd put their minds to it."

Mort hesitated. He wanted to say: you're wrong, he's not like that at all, he doesn't care if people are good or bad so long as they're punctual. And kind to cats, he added.

But he thought better of it. It occurred to him that people needed to believe things.

The wolf howled again, so near that Mort looked around apprehensively. Another one across the valley answered it. The chorus was picked up by a couple of others in the depths of the forest. Mort had never heard anything so mournful.

He glanced sideways at the still figure of Goodie Hamstring and then, with mounting panic, at the hourglass. He sprang to his feet, snatched up the scythe, and brought it around in a two-handed swing.

The witch stood up, leaving her body behind.

"Well done," she said. "I thought you'd missed it, for a minute, there."

Mort leaned against a tree, panting heavily, and watched Goodie walk around the log to look at herself.

"Hmm," she said critically. "Time has got a lot to answer for." She raised her hand and laughed to see the stars through it.

Then she changed. Mort had seen this happen before, when the soul realized it was no longer bound by the body's morphic field, but never under such control. Her hair unwound itself from its tight bun, changing color and lengthening. Her body straightened up. Wrinkles dwindled and vanished. Her gray woolen dress moved like the surface of the sea and ended up tracing entirely different and disturbing contours.

She looked down, giggled, and changed the dress into something leaf-green and clingy.

"What do you think, Mort?" she said. Her voice had sounded cracked and quavery before. Now it suggested musk and maple syrup and other things that set Mort's adam's apple bobbing like a rubber ball on an elastic band.

". . ." he managed, and gripped the scythe until his knuckles went white.

She walked towards him like a snake in a four-wheel drift.

"I didn't hear you," she purred.

"V-v-very nice," he said. "Is that who you were?"

"It's who I've always been."

"Oh." Mort stared at his feet. "I'm supposed to take you away," he said.

"I know," she said, "but I'm going to stay."

"You can't do that! I mean—" he fumbled for words—"you see, if you stay you sort of spread out and get thinner, until—"

"I shall enjoy it," she said firmly. She leaned forward and gave him a kiss as insubstantial as a mayfly's sigh, fading as she did so until only the kiss was left, just like a Cheshire cat only much more erotic.

"Have a care, Mort," said her voice in his head. "You may want to hold on to your job, but will you ever be able to let go?"

Mort stood idiotically holding his cheek. The trees around the clearing trembled for a moment, there was the sound of laughter on the breeze, and then the freezing silence closed in again.

Duty called out to him through the pink mists in his head. He grabbed the second glass and stared at it. The sand was nearly all gone.

The glass itself was patterned with lotus petals. When Mort flicked it with his finger it went "Ommm."

He ran across the crackling snow to Binky and hurled himself into the saddle. The horse threw up his head, reared, and launched itself towards the stars.

Great silent streamers of blue and green flame hung from the roof of the world. Curtains of octarine glow danced slowly and majestically over the Disc as the fire of the Aurora Coriolis, the vast discharge of magic from the Disc's standing field, earthed itself in the green ice mountains of the Hub.

The central spire of Cori Celesti, home of the gods, was a ten-mile-high column of cold coruscating fire.

It was a sight seen by few people, and Mort wasn't one of them, because he lay low over Binky's neck and clung on for his life as they pounded through the night sky ahead of a comet trail of steam.

There were other mountains clustered around Cori. By comparison they were no more than termite mounds, although in reality each one was a majestic assortment of cols, ridges, faces, cliffs, screes and glaciers that any normal mountain range would be happy to associate with.

Among the highest of them, at the end of a funnel-shaped valley, dwelt the Listeners.

They were one of the oldest of the Disc's religious sects, although even the gods themselves were divided as to whether Listening was really a proper religion, and all that prevented their temple being wiped out by a few well-aimed avalanches was the fact that even the gods were curious as to what it was that the Listeners might Hear. If there's one thing that really annoys a god, it's not knowing something.

It'll take Mort several minutes to arrive. A row of dots would fill in the time nicely, but the reader will already be noticing the strange shape of the temple—curled like a great white ammonite at the end of the valley—and will probably want an explanation.

The fact is that the Listeners are trying to work out precisely what it was that the Creator said when He made the universe.

The theory is quite straightforward.

Clearly, nothing that the Creator makes could ever be destroyed, which means that the echoes of those first syllables must still be around somewhere, bouncing and rebounding off all the matter in the cosmos but still audible to a really good listener.

Eons ago the Listeners had found that ice and chance had carved this one valley into the perfect acoustic opposite of an echo valley, and had built their multi-chambered temple in the exact position that the one comfy chair always occupies in the home of a rabid hi-fi fanatic. Complex baffles caught and amplified the sound that was funneled up the chilly valley, steering it ever inwards to the central chamber where, at any hour of the day or night, three monks always sat.

Listening.

There were certain problems caused by the fact that they didn't hear only the subtle echoes of the first words, but every other sound made on the Disc. In order to recognize the sound of the Words, they had to learn to recognize all the other noises. This called for a certain talent, and a novice was only accepted for training if he could distinguish by sound alone, at a distance of a thousand yards, which side a dropped coin landed. He wasn't actually accepted into the order until he could tell what color it was.

And although the Holy Listeners were so remote, many people took the extremely long and dangerous path to their temple, traveling through frozen, troll-haunted lands, fording swift icy rivers, climbing forbidding mountains, trekking across inhospitable tundra, in order to climb the narrow stairway that led into the hidden valley and seek with an open heart the secrets of being.

And the monks would cry unto them, "Keep the bloody noise down!"

Binky came through the mountain tops like a white blur, touching down in the snowy emptiness of a courtyard made spectral by the disco light from the sky. Mort leapt from his back and ran through the silent cloisters to the room where the 88th abbot lay dying, surrounded by his devout followers.

Mort's footsteps boomed as he hurried across the intricate mosaic floor. The monks themselves wore woolen overshoes.

He reached the bed and waited for a moment, leaning on the scythe, until he could get his breath back.

The abbot, who was small and totally bald and had more wrinkles than a sackful of prunes, opened his eyes.

"You're late," he whispered, and died.

Mort swallowed, fought for breath, and brought the scythe around in a slow arc. Nevertheless, it was accurate enough; the abbot sat up, leaving his corpse behind.

"Not a moment too soon," he said, in a voice only Mort could hear. "You had me worried for a moment there."

"Okay?" said Mort. "Only I've got to rush—"

The abbot swung himself off the bed and walked towards Mort through the ranks of his bereaved followers.

"Don't rush off," he said. "I always look forward to these talks. What's happened to the usual fellow?"

"Usual fellow?" said Mort, bewildered.

"Tall chap. Black cloak. Doesn't get enough to eat, by the look of him," said the abbot.

"*Usual* fellow? You mean *Death*?" said Mort.

"That's him," said the abbot, cheerfully. Mort's mouth hung open.

"Die a lot, do you?" he managed.

"A fair bit. A fair bit. Of course," said the abbot, "once you get the hang of it, it's only a matter of practice."

"It is?"

"We must be off," said the abbot. Mort's mouth snapped shut.

"That's what I've been trying to say," he said.

"So if you could just drop me off down in the valley," the little monk continued placidly. He swept past Mort and headed for the courtyard. Mort stared at the floor for a moment, and then ran after him in a way which he knew to be extremely unprofessional and undignified.

"Now look—" he began.

"The other one had a horse called Binky, I remember," said the abbot pleasantly. "Did you buy the round off him?"

"The round?" said Mort, now completely lost.

"Or whatever. Forgive me," said the abbot, "I don't really know how these things are organized, lad."

"Mort," said Mort, absently. "And I think you're supposed to come back with me, sir. If you don't mind," he added, in what he hoped was a firm and authoritative manner. The monk turned and smiled pleasantly at him.

"I wish I could," he said. "Perhaps one day. Now, if you could give me a lift as far as the nearest village, I imagine I'm being conceived about now."

"Conceived? But you've just died!" said Mort.

"Yes, but, you see, I have what you might call a season ticket," the abbot explained.

Light dawned on Mort, but very slowly.

"Oh," he said, "I've read about this. Reincarnation, yes?"

"That's the word. Fifty-three times so far. Or fifty-four."

Binky looked up as they approached and gave a short neigh of recognition when the abbot patted his nose. Mort mounted up and helped the abbot up behind him.

"It must be very interesting," he said, as Binky climbed away from the temple. On the absolute scale of small talk this comment must rate minus quite a lot, but Mort couldn't think of anything better.

"No, it mustn't," said the abbot. "You think it must be because you believe I can remember all my lives, but of course I can't. Not while I'm alive, anyway."

"I hadn't thought of that," Mort conceded.

"Imagine toilet training fifty times."

"Nothing to look back on, I imagine," said Mort.

"You're right. If I had my time all over again I wouldn't reincarnate. And just when I'm getting the hang of things, the lads come down from the temple looking for a boy conceived at the hour the old abbot died. Talk about unimaginative. Stop here a moment, please."

Mort looked down.

"We're in mid-air," he said doubtfully.

"I won't keep you a minute." The abbot slid down from Binky's back, walked a few steps on thin air, and shouted.

It seemed to go on for a long time. Then the abbot climbed back again.

"You don't know how long I've been looking forward to that," he said.

There was a village in a lower valley a few miles from the temple, which acted as a sort of service industry. From the air it was a random scattering of small but extremely well-soundproofed huts.

"Anywhere will do," the abbot said. Mort left him standing a few feet above the snow at a point where the huts appeared to be thickest.

"Hope the next lifetime improves," he said. The abbot shrugged.

"One can always hope," he said. "I get a nine-month break, anyway. The scenery isn't much, but at least it's in the warm."

"Goodbye, then," said Mort. "I've got to rush."

"Au revoir," said the abbot, sadly, and turned away.

The fires of the Hub Lights were still casting their flickering illumination across the landscape. Mort sighed, and reached for the third glass.

The container was silver, decorated with small crowns. There was hardly any sand left.

Mort, feeling that the night had thrown everything at him and couldn't get any worse, turned it around carefully to get a glimpse of the name. . . .

Princess Keli awoke.

There had been a sound like someone making no noise at all. Forget peas and mattresses—sheer natural selection had established over the years that the royal families that survived longest were those whose members could distinguish an assassin in the dark by the noise he was clever enough not

to make, because, in court circles, there was always someone ready to cut the heir with a knife.

She lay in bed, wondering what to do next. There was a
dagger under her pillow. She started to slide one hand up the
sheets, while peering around the room with half-closed eyes
in search of unfamiliar shadows. She was well aware that if
she indicated in any way that she was not asleep she would
never wake up again.

Some light came into the room from the big window at
the far end, but the suits of armor, tapestries and assorted
paraphernalia that littered the room could have provided
cover for an army.

The knife had dropped down behind the bedhead. She
probably wouldn't have used it properly anyway.

Screaming for the guards, she decided, was not a good
idea. If there was anyone in the room then the guards must
have been overpowered, or at least stunned by a large sum of
money.

There was a warming pan on the flagstones by the fire.
Would it make a weapon?

There was a faint metallic sound.

Perhaps screaming wouldn't be such a bad idea after
all. . . .

The window imploded. For an instant Keli saw, framed
against a hell of blue and purple flames, a hooded figure
crouched on the back of the largest horse she had ever seen.

There *was* someone standing by the bed, with a knife half
raised.

In slow motion, she watched fascinated as the arm went
up and the horse galloped at glacier speed across the floor.
Now the knife was above her, starting its descent, and the
horse was rearing and the rider was standing in the stirrups
and swinging some sort of weapon and its blade tore through
the slow air with a noise like a finger on the rim of a wet
glass—

The light vanished. There was a soft thump on the floor, followed by a metallic clatter.

Keli took a deep breath.

A hand was briefly laid across her mouth and a worried voice said, "If you scream, I'll regret it. Please? I'm in enough trouble as it is."

Anyone who could get that amount of bewildered pleading into their voice was either genuine or such a good actor they wouldn't have to bother with assassination for a living. She said, "Who are you?"

"I don't know if I'm allowed to tell you," said the voice. "You are still alive, aren't you?"

She bit down the sarcastic reply just in time. Something about the tone of the question worried her.

"Can't you tell?" she said.

"It's not easy. . . ." There was a pause. She strained to see in the darkness, to put a face around that voice. "I may have done you some terrible harm," it added.

"Haven't you just saved my life?"

"I don't know what I have saved, actually. Is there some light around here?"

"The maid sometimes leaves matches on the mantelpiece," said Keli. She felt the presence beside her move away. There were a few hesitant footsteps, a couple of thumps, and finally a clang, although the word isn't sufficient to describe the real ripe cacophony of falling metal that filled the room. It was even followed by the traditional little tinkle a couple of seconds after you thought it was all over.

The voice said, rather indistinctly, "I'm under a suit of armor. Where should I be?"

Keli slid quietly out of bed, felt her way towards the fireplace, located the bundle of matches by the faint light from the dying fire, struck one in a burst of sulfurous smoke, lit a candle, found the pile of dismembered armor, pulled its sword from its scabbard and then nearly swallowed her tongue.

Someone had just blown hot and wetly in her ear.

"That's Binky," said the heap. "He's just trying to be friendly. I expect he'd like some hay, if you've got any."

With royal self-control, Keli said, "This is the fourth floor. It's a lady's bedroom. You'd be amazed at how many horses we don't get up here."

"Oh. Could you help me up, please?"

She put the sword down and pulled aside a breastplate. A thin white face stared back at her.

"First, you'd better tell me why I shouldn't send for the guards anyway," she said. "Even being in my bedroom could get you tortured to death."

She glared at him.

Finally he said, "Well—could you let my hand free, please? Thank you—firstly, the guards probably wouldn't see me, secondly, you'll never find out why I'm here and you look as though you'd hate not to know, and thirdly. . . ."

"Thirdly what?" she said.

His mouth opened and shut. Mort wanted to say: thirdly, you're so beautiful, or at least very attractive, or anyway far more attractive than any other girl I've ever met, although admittedly I haven't met very many. From this it will be seen that Mort's innate honesty will never make him a poet; if Mort ever compared a girl to a summer's day, it would be followed by a thoughtful explanation of what day he had in mind and whether it was raining at the time. In the circumstances, it was just as well that he couldn't find his voice.

Keli held up the candle and looked at the window.

It was whole. The stone frames were unbroken. Every pane, with its stained-glass representatives of the Sto Lat coat of arms, was complete. She looked back at Mort.

"Never mind thirdly," she said, "let's get back to secondly."

An hour later dawn reached the city. Daylight on the Disc flows rather than rushes, because light is slowed right down by the world's standing magical field, and it rolled across the flat lands like a golden sea. The city on the mound stood out like a sandcastle in the tide for a moment, until the day swirled around it and crept onwards.

Mort and Keli sat side by side on her bed. The hourglass lay between them. There was no sand left in the top bulb.

From outside came the sounds of the castle waking up.

"I still don't understand this," she said. "Does it mean I'm dead, or doesn't it?"

"It means you ought to be dead," he said, "according to fate or whatever. I haven't really studied the theory."

"And you should have killed me?"

"No! I mean, no, the assassin should have killed you. I did try to explain all that," said Mort.

"Why didn't you let him?"

Mort looked at her in horror.

"Did you *want* to die?"

"Of course I didn't. But it looks as though what people want doesn't come into it, does it? I'm trying to be sensible about this."

Mort stared at his knees. Then he stood up.

"I think I'd better be going," he said coldly.

He folded up the scythe and stuck it into its sheath behind the saddle. Then he looked at the window.

"You came through that," said Keli, helpfully. "Look, when I said—"

"Does it open?"

"No. There's a balcony along the passage. But people will see you!"

Mort ignored her, pulled open the door and led Binky out into the corridor. Keli ran after them. A maid stopped, curtsied, and frowned slightly as her brain wisely dismissed the sight of a very large horse walking along the carpet.

The balcony overlooked one of the inner courtyards. Mort glanced over the parapet, and then mounted.

"Watch out for the duke," he said. "He's behind all this."

"My father always warned me about him," said the princess. "I've got a foodtaster."

"You should get a bodyguard as well," said Mort. "I must go. I have important things to do. Farewell," he added, in what he hoped was the right tone of injured pride.

"Shall I see you again?" said Keli. "There's lots I want to—"

"That might not be a good idea, if you think about it," said Mort haughtily. He clicked his tongue, and Binky leapt into the air, cleared the parapet and cantered up into the blue morning sky.

"I wanted to say thank you!" Keli yelled after him.

The maid, who couldn't get over the feeling that something was wrong and had followed her, said, "Are you all right, ma'am?"

Keli looked at her distractedly.

"What?" she demanded.

"I just wondered if—everything was all right?"

Keli's shoulders sagged.

"No," she said. "Everything's all wrong. There's a dead assassin in my bedroom. Could you please have something done about it?

"And—" she held up a hand—"I don't want you to say 'Dead, ma'am?' or 'Assassin, ma'am?' or scream or anything, I just want you to get something done about it. Quietly. I think I've got a headache. So just nod."

The maid nodded, bobbed uncertainly, and backed away.

Mort wasn't sure how he got back. The sky simply changed from ice blue to sullen gray as Binky eased himself into the gap between dimensions. He didn't land on the dark soil of Death's estate, it was simply there, underfoot, as though an aircraft carrier had gently maneuvered itself under a jumpjet to save the pilot all the trouble of touching down.

The great horse trotted into the stableyard and halted outside the double door, swishing his tail. Mort slid off and ran for the house.

And stopped, and ran back, and filled the hayrack, and ran for the house, and stopped and muttered to himself and ran back and rubbed the horse down and checked the water bucket, and ran for the house, and ran back and fetched the horseblanket down from its hook on the wall and buckled it on. Binky gave him a dignified nuzzle.

No one seemed to be about as Mort slipped in by the back door and made his way to the library, where even at this time of night the air seemed to be made of hot dry dust. It seemed to take years to locate Princess Keli's biography, but he found it eventually. It was a depressingly slim volume on a shelf only reachable by the library ladder, a wheeled rickety structure that strongly resembled an early siege engine.

With trembling fingers he opened it at the last page, and groaned.

"The princess's assassination at the age of fifteen," he read, "was followed by the union of Sto Lat with Sto Helit and, indirectly, the collapse of the city states of the central plain and the rise of—"

He read on, unable to stop. Occasionally he groaned again.

Finally he put the book back, hesitated, and then shoved it behind a few other volumes. He could still feel it there as he climbed down the ladder, shrieking its incriminating existence to the world.

There were few ocean-going ships on the Disc. No captain liked to venture out of sight of a coastline. It was a sorry fact that ships which looked from a distance as though they were going over the edge of the world weren't in fact disappearing over the horizon, they were in fact dropping over the edge of the world.

Every generation or so a few enthusiastic explorers doubted this and set out to prove it wrong. Strangely enough, none of them had ever come back to announce the result of their researches.

The following analogy would, therefore, have been meaningless to Mort.

He felt as if he'd been shipwrecked on the *Titanic* but in the nick of time had been rescued. By the *Lusitania*.

He felt as though he'd thrown a snowball on the spur of the moment and watched the ensuing avalanche engulf three ski resorts.

He felt history unraveling all around him.

He felt he needed someone to talk to, quickly.

That had to mean either Albert or Ysabell, because the thought of explaining everything to those tiny blue pinpoints was not one he cared to contemplate after a long night. On the rare occasions Ysabell deigned to look in his direction she made it clear that the only difference between Mort and a dead toad was the color. As for Albert. . . .

All right, not the perfect confidant, but definitely the best in a field of one.

Mort slid down the steps and threaded his way back through the bookshelves. A few hours' sleep would be a good idea, too.

Then he heard a gasp, the brief patter of running feet, and the slam of a door. When he peered around the nearest bookcase there was nothing there except a stool with a couple of books on it. He picked one up and glanced at the name, then read a few pages. There was a damp lace handkerchief lying next to it.

Mort rose late, and hurried towards the kitchen expecting at any moment the deep tones of disapproval. Nothing happened.

Albert was at the stone sink, gazing thoughtfully at his chip pan, probably wondering whether it was time to change the fat or let it bide for another year. He turned as Mort slid into a chair.

"You had a busy time of it, then," he said. "Gallivanting all over the place until all hours, I heard. I could do you an egg. Or there's porridge."

"Egg, please," said Mort. He'd never plucked up the courage to try Albert's porridge, which led a private life of its own in the depths of its saucepan and ate spoons.

"The master wants to see you after," Albert added, "but he said you wasn't to rush."

"Oh." Mort stared at the table. "Did he say anything else?"

"He said he hadn't had an evening off in a thousand years," said Albert. "He was humming. I don't like it. I've never seen him like this."

"Oh." Mort took the plunge. "Albert, have you been here long?"

Albert looked at him over the top of his spectacles.

"Maybe," he said. "It's hard to keep track of outside time, boy. I bin here since just after the old king died."

"Which king, Albert?"

"Artorollo, I think he was called. Little fat man. Squeaky voice. I only saw him the once, though."

"Where was this?"

"In Ankh, of course."

"What?" said Mort. "They don't have kings in Ankh-Morpork, everyone knows that!"

"This was back a bit, I said," said Albert. He poured himself a cup of tea from Death's personal teapot and sat down, a dreamy look in his crusted eyes. Mort waited expectantly.

"And they was kings in those days, real kings, not like the sort you get now. They was *monarchs*," continued Albert, carefully pouring some tea into his saucer and fanning it primly with the end of his muffler. "I mean, they was wise and fair, well, fairly wise. And they wouldn't think twice about cutting your head off soon as look at you," he added approvingly. "And all the queens were tall and pale and wore them balaclava helmet things—"

"Wimples?" said Mort.

"Yeah, them, and the princesses were beautiful as the day is long and so noble they, they could pee through a dozen mattresses—"

"What?"

Albert hesitated. "Something like that, anyway," he conceded. "And there was balls and tournaments and executions. Great days." He smiled dreamily at his memories.

"Not like the sort of days you get now," he said, emerging from his reverie with bad grace.

"Have you got any other names, Albert?" said Mort. But the brief spell had been broken and the old man wasn't going to be drawn.

"Oh, I know," he snapped, "get Albert's name and you'll go and look him up in the library, won't you? Prying and poking. I know you, skulking in there at all hours reading the lives of young wimmen—"

The heralds of guilt must have flourished their tarnished trumpets in the depths of Mort's eyes, because Albert cackled and prodded him with a bony finger.

"You might at least put them back where you find 'em," he said, "not leave piles of 'em around for old Albert to put back. Anyway, it's not right, ogling the poor dead things. It probably turns you blind."

"But I only—" Mort began, and remembered the damp lace handkerchief in his pocket, and shut up.

He left Albert grumbling to himself and doing the washing up, and slipped into the library. Pale sunlight lanced down from the high windows, gently fading the covers on the patient, ancient volumes. Occasionally a speck of dust would catch the light as it floated through the golden shafts, and flare like a miniature supernova.

Mort knew that if he listened hard enough he could hear

the insect-like scritching of the books as they wrote themselves.

Once upon a time Mort would have found it eerie. Now it was—reassuring. It demonstrated that the universe was running smoothly. His conscience, which had been looking for the opening, gleefully reminded him that, all right, it might be running smoothly but it certainly wasn't heading in the right direction.

He made his way through the maze of shelves to the mysterious pile of books, and found it was gone. Albert had been in the kitchen, and Mort had never seen Death himself enter the library. What was Ysabell looking for, then?

He glanced up at the cliff of shelves above him, and his stomach went cold when he thought of what was starting to happen. . . .

There was nothing for it. He'd have to tell someone.

Keli, meanwhile, was also finding life difficult.

This was because causality had an incredible amount of inertia. Mort's misplaced thrust, driven by anger and desperation and nascent love, had sent it down a new track but it hadn't noticed yet. He'd kicked the tail of the dinosaur, but it would be some time before the other end realized it was time to say "ouch."

Bluntly, the universe knew Keli was dead and was therefore rather surprised to find that she hadn't stopped walking and breathing yet.

It showed it in little ways. The courtiers who gave her furtive odd looks during the morning would not have been able to say why the sight of her made them feel strangely uncomfortable. To their acute embarrassment and her annoyance they found themselves ignoring her, or talking in hushed voices.

The Chamberlain found he'd instructed that the royal standard be flown at half mast and for the life of him couldn't explain why. He was gently led off to his bed with a mild nervous affliction after ordering a thousand yards of black bunting for no apparent reason.

The eerie, unreal feeling soon spread throughout the castle. The head coachman ordered the state bier to be brought out again and polished, and then stood in the stable yard and wept into his chamois leather because he couldn't remember why. Servants walked softly along the corridors. The cook had to fight an overpowering urge to prepare simple banquets of cold meat. Dogs howled and then stopped, feeling rather stupid. The two black stallions who traditionally pulled the Sto Lat funeral cortege grew restive in their stalls and nearly kicked a groom to death.

In his castle in Sto Helit, the duke waited in vain for a messenger who had in fact set out, but had stopped halfway down the street, unable to remember what it was he was supposed to be doing.

Through all this Keli moved like a solid and increasingly more irritated ghost.

Things came to a head at lunchtime. She swept into the great hall and found no place had been set in front of the royal chair. By speaking loudly and distinctly to the butler she managed to get that rectified, then saw dishes being passed in front of her before she could get a fork into them. She watched in sullen disbelief as the wine was brought in and poured first for the Lord of the Privy Closet.

It was an unregal thing to do, but she stuck out a foot and tripped the wine waiter. He stumbled, muttered something under his breath, and stared down at the flagstones.

She leaned the other way and shouted into the ear of the Yeoman of the Pantry: "Can you see me, man? Why are we reduced to eating cold pork and ham?"

He turned aside from his hushed conversation with the Lady of the Small Hexagonal Room in the North Turret, gave her a long look in which shock made way for a sort of unfocused puzzlement, and said, "Why, yes . . . I can . . . er. . . ."

"Your Royal Highness," prompted Keli.

"But . . . yes . . . Highness," he muttered. There was a heavy pause.

Then, as if switched back on, he turned his back on her and resumed his conversation.

Keli sat for a while, white with shock and anger, then pushed the chair back and stormed away to her chambers. A couple of servants sharing a quick rollup in the passage outside were knocked sideways by something they couldn't quite see.

Keli ran into her room and hauled on the rope that should have sent the duty maid running in from the sitting room at the end of the corridor. Nothing happened for some time, and then the door was pushed open slowly and a face peered in at her.

She recognized the look this time, and was ready for it. She grabbed the maid by the shoulders and hauled her bodily into the room, slamming the door shut behind her. As the frightened woman stared everywhere but at Keli she hauled off and fetched her a stinging slap across the cheek.

"Did you feel that? Did you feel it?" she shrieked.

"But . . . you . . ." the maid whimpered, staggering backwards until she hit the bed and sitting down heavily on it.

"Look at me! Look at me when I talk to you!" yelled Keli, advancing on her. "You can see me, can't you? Tell me you can see me or I'll have you executed!"

The maid stared into her terrified eyes.

"I can see you," she said, "but. . . ."

"But what? But what?"

"Surely you're . . . I heard . . . I thought. . . ."

"What did you think?" snapped Keli. She wasn't shouting any more. Her words came out like white-hot whips.

The maid collapsed into a sobbing heap. Keli stood tapping her foot for a moment, and then shook the woman gently.

"Is there a wizard in the city?" she said. "Look at me, *at me*. There's a wizard, isn't there? You girls are always skulking off to talk to wizards! Where does he live?"

The woman turned a tear-stained face towards her, fighting against every instinct that told her the princess didn't exist.

"Uh . . . wizard, yes . . . Cutwell, in Wall Street. . . ."

Keli's lips compressed into a thin smile. She wondered where her cloaks were kept, but cold reason told her it was going to be a damn sight easier to find them herself than try to make her presence felt to the maid. She waited, watching closely, as the woman stopped sobbing, looked around her in vague bewilderment, and hurried out of the room.

She's forgotten me already, she thought. She looked at her hands. She seemed solid enough.

It had to be magic.

She wandered into her robing room and experimentally opened a few cupboards until she found a black cloak and hood. She slipped them on and darted out into the corridor and down the servants' stairs.

She hadn't been this way since she was little. This was the world of linen cupboards, bare floors and dumb-waiters. It smelled of slightly stale crusts.

Keli moved through it like an earthbound spook. She was aware of the servants' quarters, of course, in the same way that people are aware at some level in their minds of the drains or the guttering, and she would be quite prepared to concede that although servants all looked pretty much alike they must have some distinguishing features by which their nearest and dearest could, presumably, identify them. But she was not prepared for sights like Moghedron the wine butler, whom she had hitherto seen only as a stately presence, moving like a galleon under full sail, sitting in his pantry with his jacket undone and smoking a pipe.

A couple of maids ran past her without a second glance, giggling. She hurried on, aware that in some strange way she was trespassing in her own castle.

And that, she realized, was because it wasn't her castle at

all. The noisy world around her, with its steaming laundries and chilly stillrooms, was its own world. She couldn't own it. Possibly it owned her.

She took a chicken leg from the table in the biggest kitchen, a cavern lined with so many pots that by the light of its fires it looked like an armory for tortoises, and felt the unfamiliar thrill of theft. Theft! In her own kingdom! And the cook looked straight through her, eyes as glazed as jugged ham.

Keli ran across the stable yards and out of the back gate, past a couple of sentries whose stern gaze quite failed to notice her.

Out in the streets it wasn't so creepy, but she still felt oddly naked. It was unnerving, being among people who were going about their own affairs and not bothering to look at one, when one's entire experience of the world hitherto was that it revolved around one. Pedestrians bumped into one and rebounded away, wondering briefly what it was they had hit, and one several times had to scurry away out of the path of wagons.

The chicken leg hadn't gone far to fill the hole left by the absence of lunch, and she filched a couple of apples from a stall, making a mental note to have the chamberlain find out how much apples cost and send some money down to the stallholder.

Disheveled, rather grubby and smelling slightly of horse dung, she came at last to Cutwell's door. The knocker gave her some trouble. In her experience doors opened for you; there were special people to arrange it.

She was so distraught she didn't even notice that the knocker winked at her.

She tried again, and thought she heard a distant crash. After some time the door opened a few inches and she caught a glimpse of a round flustered face topped with curly hair. Her right foot surprised her by intelligently inserting itself in the crack.

"I demand to see the wizard," she announced. "Pray admit me this instant."

"He's rather busy at present," said the face. "Were you after a love potion?"

"A what?"

"I've—we've got a special on Cutwell's Shield of Passion ointment," said the face, and winked in a startling fashion. "Provides your wild oats while guaranteeing a crop failure, if you know what I mean."

Keli bridled. "No," she lied coldly, "I do not."

"Ramrub? Maidens' Longstop? Belladonna eyedrops?"

"I demand—"

"Sorry, we're closed," said the face, and shut the door. Keli withdrew her foot just in time.

She muttered some words that would have amazed and shocked her tutors, and thumped on the woodwork.

The tattoo of her hammering suddenly slowed as realization dawned.

He'd seen her! He'd heard her!

She beat on the door with renewed vigor, yelling with all the power in her lungs.

A voice by her ear said, "It won't work. He 'eef very fstubborn."

She looked around slowly and met the impertinent gaze of the doorknocker. It waggled its metal eyebrows at her and spoke indistinctly through its wrought-iron ring.

"I am Princess Keli, heir to the throne of Sto Lat," she said haughtily, holding down the lid on her terror. "And I don't talk to door furniture."

"Fwell, *I'm* just a doorknocker and I can talk to fwhoever I please," said the gargoyle pleasantly. "And I can ftell you the fmaster iff having a trying day and duff fnot fwant to be disturbed. But you could ftry to use the magic word," it added. "Coming from an attractiff fwoman it works nine times out of eight."

"Magic word? What's the magic word?"

The knocker perceptibly sneered. "Haff you been taught nothing, miss?"

She drew herself up to her full height, which wasn't really worth the effort. She felt she'd had a trying day too. Her father had personally executed a hundred enemies in battle. She should be able to manage a doorknocker.

"I have been *educated*," she informed it with icy precision, "by some of the finest scholars in the land."

The doorknocker did not appear to be impressed.

"Iff they didn't teach you the magic word," it said calmly, "they couldn't haff fbeen all that fine."

Keli reached out, grabbed the heavy ring, and pounded it on the door. The knocker leered at her.

"Ftreat me rough," it lisped. "That'f the way I like it!"

"You're disgusting!"

"Yeff. Ooo, that waff nife, do it again. . . ."

The door opened a crack. There was a shadowy glimpse of curly hair.

"Madam, I said we're cl—"

Keli sagged.

"*Please* help me," she said. "Please!"

"See?" said the doorknocker triumphantly. "Sooner or later *everyone* remembers the magic word!"

Keli had been to official functions in Ankh-Morpork and had met senior wizards from Unseen University, the Disc's premier college of magic. Some of them had been tall, and most of them had been fat, and nearly all of them had been richly dressed, or at least thought they were richly dressed.

In fact there are fashions in wizardry as in more mundane arts, and this tendency to look like elderly aldermen was only temporary. Previous generations had gone in for looking pale and interesting, or druidical and grubby, or mysterious and saturnine. But Keli was used to wizards as a sort of fur-trimmed small mountain with a wheezy voice, and Igneous Cutwell didn't quite fit the mage image.

He was young. Well, that couldn't be helped; presumably even wizards had to start off young. He didn't have a beard, and the only thing his rather grubby robe was trimmed with was frayed edges.

"Would you like a drink or something?" he said, surreptitiously kicking a discarded vest under the table.

Keli looked around for somewhere to sit that wasn't occupied with laundry or used crockery, and shook her head. Cutwell noticed her expression.

"It's a bit alfresco, I'm afraid," he added hurriedly, elbowing the remains of a garlic sausage on to the floor. "Mrs. Nugent usually comes in twice a week and does for me but she's gone to see her sister who's had one of her turns. Are you sure? It's no trouble. I saw a spare cup here only yesterday."

"I have a problem, Mr. Cutwell," said Keli.

"Hang on a moment." He reached up to a hook over the fireplace and took down a pointy hat that had seen better days, although from the look of it they hadn't been *very* much better, and then said, "Right. Fire away."

"What's so important about the hat?"

"Oh, it's very essential. You've got to have the proper hat for wizarding. We wizards know about this sort of thing."

"If you say so. Look, can you see me?"

He peered at her. "Yes. Yes, I would definitely say I can see you."

"And hear me? You can hear me, can you?"

"Loud and clear. Yes. Every syllable tinkling into place. No problems."

"Then would you be surprised if I told you that no one else in this city can?"

"Except me?"

Keli snorted. "And your doorknocker."

Cutwell pulled out a chair and sat down. He squirmed a little. A thoughtful expression passed over his face. He stood up, reached behind him and produced a flat reddish mass which might have once been half a pizza*. He stared at it sorrowfully.

"I've been looking for that all morning, would you believe?" he said. "It was an All-On with extra peppers, too." He picked sadly at the squashed shape, and suddenly remembered Keli.

"Gosh, sorry," he said, "where's my manners? Whatever will you think of me? Here. Have an anchovy. Please."

"Have you been listening to me?" snapped Keli.

"Do you feel invisible? In yourself, I mean?" said Cutwell, indistinctly.

"Of course not. I just feel angry. So I want you to tell my fortune."

"Well, I don't know about that, it all sounds rather *medical* to me and—"

"I can pay."

"It's illegal, you see," said Cutwell wretchedly. "The old king expressly forbade fortune telling in Sto Lat. He didn't like wizards much."

"I can pay a *lot*."

"Mrs. Nugent was telling me this new girl is likely to be worse. A right haughty one, she said. Not the sort to look kindly on practitioners of the subtle arts, I fear."

Keli smiled. Members of the court who had seen that smile before would have hastened to drag Cutwell out of the

---

*The first pizza was created on the Disc by the Klatchian mystic Ronron "Revelation Joe" Shuwadhi, who claimed to have been given the recipe in a dream by the Creator of the Discworld Himself, Who had apparently added that it was what He had intended all along. Those desert travelers who had seen the original, which is reputedly miraculously preserved in the Forbidden City of Ee, say that what the Creator had in mind then was a fairly small cheese and pepperoni affair with a few black olives** and things like mountains and seas got added out of last-minute enthusiasm as so often happens.

**After the Schism of the Turnwise Ones and the deaths of some 25,000 people in the ensuing jihad the faithful were allowed to add one small bayleaf to the recipe.

way and into a place of safety, like the next continent, but he just sat there trying to pick bits of mushroom out of his robe.

"I understand she's got a foul temper on her," said Keli. "I wouldn't be surprised if she didn't turn you out of the city anyway."

"Oh dear," said Cutwell, "do you really think so?"

"Look," said Keli, "you don't have to tell my future, just my present. Even she couldn't object to that. I'll have a word with her if you like," she added magnanimously.

Cutwell brightened. "Oh, do you know her?" he said.

"Yes. But sometimes, I think, not very well."

Cutwell sighed and burrowed around in the debris on the table, dislodging cascades of elderly plates and the long-mummified remains of several meals. Eventually he unearthed a fat leather wallet, stuck to a cheese slice.

"Well," he said doubtfully, "these are Caroc cards. Distilled wisdom of the Ancients and all that. Or there's the Ching Aling of the Hublandish. It's all the rage in the smart set. I don't do tealeaves."

"I'll try the Ching thing."

"You throw these yarrow stalks in the air, then."

She did. They looked at the ensuing pattern.

"Hmm," said Cutwell after a while. "Well, that's one in the fireplace, one in the cocoa mug, one in the street, shame about the window, one on the table, and one, no, *two* behind the dresser. I expect Mrs. Nugent will be able to find the rest."

"You didn't say how hard. Shall I do it again?"

"No-ooo, I don't think so." Cutwell thumbed through the pages of a yellowed book that had previously been supporting the table leg. "The pattern seems to make sense. Yes, here we are, Octogram 8,887: Illegality, the Unatoning Goose. Which we cross reference here . . . hold on . . . hold on . . . yes. Got it."

"Well?"

*"Without verticality, wisely the cochineal emperor goes forth at teatime; at evening the mollusc is silent among the almond blossom."*

"Yes?" said Keli, respectfully. "What does that mean?"

"Unless you're a mollusc, probably not a lot," said Cutwell. "I think perhaps it lost something in translation."

"Are you sure you know how to do this?"

"Let's try the cards," said Cutwell hurriedly, fanning them out. "Pick a card. Any card."

"It's Death," said Keli.

"Ah. Well. Of course, the Death card doesn't actually mean *death* in all circumstances," Cutwell said quickly.

"You mean, it doesn't mean death in those circumstances where the subject is getting over-excited and you're too embarrassed to tell the truth, hmm?"

"Look, take another card."

"This one's Death as well," said Keli.

"Did you put the other one back?"

"No. Shall I take another card?"

"May as well."

"Well, there's a coincidence!"

"Death number three?"

"Right. Is this a special pack for conjuring tricks?" Keli tried to sound composed, but even she could detect the faint tinkle of hysteria in her voice.

Cutwell frowned at her and carefully put the cards back in the pack, shuffled it, and dealt them out on to the table. There was only one Death.

"Oh dear," he said, "I think this is going to be serious. May I see the palm of your hand, please?"

He examined it for a long time. Alter a while he went to the dresser, took a jeweler's eyeglass out of a drawer, wiped the porridge off it with the sleeve of his robe, and spent another few minutes examining her hand in minutest detail. Eventually he sat back, removed the glass, and stared at her.

"You're dead," he said.

Keli waited. She couldn't think of any suitable reply. "I'm not" lacked a certain style, while "Is it serious?" seemed somehow too frivolous.

"Did I say I thought this was going to be serious?" said Cutwell.

"I think you did," said Keli carefully, keeping her tone totally level.

"I was right."

"Oh."

"It could be fatal."

"How much more fatal," said Keli, "than being dead?"

"I didn't mean for you."

"Oh."

"Something very fundamental seems to have gone wrong, you see. You're dead in every sense but the, er, actual. I mean, the cards think you're dead. Your lifeline thinks you're dead. Everything and everyone thinks you're dead."

"*I* don't," said Keli, but her voice was less than confident.

"I'm afraid your opinion doesn't count."

"But people can see and hear me!"

"The first thing you learn when you enroll at Unseen University, I'm afraid, is that people don't pay much attention to that sort of thing. It's what their minds tell them that's important."

"You mean people don't see me because their minds tell them not to?"

" 'Fraid so. It's called predestination, or something." Cutwell looked at her wretchedly. "I'm a wizard. We know about these things.

"Actually it's not the *first* thing you learn when you enroll," he added, "I mean, you learn where the lavatories are and all that sort of thing before that. But after all that, it's the first thing."

"You can see me, though."

"Ah. Well. Wizards are specially trained to see things that are there and not to see things that aren't. You get these special exercises—"

Keli drummed her fingers on the table, or tried to. It turned out to be difficult. She stared down in vague horror.

Cutwell hurried forward and wiped the table with his sleeve.

"Sorry," he muttered, "I had treacle sandwiches for supper last night."

"What can I do?"

"Nothing."

*"Nothing?"*

"Well, you could certainly become a very successful burglar . . . sorry. That was tasteless of me."

"*I* thought so."

Cutwell patted her ineptly on the hand, and Keli was too preoccupied even to notice such flagrant *lèse majesté*.

"You see, everything's fixed. History is all worked out, from start to finish. What the facts actually are is beside the point; history just rolls straight over the top of them. You can't change anything because the changes are already part of it. You're dead. It's fated. You'll just have to accept it."

He gave an apologetic grin. "You're a lot luckier than most dead people, if you look at it objectively," he said. "You're alive to enjoy it."

"I don't want to accept it. Why should I accept it? It's not my fault!"

"You don't understand. History is moving on. You can't get involved in it any more. There isn't a part in it for you, don't you see? Best to let things take their course." He patted her hand again. She looked at him. He withdrew his hand.

"What am I supposed to do then?" she said. "Not eat, because the food wasn't destined to be eaten by me? Go and live in a crypt somewhere?"

"Bit of a poser, isn't it?" agreed Cutwell. "That's fate for you, I'm afraid. If the world can't sense you, you don't exist. I'm a wizard. We know—"

"Don't say it."

Keli stood up.

Five generations ago one of her ancestors had halted his

band of nomadic cutthroats a few miles from the mound of
Sto Lat and had regarded the sleeping city with a peculiarly
determined expression that said: This'll do. Just because
you're born in the saddle doesn't mean you have to die in the
bloody thing.

Strangely enough, many of his distinctive features had, by
a trick of heredity, been bequeathed to his descendant*,
accounting for her rather idiosyncratic attractiveness. They
were never more apparent than now. Even Cutwell was
impressed. When it came to determination, you could have
cracked rocks on her jaw.

In exactly the same tone of voice that her ancestor had
used when he addressed his weary, sweaty followers before
the attack†, she said:

"No. No, I'm not going to accept it. I'm not going to dwin-
dle into some sort of ghost. You're going to help me, wizard."

Cutwell's subconscious recognized that tone. It had har-
monics in it that made even the woodworms in the floor-
boards stop what they were doing and stand to attention. It
wasn't voicing an opinion, it was saying: things will be thus.

-------

*Although not the droopy moustache and round furry hat with the spike on it.

†The speech has been passed on to later generations in an epic poem com-
missioned by his son, who wasn't born in a saddle and could eat with a
knife and fork. It began:

> "See yonder the stolid foemen slumber
> Fat with stolen gold, corrupt of mind.
> Let the spears of your wrath be as the steppe fire on a
> windy day in the dry season,
> Let your honest blade thrust like the horns of
> a five-year old yok with severe toothache. . . ."

And went on for three hours. Reality, which can't usually afford to pay
poets, records that in fact the entire speech ran:

"Lads, most of them are still in bed, we should go through them like kzak
fruit through a short grandmother, and I for one have had it right up to here
with yurts, okay?"

"Me, madam?" he quavered, "I don't see what I can possibly—"

He was jerked off his chair and out into the street, his robes billowing around him. Keli marched towards the palace with her shoulders set determinedly, dragging the wizard behind her like a reluctant puppy. It was with such a walk that mothers used to bear down on the local school when their little boy came home with a black eye; it was unstoppable; it was like the March of Time.

"What is it you intend?" Cutwell stuttered, horribly aware that there was going to be nothing he could do to resist, whatever it was.

"It's your lucky day, wizard."

"Oh. Good," he said weakly.

"You've just been appointed Royal Recognizer."

"Oh. What does that entail, exactly?"

"You're going to remind everyone I'm alive. It's very simple. There's three square meals a day and your laundry done. Step lively, man."

"Royal?"

"You're a wizard. I think there's something you ought to know," said the princess.

THERE IS? said Death.

(That was a cinematic trick adapted for print. Death wasn't talking to the princess. He was actually in his study, talking to Mort. But it was quite effective, wasn't it? It's probably called a fast dissolve, or a crosscut/zoom. Or something. An industry where a senior technician is called a Best Boy might call it anything.)

AND WHAT IS THAT? he added, winding a bit of black silk around the wicked hook in a little vice he'd clamped to his desk.

Mort hesitated. Mostly this was because of fear and embarrassment, but it was also because the sight of a hooded specter peacefully tying dry flies was enough to make anyone pause.

Besides, Ysabell was sitting on the other side of the room, ostensibly doing some needlework but also watching him through a cloud of sullen disapproval. He could feel her red-rimmed eyes boring into the back of his neck.

Death inserted a few crow hackles and whistled a busy little tune through his teeth, not having anything else to whistle through. He looked up.

HMM?

"They—didn't go as smoothly as I thought," said Mort, standing nervously on the carpet in front of the desk.

YOU HAD TROUBLE? said Death, snipping off a few scraps of feather.

"Well, you see, the witch wouldn't come away, and the monk, well, he started out all over again."

THERE'S NOTHING TO WORRY ABOUT THERE, LAD—

"—Mort—"

—YOU SHOULD HAVE WORKED OUT BY NOW THAT EVERYONE GETS WHAT THEY THINK IS COMING TO THEM. IT'S SO MUCH NEATER THAT WAY.

"I know, sir. But that means bad people who think they're going to some sort of paradise actually do get there. And good people who fear they're going to some kind of horrible place really suffer. It doesn't seem like justice."

WHAT IS IT I'VE SAID YOU MUST REMEMBER, WHEN YOU'RE OUT ON THE DUTY?

"Well, you—"

HMM?

Mort stuttered into silence.

THERE'S NO JUSTICE. THERE'S JUST YOU.

"Well, I—"

YOU MUST REMEMBER THAT.

"Yes, but—"

I EXPECT IT ALL WORKS OUT PROPERLY IN THE END. I HAVE

NEVER MET THE CREATOR, BUT I'M TOLD HE'S QUITE KINDLY
DISPOSED TO PEOPLE. Death snapped the thread and started to
unwind the vice.

PUT SUCH THOUGHTS OUT OF YOUR MIND, he added. AT
LEAST THE THIRD ONE SHOULDN'T HAVE GIVEN YOU ANY TROU-
BLE.

This was the moment. Mort had thought about it for a
long time. There was no sense in concealing it. He'd upset
the whole future course of history. Such things tend to draw
themselves to people's attention. Best to get it off his chest.
Own up like a man. Take his medicine. Cards on table. Beat-
ing about bush, none of. Mercy, throw himself on.

The piercing blue eyes glittered at him.

He looked back like a nocturnal rabbit trying to outstare
the headlights of a sixteen-wheeled artic whose driver is a
twelve-hour caffeine freak outrunning the tachometers of
hell.

He failed.

"No, sir," he said.

GOOD. WELL DONE. NOW THEN, WHAT DO YOU THINK OF
THIS?

Anglers reckon that a good dry fly should cunningly
mimic the real thing. There are the right flies for morning.
There are different flies for the evening rise. And so on.

But the thing between Death's triumphant digits was a fly
from the dawn of time. It was the fly in the primordial soup.
It had bred on mammoth turds. It wasn't a fly that bangs on
window panes, it was a fly that drills through walls. It was an
insect that would crawl out from between the slats of the
heaviest swat dripping venom and seeking revenge. Strange
wings and dangling bits stuck out all over it. It seemed to
have a lot of teeth.

"What's it called?" said Mort.

I SHALL CALL IT—DEATH'S GLORY. Death gave the thing a
final admiring glance and stuck it into the hood of his robe. I
FEEL INCLINED TO SEE A LITTLE BIT OF LIFE THIS EVENING, he

said. YOU CAN TAKE THE DUTY, NOW THAT YOU'VE GOT THE
HANG OF IT. AS IT WERE.

"Yes. Sir," said Mort, mournfully. He saw his life stretching out in front of him like a nasty black tunnel with no light
at the end of it.

Death drummed his finger on the desk, muttered to himself.

AH YES, he said. ALBERT TELLS ME SOMEONE'S BEEN MED-
DLING IN THE LIBRARY.

"Pardon, sir?"

TAKING BOOKS OUT, LEAVING THEM LYING AROUND. BOOKS
ABOUT YOUNG WOMEN. HE SEEMS TO THINK IT IS AMUSING.

As has already been revealed, the Holy Listeners have
such well developed hearing that they can be deafened by a
good sunset. Just for a few seconds it seemed to Mort that
the skin on the back of his neck was developing similar
strange powers, because he could see Ysabell freeze in mid-
stitch. He also heard the little intake of breath that he'd
heard before, among the shelves. He remembered the lace
handkerchief.

He said, "Yes, sir. It won't happen again, sir."

The skin on the back of his neck started to itch like fury.

SPLENDID. NOW, YOU TWO CAN RUN ALONG. GET ALBERT TO
DO YOU A PICNIC LUNCH OR SOMETHING. GET SOME FRESH AIR.
I'VE NOTICED THE WAY YOU TWO ALWAYS AVOID EACH OTHER.
He gave Mort a conspiratorial nudge—it was like being
poked with a stick—and added, ALBERT'S TOLD ME WHAT
THAT MEANS.

"Has he?" said Mort gloomily. He'd been wrong, there
*was* a light at the end of the tunnel, and it was a flamethrower.

Death gave him another of his supernova winks.

Mort didn't return it. Instead he turned and plodded
towards the door, at a general speed and gait that made Great
A'Tuin look like a spring lamb.

He was halfway along the corridor before he heard the
soft rush of footsteps behind him and a hand caught his arm.

"Mort?"

He turned and gazed at Ysabell through a fog of depression.

"Why did you let him think it was you in the library?"

"Don't know."

"It was . . . very . . . kind of you," she said cautiously.

"Was it? I can't think what came over me." He felt in his pocket and produced the handkerchief. "This belongs to you, I think."

"Thank you." She blew her nose noisily.

Mort was already well down the corridor, his shoulders hunched like vulture's wings. She ran after him.

"I say," she said.

"What?"

"I wanted to say thank you."

"It doesn't matter," he muttered. "It'd just be best if you don't take books away again. It upsets them, or something." He gave what he considered to be a mirthless laugh. "Ha!"

"Ha what?"

"Just ha!"

He'd reached the end of the corridor. There was the door into the kitchen, where Albert would be leering knowingly, and Mort decided he couldn't face that. He stopped.

"But I only took the books for a bit of company," she said behind him.

He gave in.

"We could have a walk in the garden," he said in despair, and then managed to harden his heart a little and added, "Without obligation, that is."

"You mean you're not going to marry me?" she said. Mort was horrified. "Marry?"

"Isn't that what father brought you here for?" she said. "He doesn't need an apprentice, after all."

"You mean all those nudges and winks and little comments about some day my son all this will be yours?" said Mort. "I tried to ignore them. I don't want to get married to anyone yet," he added, suppressing a fleeting mental picture of the princess. "And certainly not to you, no offense meant."

"I wouldn't marry you if you were the last man on the Disc," she said sweetly.

Mort was hurt by this. It was one thing not to want to marry someone, but quite another to be told they didn't want to marry *you*.

"At least I don't look like I've been eating doughnuts in a wardrobe for years," he said, as they stepped out on to Death's black lawn.

"At least I walk as if my legs only had one knee each," she said.

"My eyes aren't two juugly poached eggs."

Ysabell nodded. "On the other hand, *my* ears don't look like something growing on a dead tree. What does juugly mean?"

"You know, eggs like Albert does them."

"With the white all sticky and runny and full of slimy bits?"

"Yes."

"A good word," she conceded thoughtfully. "But *my* hair, I put it to you, doesn't look like something you clean a privy with."

"Certainly, but neither does mine look like a wet hedgehog."

"Pray note that my chest does not appear to be a toast rack in a wet paper bag."

Mort glanced sideways at the top of Ysabell's dress, which contained enough puppy fat for two litters of Rottweilers, and forbore to comment.

"*My* eyebrows don't look like a pair of mating caterpillars," he hazarded.

"True. But *my* legs, I suggest, could at least stop a pig in a passageway."

"Sorry—?"

"They're not bandy," she explained.

"Ah."

They strolled through the lily beds, temporarily lost for words. Eventually Ysabell confronted Mort and stuck out her hand. He shook it in thankful silence.

"Enough?" she said.

"Just about."

"Good. Obviously we shouldn't get married, if only for the sake of the children."

Mort nodded.

They sat down on a stone seat between some neatly clipped box hedges. Death had made a pond in this corner of the garden, fed by an icy spring that appeared to be vomited into the pool by a stone lion. Fat white carp lurked in the depths, or nosed on the surface among the velvety black water lilies.

"We should have brought some breadcrumbs," said Mort gallantly, opting for a totally noncontroversial subject.

"He never comes out here, you know," said Ysabell, watching the fish. "He made it to keep me amused."

"It didn't work?"

"It's not real," she said. "Nothing's real here. Not really real. He just likes to act like a human being. He's trying really hard at the moment, have you noticed. I think you're having an effect on him. Did you know he tried to learn the banjo once?"

"I see him as more the organ type."

"He couldn't get the hang of it," said Ysabell, ignoring him. "He can't create, you see."

"You said he created this pool."

"It's a copy of one he saw somewhere. Everything's a copy."

Mort shifted uneasily. Some small insect had crawled up his leg.

"It's rather sad," he said, hoping that this was approximately the right tone to adopt.

"Yes."

She scooped a handful of gravel from the path and began to flick it absent-mindedly into the pool.

"Are my eyebrows that bad?" she said.

"Um," said Mort, "afraid so."

"Oh." Flick, flick. The carp were watching her disdainfully.

"And my legs?" he said.

"Yes. Sorry."

Mort shuffled anxiously through his limited repertoire of small talk, and gave up.

"Never mind," he said gallantly. "At least you can use tweezers."

"He's very kind," said Ysabell, ignoring him, "in a sort of absent-minded way."

"He's not exactly your real father, is he?"

"My parents were killed crossing the Great Nef years ago. There was a storm, I think. He found me and brought me here. I don't know why he did it."

"Perhaps he felt sorry for you?"

"He never feels anything. I don't mean that nastily, you understand. It's just that he's got nothing to feel with, no whatd'youcallits, no glands. He probably *thought* sorry for me."

She turned her pale round face towards Mort.

"I won't hear a word against him. He tries to do his best. It's just that he's always got so much to think about."

"My father was a bit like that. Is, I mean."

"I expect he's got glands, though."

"I imagine he has," said Mort, shifting uneasily. "It's not something I've ever really thought about, glands."

They stared side by side at the trout. The trout stared back.

"I've just upset the entire history of the future," said Mort.

"Yes?"

"You see, when he tried to kill her I killed him, but the thing is, according to the history she should have died and the duke would be king, but the *worst* bit, the worst bit is that although he's absolutely rotten to the core he'd unite the cities and eventually they'll be a federation and the books say there'll be a hundred years of peace and plenty. I mean, you'd think there'd be a reign of terror or something, but apparently history needs this kind of person sometimes and the princess would just be another monarch. I mean, not *bad*, quite good really, but just not right and now it's not going to happen and history is flapping around loose and it's all my fault."

He subsided, anxiously awaiting her reply.

"You were right, you know."

"I was?"

"We ought to have brought some breadcrumbs," she said. "I suppose they find things to eat in the water. Beetles and so on."

"Did you hear what I said?"

"What about?"

"Oh. Nothing. Nothing much, really. Sorry."

Ysabell sighed and stood up.

"I expect you'll be wanting to get off," she said. "I'm glad we got this marriage business sorted out. It was quite nice talking to you."

"We could have a sort of hate-hate relationship," said Mort.

"I don't normally get to talk with the people father works with." She appeared to be unable to draw herself away, as though she was waiting for Mort to say something else.

"Well, you wouldn't," was all he could think of.

"I expect you've got to go off to work now."

"More or less." Mort hesitated, aware that in some inde-finable way the conversation had drifted out of the shallows and was now floating over some deep bits he didn't quite understand.

There was a noise like—

It made Mort recall the old yard at home, with a pang of homesickness. During the harsh Ramtop winters the family kept hardy mountain *tharga* beasts in the yard, chucking in straw as necessary. After the spring thaw the yard was several feet deep and had quite a solid crust on it. You could walk across it if you were careful. If you weren't, and sank knee deep in the concentrated gyppo, then the sound your boot made as it came out, green and steaming, was as much the sound of the turning year as birdsong and beebuzz.

It was that noise. Mort instinctively examined his shoes.

Ysabell was crying, not in little ladylike sobs, but in great yawning gulps, like bubbles from an underwater volcano, fighting one another to be the first to the surface. They were sobs escaping under pressure, matured in humdrum misery.

Mort said, "Er?"

Her body was shaking like a waterbed in an earthquake zone. She fumbled urgently in her sleeves for the handkerchief, but it was no more use in the circumstances than a paper hat in a thunderstorm. She tried to say something, which became a stream of consonants punctuated by sobs.

Mort said, "Um?"

"I said, how old do you think I am?"

"Fifteen?" he hazarded.

"I'm sixteen," she wailed. "And do you know how long I've been sixteen *for*?"

"I'm sorry, I don't under—"

"No, you wouldn't. No one would." She blew her nose again, and despite her shaking hands nevertheless carefully tucked the rather damp hanky back up her sleeve.

"*You're* allowed out," she said. "You haven't been here long enough to notice. Time stands still here, haven't you noticed? Oh, something passes, but it's not real time. He can't create real time."

"Oh."

When she spoke again it was in the thin, careful and above all *brave* voice of someone who has pulled themselves together despite overwhelming odds but might let go again at any moment.

"I've been sixteen for thirty-five years."

"Oh?"

"It was bad enough the first year."

Mort looked back at his last few weeks, and nodded in sympathy.

"Is that why you've been reading all those books?" he said.

Ysabell looked down, and twiddled a sandaled toe in the gravel in an embarrassed fashion.

"They're very romantic," she said. "There's some really lovely stories. There was this girl who drank poison when her young man had died, and there was one who jumped off a cliff because her father insisted she should marry this old man, and another one drowned herself rather than submit to—"

Mort listened in astonishment. To judge by Ysabell's careful choice of reading matter, it was a matter of note for any Disc female to survive adolescence long enough to wear out a pair of stockings.

"—and then she thought he was dead, and she killed herself and then he woke up and so he did kill himself, and then there was this girl—"

Common sense suggested that at least a few women reached their third decade without killing themselves for love, but common sense didn't seem to get even a walk-on part in these dramas.\* Mort was already aware that love made you feel hot and cold and cruel and weak, but he hadn't realized that it could make you stupid.

"—swam the river every night, but one night there was this storm, and when he didn't arrive she—"

---

\*The Disc's greatest lovers were undoubtedly Mellius and Gretelina, whose pure, passionate and soul-searing affair would have scorched the pages of History if they had not, because of some unexplained quirk of fate, been born two hundred years apart on different continents. However, the gods took pity on them and turned him into an ironing board\*\* and her into a small brass bollard.

\*\*When you're a god, you don't have to have reasons.

Mort felt instinctively that some young couples met, say, at a village dance, and hit it off, and went out together for a year or two, had a few rows, made up, got married and didn't kill themselves at all.

He became aware that the litany of star-crossed love had wound down.

"Oh," he said, weakly. "Doesn't anyone just, you know, just get along any more?"

"To love is to suffer," said Ysabell. "There's got to be lots of dark passion."

"Has there?"

"Absolutely. And anguish."

Ysabell appeared to recall something.

"Did you say something about something flapping around loose?" she said, in the tight voice of someone pulling themselves together.

Mort considered. "No," he said.

"I'm afraid I wasn't paying much attention."

"It doesn't matter at all."

They strolled back to the house in silence.

When Mort went back to the study he found that Death had gone, leaving four hourglasses on the desk. The big leather book was lying on a lectern, securely locked shut.

There was a note tucked under the glasses.

Mort had imagined that Death's handwriting would either be gothic or else tombstone angular, but Death had in fact studied a classic work on graphology before selecting a style and had adopted a hand that indicated a balanced, well-adjusted personality.

It said:

*Gone fyshing. Theyre ys ane execution in Pseudopolis, a naturral in Krull, a faytal fall in the Carrick Mtns, ane ague in Ell-Kinte. Thee rest of thee day's your own.*

Mort thought that history was thrashing around like a steel hawser with the tension off, twanging backwards and forwards across reality in great destructive sweeps.

History isn't like that. History unravels gently, like an old sweater. It has been patched and darned many times, reknitted to suit different people, shoved in a box under the sink of censorship to be cut up for the dusters of propaganda, yet it always—eventually—manages to spring back into its old familiar shape. History has a habit of changing the people who think they are changing *it*. History always has a few tricks up its frayed sleeve. It's been around a long time.

This is what was happening:

The misplaced stroke of Mort's scythe had cut history into two separate realities. In the city of Sto Lat Princess Keli still ruled, with a certain amount of difficulty and with the full time aid of the Royal Recognizer, who was put on the court payroll and charged with the duty of remembering that she existed. In the lands outside, though—beyond the plain, in the Ramtops, around the Circle Sea and all the way to the Rim—the traditional reality still held sway and she was quite definitely dead, the duke was king and the world was proceeding sedately according to plan, whatever that was.

The point is that both realities were true.

The sort of historical event horizon was currently about twenty miles away from the city, and wasn't yet very noticeable. That's because the—well, call it the difference in historical pressures—wasn't yet very great. But it was growing. Out in the damp cabbage fields there was a shimmer in the air and a faint sizzle, like frying grasshoppers.

People don't alter history any more than birds alter the sky, they just make brief patterns in it. Inch by inch, implacable as a glacier and far colder, the real reality was grinding back towards Sto Lat.

Mort was the first person to notice.

It had been a long afternoon. The mountaineer had held on to his icy handhold until the last moment and the executee had called Mort a lackey of the monarchist state. Only the old lady of 103, who had gone to her reward surrounded

by her sorrowing relatives, had smiled at him and said he
was looking a little pale.

The Disc sun was close to the horizon by the time Binky
cantered wearily through the skies over Sto Lat, and Mort
looked down and saw the borderland of reality. It curved
away below him, a crescent of faint silver mist. He didn't
know what it was, but he had a nasty foreboding that it had
something to do with him.

He reined in the horse and allowed him to trot gently
towards the ground, touching down a few yards behind the
wall of iridescent air. It was moving at something less than
walking pace, hissing gently as it drifted ghost-like across
the stark damp cabbage fields and frozen drainage ditches.

It was a cold night, the type of night when frost and fog
fight for domination and every sound is muffled. Binky's
breath made fountains of cloud in the still air. He whinnied
gently, almost apologetically, and pawed at the ground.

Mort slid out of the saddle and crept up to the interface. It
crackled softly. Weird shapes coruscated across it, flowing
and shifting and disappearing.

After some searching he found a stick and poked it cautiously into the wall. It made strange ripples that wobbled
slowly out of sight.

Mort looked up as a shape drifted overhead. It was a black
owl, patrolling the ditches for anything small and squeaky.

It hit the wall with a splash of sparkling mist, leaving an
owl-shaped ripple that grew and spread until it joined the
boiling kaleidoscope.

Then it vanished. Mort could see through the transparent
interface, and certainly no owl reappeared on the other side.
Just as he was puzzling over this there was another sound-
less splash a few feet away and the bird burst into view
again, totally unconcerned, and skimmed away across the
fields.

Mort pulled himself together, and stepped through the
barrier which was no barrier at all. It tingled.

A moment later Binky burst through after him, eyes rolling in desperation and tendrils of interface catching on his hooves. He reared up, shaking his mane like a dog to remove clinging fibers of mist, and looked at Mort beseechingly.

Mort caught his bridle, patted him on the nose, and fumbled in his pocket for a rather grubby sugar lump. He was aware that he was in the presence of something important, but he wasn't yet quite sure what it was.

There *was* a road running between an avenue of damp and gloomy willow trees. Mort remounted and steered Binky across the field into the dripping darkness under the branches.

In the distance he could see the lights of Sto Helit, which really wasn't much more than a small town, and a faint glow on the edge of sight must be Sto Lat. He looked at it longingly.

The barrier worried him. He could see it creeping across the field behind the trees.

Mort was on the point of urging Binky back into the air when he saw the light immediately ahead of him, warm and beckoning. It was spilling from the windows of a large building set back from the road. It was probably a cheerful sort of light in any case, but in these surroundings and compared with Mort's mood it was positively ecstatic.

As he rode nearer he saw shadows moving against it, and made out a few snatches of song. It was an inn, and inside there were people having a good time, or what passed for a good time if you were a peasant who spent most of your time closely concerned with cabbages. Compared to brassicas, practically anything is fun.

There were human beings in there, doing uncomplicated human things like getting drunk and forgetting the words of songs.

Mort had never really felt homesick, possibly because his mind had been too occupied with other things. But he felt it now for the first time—a sort of longing, not for a place, but for a state of mind, for being just an ordinary human being with straightforward things to worry about, like money and sickness and other people. . . .

"I shall have a drink," he thought, "and perhaps I shall feel better."

There was an open-fronted stable at one side of the main building, and he led Binky into the warm, horse-smelling darkness that already accommodated three other horses. As Mort unfastened the nosebag he wondered if Death's horse felt the same way about other horses which had rather less supernatural lifestyles. He certainly looked impressive compared to the others, which regarded him watchfully. Binky was a real horse—the blisters of the shovel handle on Mort's hands were a testimony to that—and compared to the others he looked more real than ever. More solid. More horsey. Slightly larger than life.

In fact, Mort was on the verge of making an important deduction, and it is unfortunate that he was distracted, as he walked across the yard to the inn's low door, by the sight of the inn sign. Its artist hadn't been particularly gifted, but there was no mistaking the line of Keli's jaw or her mass of fiery hair in the portrait of The Quene's Hed.

He sighed, and pushed open the door.

As one man, the assembled company stopped talking and stared at him with the honest rural stare that suggests that for two pins they'll hit you around the head with a shovel and bury your body under a compost heap at full moon.

It might be worth taking another look at Mort, because he's changed a lot in the last few chapters. For example, while he still has plenty of knees and elbows about his person, they seem to have migrated to their normal places and he no longer moves as though his joints were loosely fastened together with elastic bands. He used to look as if he knew nothing at all; now he looks as though he knew too much. Something about his eyes suggests that he has seen things that ordinary people never see, or at least never see more than once.

Something about all the rest of him suggests to the watchers that causing an inconvenience for this boy might just be as wise as kicking a wasp nest. In short, Mort no longer looks like something the cat brought in and then brought up.

The landlord relaxed his grip on the stout blackthorn peacemaker he kept under the bar and composed his features into something resembling a cheerful welcoming grin, although not very much.

"Evening, your lordship," he said. "What's your pleasure this cold and frosty night?"

"What?" said Mort, blinking in the light.

"What he means is, what d'you want to drink?" said a small ferret-faced man sitting by the fire, who was giving Mort the kind of look a butcher gives a field full of lambs.

"Um. I don't know," said Mort. "Do you sell stardrip?"

"Never heard of it, lordship."

Mort looked around at the faces watching him, illuminated by the firelight. They were the sort of people generally called the salt of the earth. In other words, they were hard, square and bad for your health, but Mort was too preoccupied to notice.

"What do people like to drink here, then?"

The landlord looked sideways at his customers, a clever trick given that they were directly in front of him.

"Why, lordship, we drink scumble, for preference."

"Scumble?" said Mort, failing to notice the muffled sniggers.

"Aye, lordship. Made from apples. Well, mainly apples."

This seemed healthy enough to Mort. "Oh, right," he said. "A pint of scumble, then." He reached into his pocket and withdrew the bag of gold that Death had given him. It was still quite full. In the sudden hush of the inn the faint clink of the coins sounded like the legendary Brass Gongs of Leshp, which can be heard far out to sea on stormy nights as the currents stir them in their drowned towers three hundred fathoms below.

"And please serve these gentlemen with whatever they want," he added.

He was so overwhelmed by the chorus of thanks that he didn't take much notice of the fact that his new friends were served their drinks in tiny, thimble-sized glasses, while his alone turned up in a large wooden mug.

A lot of stories are told about scumble, and how it is made out on the damp marshes according to ancient recipes handed down rather unsteadily from father to son. It's not true about the rats, or the snake heads, or the lead shot. The one about the dead sheep is a complete fabrication. We can lay to rest all the variations of the one about the trouser button. But the one about not letting it come into contact with metal is absolutely true, because when the landlord flagrantly shortchanged Mort and plonked the small heap of copper in a puddle of the stuff it immediately began to froth.

Mort sniffed his drink, and then took a sip. It tasted something like apples, something like autumn mornings, and quite a lot like the bottom of a logpile. Not wishing to appear disrespectful, however, he took a swig.

The crowd watched him, counting under its breath.

Mort felt something was being demanded of him.

"Nice," he said, "very refreshing." He took another sip. "Bit of an acquired taste," he added, "but well worth the effort, I'm sure."

There were one or two mutters of discontent from the back of the crowd.

"He's been watering the scumble, that's what 'tis."

"Nay, thou knows what happens if you lets a drop of water touch scumble."

The landlord tried to ignore this. "You like it?" he said to Mort, in pretty much the same tone of voice people used when they said to St. George, "You killed a *what*?"

"It's quite tangy," said Mort. "And sort of nutty."

"Excuse me," said the landlord, and gently took the mug out of Mort's hand. He sniffed at it, then wiped his eyes.

"Uuunnyag," he said. "It's the right stuff all right."

He looked at the boy with something verging on admiration. It wasn't that he'd drunk a third of a pint of scumble in itself, it was that he was still vertical and apparently alive. He handed the pot back again: it was as if Mort was being given a trophy after some incredible contest. When the boy took another mouthful several of the watchers winced. The landlord wondered what Mort's teeth were made of, and decided it must be the same stuff as his stomach.

"You're not a wizard by any chance?" he inquired, just in case.

"Sorry, no. Should I be?"

Didn't think so, thought the landlord, he doesn't walk like a wizard and anyway he isn't smoking anything. He looked at the scumble pot again.

There was something wrong about this. There was something wrong about the boy. He didn't look right. He looked—

—more solid than he should do.

That was ridiculous, of course. The bar was solid, the floor was solid, the customers were as solid as you could wish for. Yet Mort, standing there looking rather embarrassed and casually sipping a liquid you could clean spoons with, seemed to emit a particularly potent sort of solidness, an extra dimension of realness. His hair was more hairy, his clothes more clothy, his boots the epitome of bootness. It made your head ache just to look at him.

However, Mort then demonstrated that he was human after all. The mug dropped from his stricken fingers and clattered on the flagstones, where the dregs of scumble started to eat its way through them. He pointed at the far wall, his mouth opening and shutting wordlessly.

The regulars turned back to their conversations and games of shovel-up, reassured that things were as they should be; Mort was acting perfectly normal now. The landlord, relieved that the brew had been vindicated, reached across the bar top and patted him companionably on the shoulder.

"It's all right," he said. "It often takes people like this, you'll just have a headache for a few weeks, don't worry about it, a drop of scumble'll see you all right again."

It is a fact that the best remedy for a scumble hangover is a hair of the dog, although it should more accurately be called a tooth of the shark or possibly a tread of the bulldozer.

But Mort merely went on pointing and said, in a trembling voice, "Can't you see it? It's coming through the wall! It's coming right through the wall!"

"A lot of things come through the wall after your first drink of scumble. Green hairy things, usually."

"It's the mist! Can't you hear it sizzling?"

"A sizzling mist, is it?" The landlord looked at the wall, which was quite empty and unmysterious except for a few cobwebs. The urgency in Mort's voice unsettled him. He would have preferred the normal scaly monsters. A man knew where he stood with them.

"It's coming right across the room! Can't you feel it?"

The customers looked at one another. Mort was making them uneasy. One or two of them admitted later that they did feel something, rather like an icy tingle, but it could have been indigestion.

Mort backed away, and then gripped the bar. He shivered for a moment.

"Look," said the landlord, "a joke's a joke, but—"

"You had a green shirt on before!"

The landlord looked down. There was an edge of terror in his voice.

"Before what?" he quavered. To his astonishment, and before his hand could complete its surreptitious journey towards the blackthorn stick, Mort lunged across the bar and grabbed him by the apron.

"You've got a green shirt, haven't you?" he said. "I saw it, it had little yellow buttons!"

"Well, yes. I've got two shirts." The landlord tried to draw himself up a little. "I'm a man of means," he added. "I just didn't wear it today." He didn't want to know how Mort knew about the buttons.

Mort let him go and spun round.

"They're all sitting in different places! Where's the man who was sitting by the fire? It's all changed!"

He ran out through the door and there was a muffled cry from outside. He dashed back, wild-eyed, and confronted the horrified crowd.

"Who changed the sign? Someone changed the sign!"

The landlord nervously ran his tongue across his lips.

"After the old king died, you mean?" he said.

Mort's look chilled him, the boy's eyes were two black pools of terror.

"It's the name I mean!"

"We've—it's always been the same name," said the man, looking desperately at his customers for support. "Isn't that so, lads? The Duke's Head."

There was a murmured chorus of agreement.

Mort stared at everyone, visibly shaking. Then he turned and ran outside again.

The listeners heard hoofbeats in the yard, which grew fainter and then disappeared entirely, just as though a horse had left the face of the earth.

There was no sound inside the inn. Men tried to avoid one another's gaze. No one wanted to be the first to admit to seeing what he thought he had just seen.

So it was left to the landlord to walk unsteadily across the room and reach out and run his fingers across the familiar, reassuring wooden surface of the door. It was solid, unbroken, everything a door should be.

Everyone had seen Mort run through it three times. He just hadn't opened it.

Binky fought for height, rising nearly vertically with his hooves thrashing the air and his breath curling away behind him like a vapor trail. Mort hung on with knees and hands and mostly with willpower, his face buried in the horse's mane. He didn't look down until the air around him was freezing and thin as workhouse gravy.

Overhead the Hub Lights flickered silently across the winter sky. Below—

—an upturned saucer, miles across, silvery in the starlight. He could see lights through it. Clouds were drifting through it.

No. He watched carefully. Clouds were certainly drifting into it, and there were clouds *in* it, but the clouds inside were wispier and moving in a slightly different direction and, in fact, didn't seem to have much to do with the clouds outside. There was something else . . . oh yes, the Hub Lights. They gave the night outside the ghostly hemisphere a faint green tint, but there was no sign of it under the dome.

It was like looking into a piece of another world, almost identical, that had been grafted on to the Disc. The weather was slightly different in there, and the Lights weren't on display tonight.

And the Disc was resenting it, and surrounding it, and pushing it back into non-existence. Mort couldn't see it growing smaller from up here, but in his mind's ear he could hear the locust sizzle of the thing as it ground across the land, changing things back to where they should be. Reality was healing itself.

Mort knew, without even having to think about it, who was at the center of the dome. It was obvious even from here that it was centered firmly on Sto Lat.

He tried not to think what would happen when the dome had shrunk to the size of the room, and then the size of a person, and then the size of an egg. He failed.

Logic would have told Mort that here was his salvation. In a day or two the problem would solve itself; the books in the library would be right again; the world would have sprung back into shape like an elastic bandage. Logic would have told him that interfering with the process a second time around would only make things worse. Logic would have said all that, if only Logic hadn't taken the night off too.

Light travels quite slowly on the Disc, due to the braking effect of the huge magical field, and currently that part of the Rim carrying the island of Krull was directly under the little sun's orbit and it was, therefore, still early evening. It was also quite warm, since the Rim picks up more heat and enjoys a gentle maritime climate.

In fact Krull, with a large part of what for want of a better word must be called its coastline sticking out over the Edge, was a fortunate island. The only native Krullians who did not appreciate this were those who didn't look where they were going or who walked in their sleep and, because of natural selection, there weren't very many of them any more. All societies have their share of dropouts, but on Krull they never had a chance to drop back in again.

Terpsic Mims was not a dropout. He was an angler. There is a difference; angling is more expensive. But Terpsic was happy. He was watching a feather on a cork bob gently on the gentle, reed-lined waters of the Hakrull river and his mind was very nearly a blank. The only thing that could have disturbed his mood was actually catching a fish, because catching fish was the one thing about angling that he really dreaded. They were cold and slimy and panicky and got on his nerves, and Terpsic's nerves weren't very good.

So long as he caught nothing Terpsic Mims was one of the Disc's happiest anglers, because the Hakrull river was five miles from his home and therefore five miles from Mrs. Gwladys Mims, with whom he had enjoyed six happy months of married life. That had been some twenty years previously.

Terpsic did not pay undue heed when another angler took up station further along the bank. Of course, some fishermen might have objected to this breach of etiquette, but in Terpsic's book anything that reduced his chance of actually catching any of the damned things was all right by him. Out of the corner of his eye he noted that the newcomer was fly-fishing, an interesting pastime which Terpsic had rejected because one spent altogether far too much time at home making the equipment.

He had never seen fly-fishing like this before. There were wet flies, and there were dry flies, but this fly augured into the water with a saw-toothed whine and dragged the fish out backwards.

Terpsic watched in horrified fascination as the indistinct figure behind the willow trees cast and cast again. The water boiled as the river's entire piscine population fought to get out of the way of the buzzing terror and, unfortunately, a large and maddened pike took Terpsic's hook out of sheer confusion.

One moment he was standing on the bank, and the next he was in a green, clanging gloom, bubbling his breath away and watching his life flash before his eyes and, even in the moment of drowning, dreading the thought of watching the bit between the day of his wedding and the present. It occurred to him that Gwladys would soon be a widow, which cheered him up a little bit. In fact Terpsic had always tried to look on the bright side, and it struck him, as he sank gratefully into the silt, that from this point on his whole life could only improve. . . .

And a hand grabbed his hair and dragged him to the surface, which was suddenly full of pain. Ghastly blue and black blotches swam in front of his eyes. His lungs were on fire. His throat was a pipe of agony.

Hands—cold hands, freezing hands, hands that felt like a

glove full of dice—towed him through the water and threw him down on to the bank where, after some game attempts to get on with drowning, he was eventually bullied back into what passed for his life.

Terpsic didn't often get angry, because Gwladys didn't hold with it. But he felt cheated. He'd been born without being consulted, he'd been married because Gwladys and her father had seen to it, and the only major human achievement that was uniquely his had been rudely snatched away from him. A few seconds ago it had all been so simple. Now it was all complicated again.

Not that he wanted to die, of course. The gods were very firm on the subject of suicide. He just hadn't wanted to be rescued.

Through red eyes in a mask of slime and duckweed he peered at the blurred form above him, and shouted, "Why did you have to save me?"

The answer worried him. He thought about it as he squelched all the way home. It sat at the back of his mind while Gwladys complained about the state of his clothes. It squirreled around in his head as he sat and sneezed guiltily by the fire, because being ill was another thing Gwladys didn't hold with. As he lay shivering in bed it settled in his dreams like an iceberg. In the midst of his fever he muttered, "What did he mean, 'FOR LATER'?"

Torches flared in the city of Sto Lat. Whole squads of men were charged with the task of constantly renewing them. The streets glowed. The sizzling flames pushed back shadows that had been blamelessly minding their own business every night for centuries. They illuminated ancient corners where the eyes of bewildered rats glittered in the depths of their holes. They forced burglars to stay indoors. They glowed on the night mists, forming a nimbus of yellow light that blotted out the cold high flames streaming from the

Hub. But mainly they shone on the face of Princess Keli.

It was everywhere. It plastered every flat surface. Binky cantered along the glowing streets between Princess Keli on doors, walls and gable ends. Mort gaped at posters of his beloved on every surface where workmen had been able to make paste stick.

Even stranger, no one seemed to be paying them much attention. While Sto Lat's night life was not as colorful and full of incident as that of Ankh-Morpork, in the same way that a wastepaper basket cannot compete with a municipal tip, the streets were nevertheless a-bustle with people and shrill with the cries of hucksters, gamblers, sellers of sweetmeats, pea-and-thimble men, ladies of assignation, pickpockets and the occasional honest trader who had wandered in by mistake and couldn't now raise enough money to leave. As Mort rode through them snatches of conversation in half-a-dozen languages floated into his ears; with numb acceptance he realized he could understand every one of them.

He eventually dismounted and led the horse along Wall Street, searching in vain for Cutwell's house. He found it only because a lump on the nearest poster was making muffled swearing noises.

He reached out gingerly and pulled aside a strip of paper.

"Fanks very much," said the gargoyle doorknocker. "You wouldn't credit it, would you? One minute life as normal, nexft minute a mouthful of glue."

"Where's Cutwell?"

"He's gone off to the palace." The knocker leered at him and winked a cast-iron eye. "Some men came and took all his fstuff away. Then some ovver men started pasting pictures of his girlfriend all over the place. Barftuds," it added.

Mort colored.

"His girlfriend?"

The doorknocker, being of the demonic persuasion, sniggered at his tone. It sounded like fingernails being dragged over a file.

"Yeff," it said. "They feemed in a bit of a hurry, if you ask me."

Mort was already up on Binky's back.

"I fay!" shouted the knocker at his retreating back. "I fay! Could you unftick me, boy?"

Mort tugged on Binky's reins so hard that the horse reared and danced crazily backwards across the cobbles, then reached out and grabbed the ring of the knocker. The gargoyle looked up into his face and suddenly felt like a very frightened doorknocker indeed. Mort's eyes glowed like crucibles, his expression was a furnace, his voice held enough heat to melt iron. It didn't know what he could do, but felt that it would prefer not to find out.

"What did you call me?" Mort hissed.

The doorknocker thought quickly. "Fir?" it said.

"What did you ask me to do?"

"Unftick me?"

"I don't intend to."

"Fine," said the doorknocker, "fine. That's okay by me. I'll just ftick around, then."

It watched Mort canter off along the street and shuddered with relief, knocking itself gently in its nervousness.

"A naaaarrow sqeeeak," said one of the hinges.

"Fut up!"

Mort passed night watchmen, whose job now appeared to consist of ringing bells and shouting the name of the Princess, but a little uncertainly, as if they had difficulty remembering it. He ignored them, because he was listening to voices inside his head which went:

She's only met you once, you fool. Why should she bother about you?

Yes, but I did save her life.

That means it belongs to her. Not to you. Besides, he's a wizard.

So what? Wizards aren't supposed to—to go out with girls, they're celebrate. . . . .

Celebrate?

They're not supposed to youknow. . . .

What, never any youknow at all? said the internal voice, and it sounded as if it was grinning.

It's supposed to be bad for the magic, thought Mort bitterly.

Funny place to keep magic.

Mort was shocked. Who are you? he demanded.

I'm you, Mort. Your inner self.

Well, I wish I'd get out of my head, it's quite crowded enough with me in here.

Fair enough, said the voice, I was only trying to help. But remember, if you ever need you, you're always around.

The voice faded away.

Well, thought Mort bitterly, that must have been me. I'm the only one that calls me Mort.

The shock of the realization quite obscured the fact that, while Mort had been locked into the monologue, he had ridden right through the gates of the palace. Of course, people rode through the gates of the palace every day, but most of them needed the things to be opened first.

The guards on the other side were rigid with fear, because they thought they had seen a ghost. They would have been far more frightened if they had known that a ghost was almost exactly what they hadn't seen.

The guard outside the doors of the great hall had seen it happen too, but he had time to gather his wits, or such that remained, and raise his spear as Binky trotted across the courtyard.

"Halt," he croaked. "Halt. What goes where?"

Mort saw him for the first time.

"What?" he said, still lost in thought.

The guard ran his tongue over his dry lips, and backed away. Mort slid off Binky's back and walked forward.

"I meant, what goes there?" the guard tried again, with a mixture of doggedness and suicidal stupidity that marked him for early promotion.

Mort caught the spear gently and lifted it out of the way of the door. As he did so the torchlight illuminated his face.

"Mort," he said softly.

It should have been enough for any normal soldier, but this guard was officer material.

"I mean, friend or foe?" he stuttered, trying to avoid Mort's gaze.

"Which would you prefer?" he grinned. It wasn't quite the grin of his master, but it was a pretty effective grin and didn't have a trace of humor in it.

The guard sagged with relief, and stood aside.

"Pass, friend," he said.

Mort strode across the hall towards the staircase that led to the royal apartments. The hall had changed a lot since he last saw it. Portraits of Keli were everywhere; they'd even replaced the ancient and crumbling battle banners in the shadowy heights of the roof. Anyone walking through the palace would have found it impossible to go more than a few steps without seeing a portrait. Part of Mort's mind wondered why, just as another part worried about the flickering dome that was steadily closing on the city, but most of his mind was a hot and steamy glow of rage and bewilderment and jealousy. Ysabell had been right, he thought, this must be love.

"The walk-through-walls boy!"

He jerked his head up. Cutwell was standing at the top of the stairs.

The wizard had changed a lot too, Mort thought bitterly. Perhaps not that much, though. Although he was wearing a black and white robe embroidered with sequins, although his pointy hat was a yard high and decorated with more mystic symbols than a dental chart, and although his red velvet shoes had silver buckles and toes that curled like snails, there were still a few stains on his collar and he appeared to be chewing.

He watched Mort climb the stairs towards him.

"Are you angry about something?" he said. "I started work, but I got rather tied up with other things. Very difficult, walking through—why are you looking at me like that?"

"What are you doing here?"

"I might ask you the same question. Would you like a strawberry?"

Mort glanced at the small wooden punnet in the wizard's hands.

"In mid-winter?"

"Actually, they're sprouts with a dash of enchantment."

"They taste like strawberries?"

Cutwell sighed. "No, like sprouts. The spell isn't totally efficient. I thought they might cheer the princess up, but she threw them at me. Shame to waste them. Be my guest."

Mort gaped at him.

"She threw them at you?"

"Very accurately, I'm afraid. Very strong-minded young lady."

Hi, said a voice in the back of Mort's mind, it's you again, pointing out to yourself that the chances of the princess even contemplating you know with this fellow are on the far side of remote.

Go away, thought Mort. His subconscious was worrying him. It appeared to have a direct line to parts of his body that he wanted to ignore at the moment.

"Why *are* you here?" he said aloud. "Is it something to do with all these pictures?"

"Good idea, wasn't it?" beamed Cutwell. "I'm rather proud of it myself."

"Excuse me," said Mort weakly. "I've had a busy day. I think I'd like to sit down somewhere."

"There's the Throne Room," said Cutwell. "There's no-one in there at this time of night. Everyone's asleep."

Mort nodded, and then looked suspiciously at the young wizard.

"What are you doing up, then?" he said.

"Um," said Cutwell, "um, I just thought I'd see if there was anything in the pantry."

He shrugged.*

Now is the time to report that Cutwell too notices that Mort, even a Mort weary with riding and lack of sleep, is somehow glowing from within and in some strange way unconnected with size is nevertheless larger than life. The difference is that Cutwell is, by training, a better guesser than other people and knows that in occult matters the obvious answer is usually the wrong one.

Mort can move absentmindedly through walls and drink neat widowmaker soberly not because he is turning into a ghost, but because he is becoming dangerously real.

In fact, as the boy stumbles while they walk along the silent corridors and steps through a marble pillar without noticing, it's obvious that the world is becoming a pretty insubstantial place from his point of view.

---

*There had been half a jar of elderly mayonnaise, a piece of very old cheese, and a tomato with white mold growing on it. Since during the day the pantry of the palace of Sto Lat normally contained fifteen whole stags, one hundred brace of partridges, fifty hogsheads of butter, two hundred jugs of hares, seventy-five sides of beef, two miles of assorted sausages, various fowls, eighty dozen eggs, several Circle Sea sturgeon, a vat of caviar and an elephant's leg stuffed with olives, Cutwell had learned once again that one universal manifestation of raw, natural magic throughout the universe is this: that any domestic food store, raided furtively in the middle of the night, always contains, no matter what its daytime inventory, half a jar of elderly mayonnaise, a piece of very old cheese, and a tomato with white mold growing on it.

"You just walked through a marble pillar," observed Cutwell. "How did you do it?"

"Did I?" Mort looked around. The pillar looked sound enough. He poked an arm towards it, and slightly bruised his elbow.

"I could have sworn you did," said Cutwell. "Wizards notice these things, you know." He reached into the pocket of his robe.

"Then have you noticed the mist dome around the country?" said Mort.

Cutwell squeaked. The jar in his hand dropped and smashed on the tiles; there was the smell of slightly rancid salad dressing.

*"Already?"*

"I don't know about already," said Mort, "but there's this sort of crackling wall sliding over the land and no one else seems to worry about it and—"

"How fast was it moving?"

"—it changes things!"

"You saw it? How far away is it? How fast is it moving?"

"Of course I saw it. I rode through it twice. It was like—"

"But you're not a wizard, so why—"

"What are you doing here, anyway—"

Cutwell took a deep breath. "Everyone shut up!" he screamed.

There was silence. Then the wizard grabbed Mort's arm. "Come on," he said, pulling him back along the corridor. "I don't know who you are exactly and I hope I've got time to find out one day but something really horrible is going to happen soon and I think you're involved, somehow."

"Something horrible? When?"

"That depends on how far away the interface is and how fast it's moving," said Cutwell, dragging Mort down a side passage. When they were outside a small oak door he let go of his arm and fumbled in his pocket again, removing a small hard piece of cheese and an unpleasantly squashy tomato.

"Hold these, will you? Thank you." He delved again, produced a key and unlocked the door.

"It's going to kill the princess, isn't it?" said Mort.

"Yes," said Cutwell, "and then again, no." He paused with his hand on the doorhandle. "That was pretty perspicacious of you. How did you know?"

"I—" Mort hesitated.

"She told me a very strange story," said Cutwell.

"I expect she did," said Mort. "If it was unbelievable, it was true."

"You're him, are you? Death's assistant?"

"Yes. Off duty at the moment, though."

"Pleased to hear it."

Cutwell shut the door behind them and fumbled for a candlestick. There was a pop, a flash of blue light and a whimper.

"Sorry," he said, sucking his fingers. "Fire spell. Never really got the hang of it."

"You were expecting the dome thing, weren't you?" said Mort urgently. "What will happen when it closes in?"

The wizard sat down heavily on the remains of a bacon sandwich.

"I'm not exactly sure," he said. "It'll be interesting to watch. But not from inside, I'm afraid. What I *think* will happen is that the last week will never have existed."

"She'll suddenly die?"

"You don't quite understand. She will have been dead for a week. All this—" he waved his hands vaguely in the air— "will not have happened. The assassin will have done his job. You will have done yours. History will have healed itself. Everything will be all right. From History's point of view, that is. There really isn't any other."

Mort stared out of the narrow window. He could see across the courtyard into the glowing streets outside, where a picture of the princess smiled at the sky.

"Tell me about the pictures," he said. "That looks like some sort of wizard thing."

"I'm not sure if it's working. You see, people were beginning to get upset and they didn't know why, and that made it worse. Their minds were in one reality and their bodies were in another. Very unpleasant. They couldn't get used to the idea that she was still alive. I thought the pictures might be a good idea but, you know, people just don't see what their mind tells them isn't there."

"I could have told you that," said Mort bitterly.

"I had the town criers out during the daytime," Cutwell continued. "I thought that if people could come to believe in her, then this new reality could become the real one."

"Mmmph?" said Mort. He turned away from the window. "What do you mean?"

"Well, you see—I reckoned that if enough people believed in her, they could change reality. It works for gods. If people stop believing in a god, he dies. If a lot of them believe in him, he grows stronger."

"I didn't know that. I thought gods were just gods."

"They don't like it talked about," said Cutwell, shuffling through the heap of books and parchments on his worktable.

"Well, that might work for gods, because they're special," said Mort. "People are—more solid. It wouldn't work for people."

"That's not true. Let's suppose you went out of here and prowled around the palace. One of the guards would probably see you and he'd think you were a thief and he'd fire his crossbow. I mean, in his reality you'd be a thief. It wouldn't actually be true but you'd be just as dead as if it was. Belief is powerful stuff. I'm a wizard. We know about these things. Look here."

He pulled a book out of the debris in front of him and opened it at the piece of bacon he'd used as a bookmark. Mort looked over his shoulder, and frowned at the curly magical writing. It moved around on the page, twisting and writhing in an attempt not to be read by a non-wizard, and the general effect was unpleasant.

"What's this?" he said.

"It's the Book of the Magick of Alberto Malich the Mage," said the wizard, "a sort of book of magical theory. It's not a good idea to look too hard at the words, they resent it. Look, it says here—"

His lips moved soundlessly. Little beads of sweat sprang up on his forehead and decided to get together and go down and see what his nose was doing. His eyes watered.

Some people like to settle down with a good book. No-one in possession of a complete set of marbles would like to settle down with a book of magic, because even the individual words have a private and vindictive life of their own and reading them, in short, is a kind of mental Indian wrestling. Many a young wizard has tried to read a grimoire that is too strong for him, and people who've heard the screams have found only his pointy shoes with the classic wisp of smoke coming out of them and a book which is, perhaps, just a little fatter. Things can happen to browsers in magical libraries that make having your face pulled off by tentacled monstrosities from the Dungeon Dimensions seem a mere light massage by comparison.

Fortunately Cutwell had an expurgated edition, with some of the more distressing pages clamped shut (although on quiet nights he could hear the imprisoned words scritching irritably inside their prison, like a spider trapped in a matchbox; anyone who has ever sat next to someone wearing a Walkman will be able to imagine exactly what they sounded like).

"This is the bit," said Cutwell. "It says here that even gods—"

"I've seen him before!"

"What?"

Mort pointed a shaking finger at the book.

"Him!"

Cutwell gave him an odd look and examined the left-hand page. There was a picture of an elderly wizard holding a book and a candlestick in an attitude of near-terminal dignity.

"That's not part of the magic," he said testily, "that's just the author."

"What does it say under the picture?"

"Er. It says 'Yff youe have enjoyed thiss Boke, youe maye be interestede yn othere Titles by—"

"No, right under the picture is what I meant!"

"That's easy. It's old Malich himself. Every wizard knows him. I mean, he founded the University." Cutwell chuckled. "There's a famous statue of him in the main hall, and during Rag Week once I climbed up it and put a—"

Mort stared at the picture.

"Tell me," he said quietly, "did the statue have a drip on the end of its nose?"

"I shouldn't think so," said Cutwell. "It was marble. But I don't know what you're getting so worked up about. Lots of people know what he looked like. He's famous."

"He lived a long time ago, did he?"

"Two thousand years, I think. Look, I don't know why—"

"I bet he didn't die, though," said Mort. "I bet he just disappeared one day. Did he?"

Cutwell was silent for a moment.

"Funny you should say that," he said slowly. "There was a legend I heard. He got up to some weird things, they say. They say he blew himself into the Dungeon Dimensions while trying to perform the Rite of AshkEnte backwards. All they found was his hat. Tragic, really. The whole city in mourning for a day just for a hat. It wasn't even a particularly attractive hat; it had burn marks on it."

"Alberto Malich," said Mort, half to himself. "Well. Fancy that."

He drummed his fingers on the table, although the sound was surprisingly muted.

"Sorry," said Cutwell. "I can't get the hang of treacle sandwiches, either."

"I reckon the interface is moving at a slow walking pace," said Mort, licking his fingers absentmindedly. "Can't you stop it by magic?"

Cutwell shook his head. "Not me. It'd squash me flat," he said cheerfully.

"What'll happen to you when it arrives, then?"

"Oh, I'll go back to living in Wall Street. I mean, I never will have left. All this won't have happened. Pity, though. The cooking here is pretty good, and they do my laundry for free. How far away did you say it was, by the way?"

"About twenty miles, I guess."

Cutwell rolled his eyes heavenwards and moved his lips. Eventually he said: "That means it'll arrive around midnight tomorrow, just in time for the coronation."

"Whose?"

"Hers."

"But she's queen already, isn't she?"

"In a way, but officially she's not queen until she's crowned." Cutwell grinned, his face a pattern of shade in the candlelight, and added, "If you want a way of thinking about it, then it's like the difference between stopping living and being dead."

Twenty minutes earlier Mort had been feeling tired enough to take root. Now he could feel a fizzing in his blood. It was the kind of late-night, frantic energy that you knew you would pay for around midday tomorrow, but for now he felt he had to have some action or else his muscles would snap out of sheer vitality.

"I want to see her," he said. "If you can't do anything, there might be something I can do."

"There's guards outside her room," said Cutwell. "I mention this merely as an observation. I don't imagine for one minute that they'll make the slightest difference."

* * *

It was midnight in Ankh-Morpork, but in the great twin city the only difference between night and day was, well, it was darker. The markets were thronged, the spectators were still thickly clustered around the whore pits, runners-up in the city's eternal and byzantine gang warfare drifted silently down through the chilly waters of the river with lead weights tied to their feet, dealers in various illegal and even illogical delights plied their sidelong trade, burglars burgled, knives flashed starlight in alleyways, astrologers started their day's work and in the Shades a nightwatchman who had lost his way rang his bell and cried out: "Twelve o'clock and all's arrrrrgghhhh. . . ."

However, the Ankh-Morpork Chamber of Commerce would not be happy at the suggestion that the only real difference between their city and a swamp is the number of legs on the alligators, and indeed in the more select areas of Ankh, which tend to be in the hilly districts where there is a chance of a bit of wind, the nights are gentle and scented with habiscine and cecillia blossoms.

On this particular night they were scented with saltpeter, too, because it was the tenth anniversary of the accession of the Patrician* and he had invited a few friends round for a drink, five hundred of them in this case, and was letting off fireworks. Laughter and the occasional gurgle of passion filled the palace gardens, and the evening had just got to that interesting stage where everyone had drunk too much for their own good but not enough actually to fall over. It is the kind of state in which one does things that one will recall with crimson shame in later life, such as blowing through a paper squeaker and laughing so much that one is sick.

In fact some two hundred of the Patrician's guests were now staggering and kicking their way through the Serpent

---

*Ankh-Morpork had dallied with many forms of government and had ended up with that form of democracy known as One Man, One Vote. The Patrician was the Man; he had the Vote.

Dance, a quaint Morporkian folkway which consisted of getting rather drunk, holding the waist of the person in front, and then wobbling and giggling uproariously in a long crocodile that wound through as many rooms as possible, preferably ones with breakables in, while kicking one leg vaguely in time with the beat, or at least in time with some other beat. This dance had gone on for half an hour and had wound through every room in the palace, picking up two trolls, the cook, the Patrician's head torturer, three waiters, a burglar who happened to be passing and a small pet swamp dragon.

Somewhere around the middle of the dance was fat Lord Rodley of Quirm, heir to the fabulous Quirm estates, whose current preoccupation was with the thin fingers gripping his waist. Under its bath of alcohol his brain kept trying to attract his attention.

"I say," he called over his shoulder, as they oscillated for the tenth hilarious time through the enormous kitchen, "not so tight, please."

I AM MOST TERRIBLY SORRY.

"No offense, old chap. Do I know you?" said Lord Rodley, kicking vigorously on the back beat.

I THINK IT UNLIKELY. TELL ME, PLEASE, WHAT IS THE MEANING OF THIS ACTIVITY?

"What?" shouted Lord Rodley, above the sound of someone kicking in the door of a glass cabinet amid shrieks of merriment.

WHAT IS THIS THING THAT WE DO? said the voice, with glacial patience.

"Haven't you been to a party before? Mind the glass, by the way."

I AM AFRAID I DO NOT GET OUT AS MUCH AS I WOULD LIKE TO. PLEASE EXPLAIN THIS. DOES IT HAVE TO DO WITH SEX?

"Not unless we pull up sharp, old boy, if you know what I mean?" said his lordship, and nudged his unseen fellow guest with his elbow.

"Ouch," he said. A crash up ahead marked the demise of the cold buffet.

No.

"What?"

I DO NOT KNOW WHAT YOU MEAN.

"Mind the cream there, it's slippery—look, it's just a dance, all right? You do it for fun."

FUN.

"That's right. Dada, dada, da—kick!" There was an audible pause.

WHO IS THIS FUN?

"No, fun isn't anybody, fun is what you have."

WE ARE HAVING FUN?

"I thought I was," said his lordship uncertainly. The voice by his ear was vaguely worrying him; it appeared to be arriving directly into his brain.

WHAT IS THIS FUN?

"This is!"

TO KICK VIGOROUSLY IS FUN?

"Well, part of the fun. Kick!"

TO HEAR LOUD MUSIC IN HOT ROOMS IS FUN?

"Possibly."

HOW IS THIS FUN MANIFEST?

"Well, it—look, either you're having fun or you're not, you don't have to ask me, you just know, all right? How did you get in here, anyway?" he added. "Are you a friend of the Patrician?"

LET US SAY, HE PUTS BUSINESS MY WAY. I FELT I OUGHT TO LEARN SOMETHING OF HUMAN PLEASURES.

"Sounds like you've got a long way to go."

I KNOW. PLEASE EXCUSE MY LAMENTABLE IGNORANCE. I WISH ONLY TO LEARN. ALL THESE PEOPLE, PLEASE—THEY ARE HAVING FUN?

"Yes!"

THEN THIS IS FUN.

"I'm glad we've got that sorted out. Mind the chair,"

snapped Lord Rodley, who was now feeling very unfunny and unpleasantly sober.

A voice behind him said quietly: THIS IS FUN. TO DRINK EXCESSIVELY IS FUN. WE ARE HAVING FUN. HE IS HAVING FUN. THIS IS SOME FUN.

WHAT FUN.

Behind Death the Patrician's small pet swamp dragon held on grimly to the bony hips and thought: guards or no guards, next time we pass an open window I'm going to run like buggery.

Keli sat bolt upright in bed.

"Don't move another step," she said. "Guards!"

"We couldn't stop him," said the first guard, poking his head shame-facedly around the doorpost.

"He just pushed in . . ." said the other guard, from the other side of the doorway.

"And the wizard said it was all right, and we were told everyone must listen to him because. . . ."

"All right, all right. People could get murdered around here," said Keli testily, and put the crossbow back on the bedside table without, unfortunately, operating the safety catch.

There was a click, the thwack of sinew against metal, a zip of air, and a groan. The groan came from Cutwell. Mort spun round to him.

"Are you all right?" he said. "Did it hit you?"

"No," said the wizard, weakly. "No, it didn't. How do you feel?"

"A bit tired. Why?"

"Oh, nothing. Nothing. No draughts anywhere? No slight leaking feelings?"

"No. Why?"

"Oh, nothing, nothing." Cutwell turned and looked closely at the wall behind Mort.

"Aren't the dead allowed any peace?" said Keli bitterly. "I

thought one thing you could be sure of when you were dead was a good night's sleep." She looked as though she had been crying. With an insight that surprised him, Mort realized that she knew this and that it was making her even angrier than before.

"That's not really fair," he said. "I've come to help. Isn't that right, Cutwell?"

"Hmm?" said Cutwell, who had found the crossbow bolt buried in the plaster and was looking at it with deep suspicion. "Oh, yes. He has. It won't work, though. Excuse me, has anyone got any string?"

"Help?" snapped Keli. "Help? If it wasn't for you—"

"You'd still be dead," said Mort. She looked at him with her mouth open.

"I wouldn't know about it, though," she said. "That's the worst part."

"I think you two had better go," said Cutwell to the guards, who were trying to appear inconspicuous. "But I'll have that spear, please. Thank you."

"Look," said Mort, "I've got a horse outside. You'd be amazed. I can take you anywhere. You don't have to wait around here."

"You don't know much about monarchy, do you," said Keli.

"Um. No?"

"She means better to be a dead queen in your own castle than a live commoner somewhere else," said Cutwell, who had stuck the spear into the wall by the bolt and was trying to sight along it. "Wouldn't work, anyway. The dome isn't centered on the palace, it's centered on her."

"On *who*?" said Keli. Her voice could have kept milk fresh for a month.

"On her Highness," said Cutwell automatically, squinting along the shaft.

"Don't you forget it."

"I won't forget it, but that's not the point," said the wizard. He pulled the bolt out of the plaster and tested the point with his finger.

"But if you stay here you'll die!" said Mort.

"Then I shall have to show the Disc how a queen can die," said Keli, looking as proud as was possible in a pink knitted bed jacket.

Mort sat down on the end of the bed with his head in his hands.

"I know how a queen can die," he muttered. "They die just like other people. And some of us would rather not see it happen."

"Excuse me, I just want to look at this crossbow," said Cutwell conversationally, reaching across them. "Don't mind me."

"I shall go proudly to meet my destiny," said Keli, but there was the barest flicker of uncertainty in her voice.

"No you won't. I mean, I know what I'm talking about. Take it from me. There's nothing proud about it. You just die."

"Yes, but it's how you do it. I shall die nobly, like Queen Ezeriel."

Mort's forehead wrinkled. History was a closed book to him.

"Who's she?"

"She lived in Klatch and she had a lot of lovers and she sat on a snake," said Cutwell, who was winding up the crossbow.

"She meant to! She was crossed in love!"

"All I can remember was that she used to take baths in asses' milk. Funny thing, history," said Cutwell reflectively. "You become a queen, reign for thirty years, make laws, declare war on people and then the only thing you get remembered for is that you smelled like yogurt and were bitten in the—"

"She's a distant ancestor of mine," snapped Keli. "I won't listen to this sort of thing."

"Will you both be quiet and listen to me!" shouted Mort.

Silence descended like a shroud.

Then Cutwell sighted carefully and shot Mort in the back.

The night shed its early casualties and journeyed onwards. Even the wildest parties had ended, their guests lurching home to their beds, or someone's bed at any rate. Shorn of these fellow travelers, mere daytime people who had strayed out of their temporal turf, the true survivors of the night got down to the serious commerce of the dark.

This wasn't so very different from Ankh-Morpork's daytime business, except that the knives were more obvious and people didn't smile so much.

The Shades were silent, save only for the whistled signals of thieves and the velvety hush of dozens of people going about their private business in careful silence.

And, in Ham Alley, Cripple Wa's famous floating crap game was just getting under way. Several dozen cowled figures knelt or squatted around the little circle of packed earth where Wa's three eight-sided dice bounced and spun their misleading lesson in statistical probability.

"Three!"

"Tuphal's Eyes, by Io!"

"He's got you there, Hummok! This guy knows how to roll his bones!"

IT'S A KNACK.

Hummok M'guk, a small flat-faced man from one of the Hublandish tribes whose skill at dice was famed wherever two men gathered together to fleece a third, picked up the dice and glared at them. He silently cursed Wa, whose own skill at switching dice was equally notorious among the cognoscenti but had, apparently, failed him, wished a painful and untimely death on the shadowy player seated opposite and hurled the dice into the mud.

"Twenty-one the hard way!"

Wa scooped up the dice and handed them to the stranger.

As he turned to Hummok one eye flickered ever so slightly. Hummok was impressed—he'd barely noticed the blur in Wa's deceptively gnarled fingers, and he'd been watching for it.

It was disconcerting the way the things rattled in the stranger's hand and then flew out of it in a slow arc that ended with twenty-four little spots pointing at the stars.

Some of the more streetwise in the crowd shuffled away from the stranger, because luck like that can be very unlucky in Cripple Wa's floating crap game.

Wa's hand closed over the dice with a noise like the click of a trigger.

"All the eights," he breathed. "Such luck is uncanny, mister."

The rest of the crowd evaporated like dew, leaving only those heavy-set, unsympathetic-looking men who, if Wa had ever paid tax, would have gone down on his return as Essential Plant and Business Equipment.

"Maybe it's not luck," he added. "Maybe it's wizarding?"

I MOST STRONGLY RESENT THAT.

"We had a wizard once who tried to get rich," said Wa. "Can't seem to remember what happened to him. Boys?"

"We give him a good talking-to—"

"—and left him in Pork Passage—"

"—and in Honey Lane—"

"—and a couple other places I can't remember."

The stranger stood up. The boys closed in around him.

THIS IS UNCALLED FOR. I SEEK ONLY TO LEARN. WHAT PLEASURE CAN HUMANS FIND IN A MERE REITERATION OF THE LAWS OF CHANCE?

"Chance doesn't come into it. Let's have a look at him, boys."

The events that followed were recalled by no living soul except the one belonging to a feral cat, one of the city's thousands, that was crossing the alley en route to a tryst. It stopped and watched with interest.

The boys froze in mid-stab. Painful purple light flickered around them. The stranger pushed his hood back and picked up the dice, and then pushed them into Wa's unresisting hand. The man was opening and shutting his mouth, his eyes unsuccessfully trying not to see what was in front of them. Grinning.

THROW.

Wa managed to look down at his hand.

"What are the stakes?" he whispered.

IF YOU WIN, YOU WILL REFRAIN FROM THESE RIDICULOUS ATTEMPTS TO SUGGEST THAT CHANCE GOVERNS THE AFFAIRS OF MEN.

"Yes. Yes. And . . . if I lose?"

YOU WILL WISH YOU HAD WON.

Wa tried to swallow, but his throat had gone dry. "I know I've had lots of people murdered—"

TWENTY-THREE, TO BE PRECISE.

"Is it too late to say I'm sorry?"

SUCH THINGS DO NOT CONCERN ME. NOW THROW THE DICE.

Wa shut his eyes and dropped the dice on to the ground, too nervous even to try the special flick-and-twist throw. He kept his eyes shut.

ALL THE EIGHTS. THERE, THAT WASN'T TOO DIFFICULT, WAS IT?

Wa fainted.

Death shrugged and walked away, pausing only to tickle the ears of an alley cat that happened to be passing. He hummed to himself. He didn't quite know what had come over him, but he was enjoying it.

"You couldn't be sure it would work!"

Cutwell spread his hands in a conciliatory gesture.

"Well, no," he conceded, "but I thought, what have I got to lose?" He backed away.

"What have you got to lose?" shouted Mort.

He stamped forward and tugged the bolt out of one of the posts in the princess's bed.

"You're not going to tell me this went through me?" he snapped.

"I was particularly watching it," said Cutwell.

"I saw it too," said Keli. "It was horrible. It came right out of where your heart is."

"And I saw you walk through a stone pillar," said Cutwell.

"And *I* saw you ride straight through a window."

"Yes, but that *was* on business," declared Mort, waving his hands in the air. "That wasn't everyday, that's different. And—"

He paused. "The way you're looking at me," he said. "They looked at me the same way in the inn this evening. What's wrong?"

"It was the way you waved your arm straight through the bedpost," said Keli faintly.

Mort stared at his hand, and then rapped it on the wood.

"See?" he said. "Solid. Solid arm, solid wood."

"You said people looked at you in an inn?" said Cutwell. "What did you do, then? Walk through the wall?"

"No! I mean, no, I just drank this drink, I think it was called scrumble—"

"Scumble?"

"Yes. Tastes like rotten apples. You'd have thought it was some sort of poison the way they kept staring."

"How much did you drink, then?" said Cutwell.

"A pint, perhaps, I wasn't really paying much attention—"

"Did you know scumble is the strongest alcoholic drink between here and the Ramtops?" the wizard demanded.

"No. No one said," said Mort. "What's it got to do with—"

"No," said Cutwell, slowly, "you didn't know. Hmm. That's a clue, isn't it?"

"Has it got anything to do with saving the princess?"

"Probably not. I'd like to have a look at my books, though."

"In that case it's not important," said Mort firmly.

He turned to Keli, who was looking at him with the faint beginnings of admiration.

"I think I can help," he said. "I think I can lay my hands on some powerful magic. Magic will hold back the dome, won't it, Cutwell?"

"My magic won't. It'd have to be pretty strong stuff, and I'm not sure about it even then. Reality is tougher than—"

"I shall go," said Mort. "Until tomorrow, farewell!"

"It is tomorrow," Keli pointed out.

Mort deflated slightly.

"All right, tonight then," he said, slightly put out, and added, "I will begone!"

"Begone what?"

"It's hero talk," said Cutwell, kindly. "He can't help it." Mort scowled at him, smiled bravely at Keli and walked out of the room.

"He might have opened the door," said Keli, after he had gone.

"I think he was a bit embarrassed," said Cutwell. "We all go through that stage."

"What, of walking through things?"

"In a manner of speaking. Walking into them, anyway."

"I'm going to get some sleep," Keli said. "Even the dead need some rest. Cutwell, stop fiddling with that crossbow, please. I'm sure it's not wizardly to be alone in a lady's boudoir."

"Hmm? But I'm not alone, am I? You're here."

"That," she said, "is the point, isn't it?"

"Oh. Yes. Sorry. Um. I'll see you in the morning, then."

"Goodnight, Cutwell. Shut the door behind you."

The sun crept over the horizon, decided to make a run for it, and began to rise.

But it would be some time before its slow light rolled

across the sleeping Disc, herding the night ahead of it, and nocturnal shadows still ruled the city.

They clustered now around The Mended Drum in Filigree Street, foremost of the city's taverns. It was famed not for its beer, which looked like maiden's water and tasted like battery acid, but for its clientele. It was said that if you sat long enough in the Drum, then sooner or later every major hero on the Disc would steal your horse.

The atmosphere inside was still loud with talk and heavy with smoke although the landlord was doing all those things landlords do when they think it's time to close, like turn some of the lights out, wind up the clock, put a cloth over the pumps and, just in case, check the whereabouts of their club with the nails hammered in it. Not that the customers were taking the slightest bit of notice, of course. To most of the Drum's clientele even the nailed club would have been considered a mere hint.

However, they were sufficiently observant to be vaguely worried by the tall dark figure standing by the bar and drinking his way through its entire contents.

Lonely, dedicated drinkers always generate a mental field which insures complete privacy, but this particular one was radiating a kind of fatalistic gloom that was slowly emptying the bar.

This didn't worry the barman, because the lonely figure was engaged in a very expensive experiment.

Every drinking place throughout the multiverse has them—those shelves of weirdly-shaped, sticky bottles that not only contain exotically-named liquid, which is often blue or green, but also odds and ends that bottles of real drink would never stoop to contain, such as whole fruits, bits of twig and, in extreme cases, small drowned lizards. No-one knows why barmen stock so many, since they all taste like treacle dissolved in turpentine. It has been speculated that they dream of a day when someone will walk in off the street unbidden and ask for a glass of Peach Corniche with A

Hint Of Mint and overnight the place will become somewhere To Be Seen At.

The stranger was working his way along the row.

WHAT IS THAT GREEN ONE?

The landlord peered at the label.

"It says it's Melon Brandy," he said doubtfully. "It says it's bottled by some monks to an ancient recipe," he added.

I WILL TRY IT.

The man looked sideways at the empty glasses on the counter, some of them still containing bits of fruit salad, cherries on a stick and small paper umbrellas.

"Are you sure you haven't had enough?" he said. It worried him vaguely that he couldn't seem to make out the stranger's face.

The glass, with its drink crystallizing out on the sides, disappeared into the hood and came out again empty.

NO. WHAT IS THE YELLOW ONE WITH THE WASPS IN IT?

"Spring Cordial, it says. Yes?"

YES. AND THEN THE BLUE ONE WITH THE GOLD FLECKS.

"Er. Old Overcoat?"

YES. AND THEN THE SECOND ROW.

"Which one did you have in mind?"

ALL OF THEM.

The stranger remained bolt upright, the glasses with their burdens of syrup and assorted vegetation disappearing into the hood on a production line basis.

This is it, the landlord thought, this is style, this is where I buy a red jacket and maybe put some monkey nuts and a few gherkins on the counter, get a few mirrors around the place, replace the sawdust. He picked up a beer-soaked cloth and gave the woodwork a few enthusiastic wipes, speading the drips from the cordial glasses into a rainbow smear that took the varnish off. The last of the usual customers put on his hat and staggered out, muttering to himself.

"I DON'T SEE THE POINT, the stranger said.

"Sorry?"

WHAT IS SUPPOSED TO HAPPEN?

"How many drinks have you had?"

FORTY-SEVEN.

"Just about anything, then," said the barman and, because he knew his job and knew what was expected of him when people drank alone in the small hours, he started to polish a glass with the slops cloth and said, "Your lady thrown you out, has she?"

PARDON?

"Drowning your sorrows, are you?"

I HAVE NO SORROWS.

"No, of course not. Forget I mentioned it." He gave the glass a few more wipes. "Just thought it helps to have someone to talk to," he said.

The stranger was silent for a moment, thinking. Then he said: YOU WANT TO TALK TO ME?

"Yes. Sure. I'm a good listener."

NO ONE EVER WANTED TO TALK TO ME BEFORE.

"That's a shame."

THEY NEVER INVITE ME TO PARTIES, YOU KNOW.

"Tch."

THEY ALL HATE ME. EVERYONE HATES ME. I DON'T HAVE A SINGLE FRIEND.

"Everyone ought to have a friend," said the barman sagely.

I THINK—

"Yes?"

I THINK . . . I THINK I COULD BE FRIENDS WITH THE GREEN BOTTLE.

The landlord slid the octagon-bottle along the counter. Death took it and tilted it over the glass. The liquid tinkled on the rim.

YOU DRUNK I'M THINK, DON'T YOU?

"I serve anyone who can stand upright best out of three," said the landlord.

YOURRRE ABSOROOTLY RIGHT. BUT I—

The stranger paused, one declamatory finger in the air.

WAS WHAT I SAYING?

"You said I thought you were drunk."

AH. YES, *BUT* I CAN BE SHOBER ANY TIME I LIKE. THIS ISH
AN EXPERIMENT. AND NOW I WOULD LIKES TO EXPERIMENT
WITH THE ORANGE BRANDY AGAIN.

The landlord sighed, and glanced at the clock. There was
no doubt that he was making a lot of money, especially since
the stranger didn't seem inclined to worry about overcharg-
ing or short change. But it was getting late; in fact it was getting so late that it was getting early. There was also
something about the solitary customer that unsettled him.
People in The Mended Drum often drank as though there
was no tomorrow, but this was the first time he'd actually
felt they might be right.

I MEAN, WHAT HAVE I GOT TO LOOK FORWARD TO? WHERE'S
THE SENSE IN IT ALL? WHAT IS IT REALLY ALL ABOUT?

"Can't say, my friend. I expect you'll feel better after a
good night's sleep."

SLEEP? SLEEP? I NEVER SLEEP. I'M WOSSNAME, PROVERBIAL
FOR IT.

"Everyone needs their sleep. Even me," he hinted.

THEY ALL HATE ME, YOU KNOW.

"Yes, you said. But it's a quarter to three."

The stranger turned unsteadily and looked around the
silent room.

THERE'S NO ONE IN THE PLACE BUT YOU AND I, he said.

The landlord lifted up the flap and came around the bar,
helping the stranger down from his stool.

I HAVEN'T GOT A SINGLE FRIEND. EVEN CATS FIND ME AMUS-
ING.

A hand shot out and grabbed a bottle of Amanita Liquor
before the man managed to propel its owner to the door,
wondering how someone so thin could be so heavy.

I DON'T HAVE TO BE DRUNK, I SAID. WHY DO PEOPLE LIKE TO
BE DRUNK? IS IT FUN?

"Helps them forget about life, old chap. Now just you
lean there while I get the door open—"

FORGET ABOUT LIFE. HA. HA.

"You come back any time you like, y'hear?"

YOU'D REALLY LIKE TO SEE ME AGAIN?

The landlord looked back at the small heap of coins on the
bar. That was worth a little weirdness. At least this one was a
quiet one, and seemed to be harmless.

"Oh, yes," he said, propelling the stranger into the street
and retrieving the bottle in one smooth movement. "Drop in
anytime."

THAT'S THE NICEHEST THING—

The door slammed on the rest of the sentence.

Ysabell sat up in bed.

The knocking came again, soft and urgent. She pulled the
covers up to her chin.

"Who is it?" she whispered.

"It's me, Mort," came the hiss under the door. "Let me in,
please!"

"Wait!"

Ysabell scrambled frantically on the bedside table for the
matches, knocking over a bottle of toilet water and dislodging
a box of chocolates that was now mostly discarded wrappers.
Once she'd got the candle alight she adjusted its position for
maximum effect, tweaked the line of her nightdress into
something more revealing, and said: "It's not locked."

Mort staggered into the room, smelling of horses and frost
and scumble.

"I hope," said Ysabell archly, "that you have not forced
your way in here in order to take advantage of your position
in this household."

Mort looked around him. Ysabell was heavily into frills.

Even the dressing table seemed to be wearing a petticoat. The whole room wasn't so much furnished as lingeried.

"Look, I haven't got time to mess around," he said. "Bring that candle into the library. And for heaven's sake put on something sensible, you're overflowing."

Ysabell looked down, and then her head snapped up.

"Well!"

Mort poked his head back round the door. "It's a matter of life and death," he added, and disappeared.

Ysabell watched the door creak shut after him, revealing the blue dressing gown with the tassels that Death had thought up for her as a present last Hogswatch and which she hadn't the heart to throw away, despite the fact that it was a size too small and had a rabbit on the pocket.

Finally she swung her legs out of bed, slipped into the shameful dressing gown, and padded out into the corridor. Mort was waiting for her.

"Won't father hear us?" she said.

"He's not back. Come on."

"How can you tell?"

"The place feels different when he's here. It's—it's like the difference between a coat when it's being worn and when it's hanging on a hook. Haven't you noticed?"

"What are we doing that's so important?"

Mort pushed open the library door. A gust of warm, dry air drifted out, and the door hinges issued a protesting creak.

"We're going to save someone's life," he said. "A princess, actually."

Ysabell was instantly fascinated.

"A real princess? I mean can she feel a pea through a dozen mattresses?"

"Can she—?" Mort felt a minor worry disappear. "Oh. Yes. I thought Albert had got it wrong."

"Are you in love with her?"

Mort came to a standstill between the shelves, aware of the busy little scritchings inside the book covers.

"It's hard to be sure," he said. "Do I look it?"

"You look a bit flustered. How does she feel about you?"

"Don't know."

"Ah," said Ysabell knowingly, in the tones of an expert. "Unrequited love is the worst kind. It's probably not a good idea to go taking poison or killing yourself, though," she added thoughtfully. "What are we doing here? Do you want to find her book to see if she marries you?"

"I've read it, and she's dead," said Mort. "But only technically. I mean, not really dead."

"Good, otherwise that would be necromancy. What are we looking for?"

"Albert's biography."

"What for? I don't think he's got one."

"Everyone's got one."

"Well, he doesn't like people asking personal questions. I looked for it once and I couldn't find it. Albert by itself isn't much to go on. Why is he so interesting?" Ysabell lit a couple of candles from the one in her hand and filled the library with dancing shadows.

"I need a powerful wizard and I think he's one."

"What, Albert?"

"Yes. Only we're looking for Alberto Malich. He's more than two thousand years old, I think."

"What, Albert?"

"Yes. Albert."

"He never wears a wizard's hat," said Ysabell doubtfully.

"He lost it. Anyway, the hat isn't compulsory. Where do we start looking?"

"Well, if you're sure . . . the Stack, I suppose. That's where father puts all the biographies that are more than five hundred years old. It's this way."

She led the way past the whispering shelves to a door set in a cul-de-sac. It opened with some effort and the groan of the hinges reverberated around the library; Mort fancied for a moment that all the books paused momentarily in their work just to listen.

Steps led down into the velvet gloom. There were cobwebs and dust, and air that smelled as though it had been locked in a pyramid for a thousand years.

"People don't come down here very often," said Ysabell. "I'll lead the way."

Mort felt something was owed.

"I must say," he said, "you're a real brick."

"You mean pink, square and dumpy? You really know how to talk to a girl, my boy."

"Mort," said Mort automatically.

The Stack was as dark and silent as a cave deep underground. The shelves were barely far enough apart for one person to walk between them, and towered up well beyond the dome of candlelight. They were particularly eerie because they were silent. There were no more lives to write; the books slept. But Mort felt that they slept like cats, with one eye open. They were aware.

"I came down here once," said Ysabell, whispering. "If you go far enough along the shelves the books run out and there's clay tablets and lumps of stone and animal skins and everyone's called Ug and Zog."

The silence was almost tangible. Mort could feel the books watching them as they tramped through the hot, silent passages. Everyone who had ever lived was here somewhere, right back to the first people that the gods had baked out of mud or whatever. They didn't exactly resent him, they were just wondering about why he was here.

"Did you get past Ug and Zog?" he hissed. "There's a lot of people would be very interested to know what's there."

"I got frightened. It's a long way and I didn't have enough candles."

"Pity."

Ysabell stopped so sharply that Mort cannoned into the back of her.

"This would be about the right area," she said. "What now?"

Mort peered at the faded names on the spines.

"They don't seem to be in any order!" he moaned.

They looked up. They wandered down a couple of side alleys. They pulled a few books off the lowest shelves at random, raising pillows of dust.

"This is silly," said Mort at last. "There's millions of lives here. The chances of finding his are worse than—"

Ysabell laid her hand against his mouth.

"Listen!"

Mort mumbled a bit through her fingers and then got the message. He strained his ears, striving to hear anything above the heavy hiss of absolute silence.

And then he found it. A faint, irritable scratching. High, high overhead, somewhere in the impenetrable darkness on the cliff of shelves, a life was still being written.

They looked at each other, their eyes widening. Then Ysabell said, "We passed a ladder back there. On wheels."

The little casters on the bottom squeaked as Mort rolled it back. The top end moved too, as if it was fixed to another set of wheels somewhere up in the darkness.

"Right," he said. "Give me the candle, and—"

"If the candle's going up, then so am I," said Ysabell firmly. "You stop down here and move the ladder when I say. And don't argue."

"It might be dangerous up there," said Mort gallantly.

"It might be dangerous down here," Ysabell pointed out. "So I'll be up the ladder with the candle, thank you."

She set her foot on the bottom rung and was soon no more than a frilly shadow outlined in a halo of candlelight that soon began to shrink.

Mort steadied the ladder and tried not to think of all the lives pressing in on him. Occasionally a meteor of hot wax would thump into the floor beside him, raising a crater in the dust. Ysabell was now a faint glow far above, and he could feel every footstep as it vibrated down the ladder.

She stopped. It seemed to be for quite a long time.

Then her voice floated down, deadened by the weight of silence around them.

"Mort, I've found it."

"Good. Bring it down."

"Mort, you were right."

"Okay, thanks. Now bring it down."

"Yes, Mort, but which one?"

"Don't mess about, that candle won't last much longer."

"Mort!"

"What?"

"Mort, there's a whole *shelf*!"

Now it really was dawn, that cusp of the day that belonged to no one except the seagulls in Morpork docks, the tide that rolled in up the river, and a warm turnwise wind that added a smell of spring to the complex odor of the city.

Death sat on a bollard, looking out to sea. He had decided to stop being drunk. It made his head ache.

He'd tried fishing, dancing, gambling and drink, allegedly four of life's greatest pleasures, and wasn't sure that he saw the point. Food he was happy with—Death liked a good meal as much as anyone else. He couldn't think of any other pleasures of the flesh or, rather, he could, but they were, well, *fleshy*, and he couldn't see how it would be possible to go about them without some major bodily restructuring, which he wasn't going to contemplate. Besides, humans seemed to leave off doing them as they grew older, so presumably they couldn't be that attractive.

Death began to feel that he wouldn't understand people as long as he lived.

The sun made the cobbles steam and Death felt the faintest

tingling of that little springtime urge that can send a thousand tons of sap pumping through fifty feet of timber in a forest.

The seagulls swooped and dived around him. A one-eyed cat, down to its eighth life and its last ear, emerged from its lair in a heap of abandoned fish boxes, stretched, yawned, and rubbed itself against his legs. The breeze, cutting through Ankh's famous smell, brought a hint of spices and fresh bread.

Death was bewildered. He couldn't fight it. He was actually feeling glad to be alive, and very reluctant to be Death.

I MUST BE SICKENING FOR SOMETHING, he thought.

Mort eased himself up the ladder alongside Ysabell. It was shaky, but seemed to be safe. At least the height didn't bother him; everything below was just blackness.

Some of Albert's earlier volumes were very nearly falling apart. He reached out for one at random, feeling the ladder tremble underneath them as he did so, brought it back and opened it somewhere in the middle.

"Move the candle this way," he said.

"Can you read it?"

"Sort of—"

—'turnered hys hand, butt was sorelie vexed that alle menne at laste comme to nort, viz. Deathe, and vowed hymme to seke Imortalitie yn his pride. "Thus," he tolde the younge wizzerds, "we may take unto ourselfes the mantel of Goddes." Thee next day, yt being raining, Alberto'—

"It's written in Old," he said. "Before they invented spelling. Let's have a look at the latest one."

It was Albert all right. Mort caught several references to fried bread.

"Let's have a look at what he's doing now," said Ysabell.

"Do you think we should? It's a bit like spying."

"So what? Scared?"

"All right."

He flicked through until he came to the unfilled pages,

and then turned back until he found the story of Albert's life, crawling across the page at surprising speed considering it was the middle of the night; most biographies didn't have much to say about sleep, unless the dreams were particularly vivid.

"Hold the candle properly, will you? I don't want to get grease on his life."

"Why not? He likes grease."

"Stop giggling, you'll have us both off. Now look at this bit. . . ."

—"He crept through the dusty darkness of the Stack—" Ysabell read—"his eyes fixed on the tiny glow of candle-light high above. Prying, he thought, poking away at things that shouldn't concern them, the little devils"—

"Mort! He's—"

"Shut up! I'm reading!"

—"soon put a stop to this. Albert crept silently to the foot of the ladder, spat on his hands, and got ready to push. The master'd never know; he was acting strange these days and it was all that lad's fault, and"—

Mort looked up into Ysabell's horrified eyes.

Then the girl took the book out of Mort's hand, held it at arm's length while her gaze remained fixed woodenly on his, and let it go.

Mort watched her lips move and then realized that he, too, was counting under his breath.

Three, four—

There was a dull thump, a muffled cry, and silence.

"Do you think you've killed him?" said Mort, after a while.

"What, *here*? Anyway, I didn't notice any better ideas coming from you."

"No, but—he is an old man, after all."

"No, he's not," said Ysabell sharply, starting down the ladder.

"Two thousand years?"

"Not a day over sixty-seven."

"The books said—"

"I told you, time doesn't apply here. Not *real* time. Don't you listen, boy?"

"Mort," said Mort.

"And stop treading on my fingers, I'm going as fast as I can."

"Sorry."

"And don't act so wet. Have you any idea how boring it is living here?"

"Probably not," said Mort, adding with genuine longing, "I've heard about boredom but I've never had a chance to try it."

"It's dreadful."

"If it comes to that, excitement isn't all it's cracked up to be."

"Anything's got to be better than this."

There was a groan from below, and then a stream of swearwords.

Ysabell peered into the gloom.

"Obviously I didn't damage his cursing muscles," she said. "I don't think I ought to listen to words like that. It could be bad for my moral fiber."

They found Albert slumped against the foot of the bookshelf, muttering and holding his arm.

"There's no need to make that kind of fuss," said Ysabell briskly. "You're not hurt; father simply doesn't allow that kind of thing to happen."

"What did you have to go and do that for?" he moaned. "I didn't mean any harm."

"You were going to push us off," said Mort, trying to help him up. "I read it. I'm surprised you didn't use magic."

Albert glared at him.

"Oh, so you've found out, have you?" he said quietly. "Then much good may it do you. You've no right to go prying."

He struggled to his feet, shook off Mort's hand, and stumbled back along the hushed shelves.

"No, wait," said Mort, "I need your help!"

"Well, of course," said Albert over his shoulder. "It stands to reason, doesn't it? You thought, I'll just go and pry into someone's private life and then I'll drop it on him and then I'll ask him to help me."

"I only wanted to find out if you were really you," said Mort, running after him.

"I am. Everyone is."

"But if you don't help me something terrible will happen! There's this princess, and she—"

"Terrible things happen all the time, boy—"

"—Mort—"

"—and no one expects me to do anything about it."

"But you were the greatest!"

Albert stopped for a moment, but did not look around.

"*Was* the greatest, *was* the greatest. And don't you try to butter me up. I ain't butterable."

"They've got statues to you and everything," said Mort, trying not to yawn.

"More fool them, then." Albert reached the foot of the steps into the library proper, stamped up them and stood outlined against the candlelight from the library.

"You mean you won't help?" said Mort. "Not even if you can?"

"Give the boy a prize," growled Albert. "And it's no good thinking you can appeal to my better nature under this here crusty exterior," he added, " 'cos my interior's pretty damn crusty too."

They heard him cross the library floor as though he had a grudge against it, and slam the door behind him.

"Well," said Mort, uncertainly.

"What did you expect?" snapped Ysabell. "He doesn't care for anyone much except father."

"It's just that I thought someone like him would help if I explained it properly," said Mort. He sagged. The rush of energy that had propelled him through the long night had evaporated, filling his mind with lead. "You know he was a famous wizard?"

"That doesn't mean anything, wizards aren't necessarily nice. Do not meddle in the affairs of wizards because a refusal often offends, I read somewhere." Ysabell stepped closer to Mort and peered at him with some concern. "You look like something left on a plate," she said.

" 'M okay," said Mort, walking heavily up the steps and into the scratching shadows of the library.

"You're not. You could do with a good night's sleep, my lad."

"M't," murmured Mort.

He felt Ysabell slip his arm over her shoulder. The walls were moving gently, even the sound of his own voice was coming from a long way off, and he dimly felt how nice it would be to stretch out on a nice stone slab and sleep forever.

Death'd be back soon, he told himself, feeling his unprotesting body being helped along the corridors. There was nothing for it, he'd have to tell Death. He wasn't such a bad old stick. Death would help; all he needed to do was explain things. And then he could stop all this worrying and go to slee. . . .

"And what was your previous position?"

I BEG YOUR PARDON?

"What did you do for a living?" said the thin young man behind the desk.

The figure opposite him shifted uneasily.

I USHERED SOULS INTO THE NEXT WORLD. I WAS THE GRAVE OF ALL HOPE. I WAS THE ULTIMATE REALITY. I WAS THE ASSASSIN AGAINST WHOM NO LOCK WOULD HOLD.

"Yes, point taken, but do you have any particular skills?"

Death thought about it.

I SUPPOSE A CERTAIN AMOUNT OF EXPERTISE WITH AGRICULTURAL IMPLEMENTS? he ventured after a while.

The young man shook his head firmly.

No?

"This is a city, Mr.—" he glanced down, and once again felt a faint unease that he couldn't quite put his finger on—"Mr.—Mr.—Mr., and we're a bit short of fields."

He laid down his pen and gave the kind of smile that suggested he'd learned it from a book.

Ankh-Morpork wasn't advanced enough to possess an employment exchange. People took jobs because their fathers made room for them, or because their natural talent found an opening, or by word-of-mouth. But there was a call for servants and menial workers, and with the commercial sections of the city beginning to boom the thin young man—a Mr. Liona Keeble—had invented the profession of job broker and was, right at this moment, finding it difficult.

"My dear Mr.—" he glanced down—"Mr., we get many people coming into the city from outside because, alas, they believe life is richer here. Excuse me for saying so, but you seem to me to be a gentleman down on his luck. I would have thought you would have preferred something rather more refined than—" he glanced down again, and frowned—" 'something nice working with cats or flowers.' "

I'M SORRY. I FELT IT WAS TIME FOR A CHANGE.

"Can you play a musical instrument?"

No.

"Can you do carpentry?"

I DO NOT KNOW, I HAVE NEVER TRIED. Death stared at his feet. He was beginning to feel deeply embarrassed.

Keeble shuffled the paper on his desk, and sighed.

I CAN WALK THROUGH WALLS, Death volunteered, aware that the conversation had reached an impasse.

Keeble looked up brightly. "I'd like to see that," he said. "That could be quite a qualification."

RIGHT.

Death pushed his chair back and stalked confidently towards the nearest wall.

OUCH.

Keeble watched expectantly. "Go on, then," he said.

UM. THIS IS AN ORDINARY WALL, IS IT?

"I assume so. I'm not an expert."

IT SEEMS TO BE PRESENTING ME WITH SOME DIFFICULTY.

"So it would appear."

WHAT DO YOU CALL THE FEELING OF BEING VERY SMALL AND HOT?

Keeble twiddled his pencil.

"Pygmy?"

BEGINS WITH AN M.

"Embarrassing?"

"Yes," said Death, I MEAN YES.

"It would seem that you have no useful skill or talent whatsoever," he said. "Have you thought of going into teaching?"

Death's face was a mask of terror. Well, it was always a mask of terror, but this time he meant it to be.

"You see," said Keeble kindly, putting down his pen and steepling his hands together, "it's very seldom I ever have to find a new career for an—what was it again?"

ANTHROPOMORPHIC PERSONIFICATION.

"Oh, yes. What is that, exactly?"

Death had had enough.

THIS, he said.

For a moment, just for a moment, Mr. Keeble saw him clearly. His face went nearly as pale as Death's own. His hands jerked convulsively. His heart gave a stutter.

Death watched him with mild interest, then drew an hourglass from the depths of his robe and held it up to the light and examined it critically.

SETTLE DOWN, he said, YOU'VE GOT A GOOD FEW YEARS YET.

"Bbbbbbb—"

I COULD TELL YOU HOW MANY IF YOU LIKE.

Keeble, fighting to breathe, managed to shake his head.

DO YOU WANT ME TO GET YOU A GLASS OF WATER, THEN?

"nnN—nnN."

The shop bell jangled. Keeble's eyes rolled. Death decided that he owed the man something. He shouldn't be allowed to lose custom, which was clearly something humans valued dearly.

He pushed aside the bead curtain and stalked into the outer shop, where a small fat woman, looking rather like an angry cottage loaf, was hammering on the counter with a haddock.

"It's about that cook's job up at the University," she said. "You told me it was a good position and it's a disgrace up there, the tricks them students play, and I demand—I want you to—I'm not. . . ."

Her voice trailed off.

" 'Ere," she said, but you could tell her heart wasn't in it, "you're not Keeble, are you?"

Death stared at her. He'd never before experienced an unsatisfied customer. He was at a loss. Finally he gave up.

BEGONE, YOU BLACK AND MIDNIGHT HAG, he said.

The cook's small eyes narrowed.

" 'Oo are you calling a midnight bag?" she said accusingly, and hit the counter with the fish again. "Look at this," she said. "Last night it was my bedwarmer, in the morning it's a fish. I ask you."

MAY ALL THE DEMONS OF HELL REND YOUR LIVING SPIRIT IF YOU DON'T GET OUT OF THE SHOP THIS MINUTE, Death tried.

"I don't know about that, but what about my bedwarmer? It's no place for a respectable woman up there, they tried to—"

IF YOU WOULD CARE TO GO AWAY, said Death desperately, I WILL GIVE YOU SOME MONEY.

"How much?" said the cook, with a speed that would have outdistanced a striking rattlesnake and given lightning a nasty shock.

Death pulled out his coin bag and tipped a heap of verdigrised and darkened coins on the counter. She regarded them with deep suspicion.

NOW LEAVE UPON THE INSTANT, said Death, and added, BEFORE THE SEARING WINDS OF INFINITY SCORCH THY WORTHLESS CARCASS.

"My husband will be told about this," said the cook darkly, as she left the shop. It seemed to Death that no threat of his could possibly be as dire.

He stalked back through the curtains. Keeble, still slumped in his chair, gave a kind of strangled gurgle.

"It was true!" he said. "I thought you were a nightmare!"

I COULD TAKE OFFENSE AT THAT, said Death.

"You really are Death?" said Keeble.

YES.

"Why didn't you say?"

PEOPLE USUALLY PREFER ME NOT TO.

Keeble scrabbled among his papers, giggling hysterically.

"You want to do something else?" he said. "Tooth fairy? Water sprite? Sandman?"

DO NOT BE FOOLISH. I SIMPLY—FEEL I WANT A CHANGE.

Keeble's frantic rustling at last turned up the paper he'd been searching for. He gave a maniacal laugh and thrust it into Death's hands.

Death read it.

THIS IS A JOB? PEOPLE ARE PAID TO DO THIS?

"Yes, yes, go and see him, you're just the right type. Only don't tell him I sent you."

Binky moved at a hard gallop across the night, the Disc unrolling far below his hooves. Now Mort found that the sword could reach out further than he had thought, it could reach the stars themselves, and he swung it across the deeps of space and into the heart of a yellow dwarf which went nova most satisfactorily. He stood in the saddle and whirled the blade around his head, laughing as the blue flame fanned across the sky leaving a trail of darkness and embers.

And didn't stop. Mort struggled as the sword cut through the horizon, grinding down the mountains, drying up the seas, turning green forests into punk and ashes. He heard voices behind him, and the brief screams of friends and relatives as he turned desperately. Dust storms whirled from the dead earth as he fought to release his own grip, but the sword burned icy cold in his hand, dragging him on in a dance that would not end until there was nothing left alive.

And that time came, and Mort stood alone except for Death, who said, "A fine job, boy."

And Mort said, MORT.

"Mort! Mort! Wake up!"

Mort surfaced slowly, like a corpse in a pond. He fought against it, clinging to his pillow and the horrors of sleep, but someone was tugging urgently at his ear.

"Mmmph?" he said.

*"Mort!"*

*"Wsst?"*

"Mort, it's father!"

He opened his eyes and stared up blankly into Ysabell's face. Then the events of the previous night hit him like a sock full of damp sand.

Mort swung his legs out of bed, still wreathed in the remains of his dream.

"Yeah, okay," he said. "I'll go and see him directly."

"He's not here! Albert's going crazy!" Ysabell stood by the bed, tugging a handkerchief between her hands. "Mort, do you think something bad has happened to him?"

He gave her a blank look. "Don't be bloody stupid," he said, "he's Death." He scratched his skin. He felt hot and dry and itchy.

"But he's never been away this long! Not even when there was that big plague in Pseudopolis! I mean, he has to be here in the mornings to do the books and work out the nodes and—"

Mort grabbed her arms. "All right, all right," he said, as soothingly as he could manage. "I'm sure everything's okay. Just settle down, I'll go and check . . . why have you got your eyes shut?"

"Mort, please put some clothes on," said Ysabell in a tight little voice.

Mort looked down.

"Sorry," he said meekly, "I didn't realize . . . Who put me to bed?"

"I did," she said. "But I looked the other way."

Mort dragged on his breeches, shrugged into his shirt and hurried out towards Death's study with Ysabell on his heels. Albert was in there, jumping from foot to foot like a duck on a griddle. When Mort came in the look on the old man's face could almost have been gratitude.

Mort saw with amazement that there were tears in his eyes.

"His chair hasn't been sat in," Albert whined.

"Sorry, but is that important?" said Mort. "My grandad didn't used to come home for days if he'd had a good sale at the market."

"But he's always here," said Albert. "Every morning, as long as I've known him, sitting here at his desk a-working on the nodes. It's his job. He wouldn't miss it."

"I expect the nodes can look after themselves for a day or two," said Mort.

The drop in temperature told him he was wrong. He looked at their faces.

"They can't?" he said.

Both heads shook.

"If the nodes aren't worked out properly all the Balance is destroyed," said Ysabell. "Anything could happen."

"Didn't he explain?" said Albert.

"Not really. I've really only done the practical side. He said he'd tell me about the theoretical stuff later," said Mort. Ysabell burst into tears.

Albert took Mort's arm and, with considerable dramatic waggling of his eyebrows, indicated that they should have a little talk in the corner. Mort trailed after him reluctantly.

The old man rummaged in his pockets and at last produced a battered paper bag.

"Peppermint?" he inquired.

Mort shook his head.

"He never tell you about the nodes?" said Albert.

Mort shook his head again. Albert gave his peppermint a suck; it sounded like the plughole in the bath of God.

"How old are you, lad?"

"Mort. I'm sixteen."

"There's some things a lad ought to be tole before he's sixteen," said Albert, looking over his shoulder at Ysabell, who was sobbing in Death's chair.

"Oh, I know about *that*. My father told me all about that when we used to take the thargas to be mated. When a man and a woman—"

"About the universe is what I meant," said Albert hurriedly. "I mean, have you ever thought about it?"

"I know the Disc is carried through space on the backs of four elephants that stand on the shell of Great A'Tuin," said Mort.

"That's just part of it. I meant the whole universe of time and space and life and death and day and night and everything."

"Can't say I've ever given it much thought," said Mort.

"Ah. You ought. The point is, the nodes are part of it. They stop death from getting out of control, see. Not him, not Death. Just death itself. Like, uh—" Albert struggled for words—"like, death should come exactly at the end of life, see, and not before or after, and the nodes have to be worked out so that the key figures . . . you're not taking this in, are you?"

"Sorry."

"They've got to be worked out," said Albert flatly, "and

then the correct lives have got to be got. The hourglasses, you call them. The actual Duty is the easy job."

"Can you do it?"

"No. Can you?"

"No!"

Albert sucked reflectively at his peppermint. "That's the whole world in the gyppo, then," he said.

"Look, I can't see why you're so worried. I expect he's just got held up somewhere," said Mort, but it sounded feeble even to him. It wasn't as though people buttonholed Death to tell him another story, or clapped him on the back and said things like "You've got time for a quick half in there, my old mate, no need to rush off home" or invited him to make up a skittles team and come out for a Klatchian take-away afterwards, or . . . It struck Mort with sudden, terrible poignancy that Death must be the loneliest creature in the universe. In the great party of Creation, he was always in the kitchen.

"I'm sure I don't know what's come over the master lately," mumbled Albert. "Out of the chair, my girl. Let's have a look at these nodes."

They opened the ledger.

They looked at it for a long time.

Then Mort said, "What do all those symbols mean?"

"Sodomy non sapiens," said Albert under his breath.

"What does that mean?"

"Means I'm buggered if I know."

"That was wizard talk, wasn't it?" said Mort.

"You shut up about wizard talk. I don't know anything about wizard talk. You apply your brain to this here."

Mort looked down again at the tracery of lines. It was as if a spider had spun a web on the page, stopping at every junction to make notes. Mort stared until his eyes hurt, waiting for some spark of inspiration. None volunteered.

"Any luck?"

"It's all Klatchian to me," said Mort. "I don't even know whether it should be read upside down or sideways."

"Spiralling from the center outwards," sniffed Ysabell from her seat in the corner.

Their heads collided as they both peered at the center of the page. They stared at her. She shrugged.

"Father taught me how to read the node chart," she said, "when I used to do my sewing in here. He used to read bits out."

"You can help?" said Mort.

"No," said Ysabell. She blew her nose.

"What do you mean, no?" growled Albert. "This is too important for any flighty—"

"I mean," said Ysabell, in razor tones, "that I can do them and you can help."

The Ankh-Morpork Guild of Merchants has taken to hiring large gangs of men with ears like fists and fists like large bags of walnuts whose job it is to re-educate those misguided people who publicly fail to recognize the many attractive points of their fine city. For example the philosopher Catroaster was found floating face downward in the river within hours of uttering the famous line, "When a man is tired of Ankh-Morpork, he is tired of ankle-deep slurry."

Therefore it is prudent to dwell on one—of the very many, of course—on one of the things that makes Ankh-Morpork renowned among the great cities of the multiverse.

This is its food.

The trade routes of half the Disc pass through the city or down its rather sluggish river. More than half the tribes and races of the Disc have representatives dwelling within its sprawling acres. In Ankh-Morpork the cuisines of the world collide: on the menu are one thousand types of vegetable, fifteen hundred cheeses, two thousand spices, three hundred types of meat, two hundred fowl, five hundred different kinds of fish, one hundred variations on the theme of pasta, seventy eggs of one kind or another, fifty insects, thirty molluscs, twenty assorted snakes and other reptiles, and something pale brown and warty known as the Klatchian migratory bog truffle.

Its eating establishments range from the opulent, where the portions are tiny but the plates are silver, to the secretive, where some of the Disc's more exotic inhabitants are rumored to eat anything they can get down their throat best out of three.

Harga's House of Ribs down by the docks is probably not numbered among the city's leading eateries, catering as it does for the type of beefy clientele that prefers quantity and breaks up the tables if it doesn't get it. They don't go in for the fancy or exotic, but stick to conventional food like flightless bird embryos, minced organs in intestine skins, slices of hog flesh and burnt ground grass seeds dipped in animal fats; or, as it is known in their patois, egg, soss and bacon and a fried slice.

It was the kind of eating house that didn't need a menu. You just looked at Harga's vest.

Still, he had to admit, this new cook seemed to be the business. Harga, an expansive advert for his own high carbohydrate merchandise, beamed at a room full of satisfied customers. And a fast worker, too! In fact, disconcertingly fast.

He rapped on the hatch.

"Double egg, chips, beans, and a trollburger, hold the onions," he rasped.

RIGHT.

The hatch slid up a few seconds later and two plates were pushed through. Harga shook his head in gratified amazement.

It had been like that all evening. The eggs were bright and shiny, the beans glistened like rubies, and the chips were the crisp golden brown of sunburned bodies on expensive beaches. Harga's last cook had turned out chips like little paper bags full of pus.

Harga looked around the steamy cafe. No one was watching him. He was going to get to the bottom of this. He rapped on the hatch again.

"Alligator sandwich," he said. "And make it sna—"

The hatch shot up. After a few seconds to pluck up enough courage, Harga peered under the top slice of the long sarny in front of him. He wasn't saying that it was alligator, and he wasn't saying it wasn't. He knuckled the hatch again.

"Okay," he said, "I'm not complaining, I just want to know how you did it so fast."

TIME IS NOT IMPORTANT.

"You say?"

RIGHT.

Harga decided not to argue.

"Well, you're doing a damn fine job in there, boy," he said.

WHAT IS IT CALLED WHEN YOU FEEL WARM AND CONTENT AND WISH THINGS WOULD STAY THAT WAY?

"I guess you'd call it happiness," said Harga.

Inside the tiny, cramped kitchen, strata'd with the grease of decades, Death spun and whirled, chopping, slicing and flying. His skillet flashed through the fetid steam.

He'd opened the door to the cold night air, and a dozen neighborhood cats had strolled in, attracted by the bowls of milk and meat—some of Harga's best, if he'd known—that had been strategically placed around the floor. Occasionally Death would pause in his work and scratch one of them behind the ears.

"Happiness," he said, and puzzled at the sound of his own voice.

Cutwell, the wizard and Royal Recognizer by appointment, pulled himself up the last of the tower steps and leaned against the wall, waiting for his heart to stop thumping.

Actually it wasn't particularly high, this tower, just high for Sto Lat. In general design and outline it looked the standard sort of tower for imprisoning princesses in; it was mainly used to store old furniture.

However, it offered unsurpassed views of the city and the Sto plain, which is to say, you could see an awful lot of cabbages.

Cutwell made it as far as the crumbling crenellations atop the wall and looked out at the morning haze. It was, maybe, a little hazier than usual. If he tried hard he could imagine a flicker in the sky. If he really strained his imagination he could hear a buzzing out over the cabbage fields, a sound like someone frying locusts. He shivered.

At a time like this his hands automatically patted his pockets, and found nothing but half a bag of jelly babies, melted into a sticky mass, and an apple core. Neither offered much consolation.

What Cutwell wanted was what any normal wizard wanted at a time like this, which was a smoke. He'd have killed for a cigar, and would have gone as far as a flesh wound for a squashed dog-end. He pulled himself together. Resolution was good for the moral fiber; the only trouble was the fiber didn't appreciate the sacrifices he was making for it. They said that a truly great wizard should be permanently under tension. You could have used Cutwell for a bowstring.

He turned his back on the brassica-ed landscape and made his way back down the winding steps to the main part of the palace.

Still, he told himself, the campaign appeared to be working. The population didn't seem to be resisting the fact that there was going to be a coronation, although they weren't exactly clear about who was going to be crowned. There was going to be bunting in the streets and Cutwell had arranged for the town square's main fountain to run, if not with wine, then at least with an acceptable beer made from broccoli. There was going to be folk dancing, at sword point if necessary. There would be races for children. There would be an ox roast. The royal coach had been regilded and Cutwell was optimistic that people could be persuaded to notice it as it went by.

The High Priest at the Temple of Blind Io was going to be a problem. Cutwell had marked him down as a dear old soul whose expertise with the knife was so unreliable that half of the sacrifices got tired of waiting and wandered away. The last time he'd tried to sacrifice a goat it had time to give birth to twins before he could focus, and then the courage of motherhood had resulted in it chasing the entire priesthood out of the temple.

The chances of him succeeding in putting the crown on the right person even in normal circumstances were only average, Cutwell had calculated; he'd have to stand alongside the old boy and try tactfully to guide his shaking hands.

Still, even that wasn't the big problem. The big problem was much bigger than that. The big problem had been sprung on him by the Chancellor after breakfast.

"Fireworks?" Cutwell had said.

"That's the sort of thing you wizard fellows are supposed to be good at, isn't it?" said the Chancellor, as crusty as a week-old loaf. "Flashes and bangs and whatnot. I remember a wizard when I was a lad—"

"I'm afraid I don't know anything about fireworks," said Cutwell, in tones designed to convey that he cherished this ignorance.

"Lots of rockets," the Chancellor reminisced happily. "Ankhian candles. Thunderflashes. And thingies that you can hold in your hand. It's not a proper coronation without fireworks."

"Yes, but, you see—"

"Good man," said the Chancellor briskly, "knew we could rely on you. Plenty of rockets, you understand, and to finish with there must be a set-piece, mind you, something really breathtaking like a portrait of—of—" his eyes glazed over in a way that was becoming depressingly familiar to Cutwell.

"The Princess Keli," he said wearily.

"Ah. Yes. Her," said the Chancellor. "A portrait of—who you said—in fireworks. Of course, it's probably all pretty simple stuff to you wizards, but the people like it. Nothing like a good blowout and a blowup and a bit of balcony waving to keep the loyalty muscles in tip-top shape, that's what I always say. See to it. Rockets. With runes on."

An hour ago Cutwell had thumbed through the index of *The Monster Fun Grimoire* and had cautiously assembled a number of common household ingredients and put a match to them.

Funny thing about eyebrows, he mused. You never really noticed them until they'd gone.

Red around the eyes, and smelling slightly of smoke, Cutwell ambled towards the royal apartments past bevies of maids engaged in whatever it was maids did, which always seemed to take at least three of them. Whenever they saw Cutwell they would usually go silent, hurry past with their heads down and then break into muffled giggles along the corridor. This annoyed Cutwell. Not—he told himself quickly—because of any personal considerations, but because wizards ought to be shown more respect. Besides, some of the maids had a way of looking at him which caused him to think distinctly unwizardly thoughts.

Truly, he thought, the way of enlightenment is like unto half a mile of broken glass.

He knocked on the door of Keli's suite. A maid opened it.

"Is your mistress in?" he said, as haughtily as he could manage.

The maid put her hand to her mouth. Her shoulders shook. Her eyes sparkled. A sound like escaping steam crept between her fingers.

I can't help it, Cutwell thought, I just seem to have this amazing effect on women.

"Is it a man?" came Keli's voice from within. The maid's

eyes glazed over and she tilted her head, as if not sure of
what she had heard.

"It's me, Cutwell," said Cutwell.

"Oh, that's all right, then. You can come in."

Cutwell pushed past the girl and tried to ignore the muffled laughter as the maid fled the room. Of course, everyone
knew a wizard didn't need a chaperon. It was just the tone of
the princess's "Oh, that's all right then" that made him
writhe inside.

Keli was sitting at her dressing table, brushing her hair.
Very few men in the world ever find out what a princess
wears under her dresses, and Cutwell joined them with
extreme reluctance but with remarkable self-control. Only
the frantic bobbing of his adam's apple betrayed him.
There was no doubt about it, he'd be no good for magic
for *days*.

She turned and he caught a whiff of talcum powder. For
*weeks*, dammit, for *weeks*.

"You look a bit hot, Cutwell. Is something the matter?"

"Naarg."

"I'm sorry?"

He shook himself. Concentrate on the hairbrush, man, the
hairbrush. "Just a bit of magical experimenting, ma'am.
Only superficial burns."

"Is it still moving?"

"I am afraid so."

Keli turned back to the mirror. Her face was set.

"Have we got time?"

This was the bit he'd been dreading. He'd done everything he could. The Royal Astrologer had been sobered up
long enough to insist that tomorrow was the only possible
day the ceremony could take place, so Cutwell had arranged
for it to begin one second after midnight. He'd ruthlessly cut
the score of the royal trumpet fanfare. He'd timed the High
Priest's invocation to the gods and then sub-edited heavily;
there was going to be a row when the gods found out. The

ceremony of the anointing with sacred oils had been cut to a quick dab behind the ears. Skateboards were an unknown invention on the Disc; if they hadn't been, Keli's trip up the aisle would have been unconstitutionally fast. And it still wasn't enough. He nerved himself.

"I think possibly not," he said. "It could be a very close thing."

He saw her glare at him in the mirror.

"How close?"

"Um. Very."

"Are you trying to say it might reach us at the same time as the ceremony?"

"Um. More sort of, um, before it," said Cutwell wretchedly. There was no sound but the drumming of Keli's fingers on the edge of the table. Cutwell wondered if she was going to break down, or smash the mirror. Instead she said:

"How do you know?"

He wondered if he could get away with saying something like, I'm a wizard, we know these things, but decided against it. The last time he'd said that she'd threatened him with the axe.

"I asked one of the guards about that inn Mort talked about," he said. "Then I worked out the approximate distance it had to travel. Mort said it was moving at a slow walking pace, and I reckon his stride is about—"

"As simple as that? You didn't use magic?"

"Only common sense. It's a lot more reliable in the long run."

She reached out and patted his hand.

"Poor old Cutwell," she said.

"I am only twenty, ma'am."

She stood up and walked over to her dressing room. One of the things you learn when you're a princess is always to be older than anyone of inferior rank.

"Yes, I suppose there must be such things as young wizards," she said over her shoulder. "It's just that people always think of them as old. I wonder why this is?"

"Rigors of the calling, ma'am," said Cutwell, rolling his eyes. He could hear the rustle of silk.

"What made you decide to become a wizard?" Her voice was muffled, as if she had something over her head.

"It's indoor work with no heavy lifting," said Cutwell. "And I suppose I wanted to learn how the world worked."

"Have you succeeded, then?"

"No." Cutwell wasn't much good at small talk, otherwise he'd never have let his mind wander sufficiently to allow him to say: "What made you decide to become a princess?"

After a thoughtful silence she said, "It was decided for me, you know."

"Sorry, I—"

"Being royal is a sort of family tradition. I expect it's the same with magic; no doubt your father was a wizard?"

Cutwell gritted his teeth. "Um. No," he said, "not really. Absolutely not, in fact."

He knew what she would say next, and here it came, reliable as the sunset, in a voice tinged with amusement and fascination.

"Oh? Is it really true that wizards aren't allowed to—"

"Well, if that's all I really should be going," said Cutwell loudly. "If anyone wants me, just follow the explosions. I—*gnnnh!*"

Keli had stepped out of the dressing room.

Now, women's clothes were not a subject that preoccupied Cutwell much—in fact, usually when he thought about women his mental pictures seldom included any clothes at all—but the vision in front of him really did take his breath away. Whoever had designed the dress didn't know when to stop. They'd put lace over the silk, and trimmed it with black vermine, and strung pearls anywhere that looked bare, and puffed and starched the sleeves and then added silver filigree and then started again with the silk.

In fact it really was amazing what could be done with several ounces of heavy metal, some irritated molluscs, a few dead rodents and a lot of thread wound out of insects' bottoms. The dress wasn't so much worn as occupied; if the outlying flounces weren't supported on wheels, then Keli was stronger than he'd given her credit for.

"What do you think?" she said, turning slowly. "This was worn by my mother, and my grandmother, and her mother."

"What, all together?" said Cutwell, quite prepared to believe it. How can she get into it? he wondered. There must be a door round the back. . . .

"It's a family heirloom. It's got real diamonds on the bodice."

"Which bit's the bodice?"

"This bit."

Cutwell shuddered. "It's very impressive," he said, when he could trust himself to speak. "You don't think it's perhaps a bit mature, though?"

"It's queenly."

"Yes, but perhaps it won't allow you to move very fast?"

"I have no intention of running. There must be dignity." Once again the set of her jaw traced the line of her descent all the way to her conquering ancestor, who preferred to move very fast at all times and knew as much about dignity as could be carried on the point of a sharp spear.

Cutwell spread his hands.

"All right," he said. "Fine. We all do what we can. I just hope Mort has come up with some ideas."

"It's hard to have confidence in a ghost," said Keli. "He walks through walls!"

"I've been thinking about that," said Cutwell. "It's a puzzle, isn't it? He walks through things only if he doesn't know he's doing it. I think it's an industrial disease."

"What?"

"I was nearly sure last night. He's becoming real."

"But we're all real! At least, you are, and I suppose I am."

"But he's becoming more real. Extremely real. Nearly as real as Death, and you don't get much realler. Not much realler at all."

"Are you sure?" said Albert, suspiciously.

"Of course," said Ysabell. "Work it out yourself if you like."

Albert looked back at the big book, his face a portrait of uncertainty.

"Well, they could be about right," he conceded with bad grace, and copied out the two names on a scrap of paper. "There's one way to find out, anyway."

He pulled open the top drawer of Death's desk and extracted a big iron keyring. There was only one key on it.

WHAT HAPPENS NOW? said Mort.

"We've got to fetch the lifetimers," said Albert. "You have to come with me."

"Mort!" hissed Ysabell.

"What?"

"What you just said—" She lapsed into silence, and then added, "Oh, nothing. It just sounded . . . odd."

"I only asked what happens now," said Mort.

"Yes, but—oh, never mind."

Albert brushed past them and sidled out into the hallway like a two-legged spider until he reached the door that was always kept locked. The key fitted perfectly. The door swung open. There wasn't so much as a squeak from its hinges, just a swish of deeper silence.

And the roar of sand.

Mort and Ysabell stood in the doorway, transfixed, as Albert stamped off between the aisles of glass. The sound didn't just enter the body via the ears, it came up through the legs and down through the skull and filled up the brain until all that it could think of was the rushing, hissing gray noise, the sound of millions of lives being lived. And rushing towards their inevitable destination.

They stared up and out at the endless ranks of lifetimers, every one different, every one named. The light from torches ranged along the walls picked highlights off them, so that a star gleamed on every glass. The far walls of the room were lost in the galaxy of light.

Mort felt Ysabell's fingers tighten on his arm. When she spoke, her voice was strained.

"Mort, some of them are so *small*."

I KNOW.

Her grip relaxed, very gently, like someone putting the top ace on a house of cards and taking their hand away gingerly so as not to bring the whole edifice down.

"Say that again?" she said quietly.

"I said I know. There's nothing I can do about it. Haven't you been in here before?"

"No." She had withdrawn slightly, and was staring at his eyes.

"It's no worse than the library," said Mort, and almost believed it. But in the library you only read about it; in here you could see it happening.

"Why are you looking at me like that?" he added.

"I was just trying to remember what color your eyes were," she said, "because—"

"If you two have quite had enough of each other!" bellowed Albert above the roar of the sand. "This way!"

"Brown," said Mort to Ysabell. "They're brown. Why?"

"Hurry up!"

"You'd better go and help him," said Ysabell. "He seems to be getting quite upset."

Mort left her, his mind a sudden swamp of uneasiness, and stalked across the tiled floor to where Albert stood impatiently tapping a foot.

"What do I have to do?" he said.

"Just follow me."

The room opened out into a series of passages, each one lined with the hourglasses. Here and there the shelves were divided by stone pillars inscribed with angular markings. Albert glanced at them occasionally; mainly he strode through the maze of sand as though he knew every turn by heart.

"Is there one glass for everyone, Albert?"

"Yes."

"This place doesn't look big enough."

"Do you know anything about m-dimensional topography?"

"Um. No."

"Then I shouldn't aspire to hold any opinions, if I was you," said Albert.

He paused in front of a shelf of glasses, glanced at the paper again, ran his hand along the row and suddenly snatched up a glass. The top bulb was almost empty.

"Hold this," he said. "If this is right, then the other should be somewhere near. Ah. Here."

Mort turned the two glasses around in his hands. One had all the markings of an important life, while the other one was squat and quite unremarkable.

Mort read the names. The first seemed to refer to a nobleman in the Agatean Empire regions. The second was a collection of pictograms that he recognized as originating in Turnwise Klatch.

"Over to you," Albert sneered. "The sooner you get started, the sooner you'll be finished. I'll bring Binky round to the front door."

"Do my eyes look all right to you?" said Mort, anxiously.

"Nothing wrong with them that I can see," said Albert. "Bit red round the edges, bit bluer than usual, nothing special."

Mort followed him back past the long shelves of glass, looking thoughtful. Ysabell watched him take the sword from the rack by the door and test its edge by swishing it through the air, just as Death did, and grinning mirthlessly at the satisfactory sound of the thunderclap.

She recognized the walk. He was *stalking*.

"Mort?" she whispered.

YES?

"Something's happening to you."

I KNOW, said Mort. "But I think I can control it."

They heard the sound of hooves outside, and Albert pushed the door open and came in rubbing his hands.

"Right, lad, no time to—"

Mort swung the sword at arm's length. It scythed through the air with a noise like ripping silk and buried itself in the doorpost by Albert's ear.

ON YOUR KNEES, ALBERTO MALICH.

Albert's mouth dropped open. His eyes rolled sideways to the shimmering blade a few inches from his head, and then narrowed to tight little lines.

"You surely wouldn't dare, boy," he said.

MORT. The syllable snapped out as fast as a whiplash and twice as vicious.

"There was a pact," said Albert, but there was the barest gnat-song of doubt in his voice. "There was an agreement."

"Not with me."

"There was an agreement! Where would we be if we could not honor an agreement?"

"I don't know where I would be," said Mort softly. BUT I KNOW WHERE YOU WOULD GO.

"That's not fair!" Now it was a whine.

THERE'S NO JUSTICE. THERE'S JUST ME.

"Stop it," said Ysabell. "Mort, you're being silly. You can't kill anyone here. Anyway, you don't really want to kill Albert."

"Not here. But I could send him back to the world."

Albert went pale.

"You wouldn't!"

"No? I can take you back and leave you there. I shouldn't think you've got much time left, have you?" HAVE YOU?

"Don't talk like that," said Albert, quite failing to meet his gaze. "You sound like the master when you talk like that."

"I could be a lot worse than the master," said Mort evenly. "Ysabell, go and get Albert's book, will you?"

"Mort, I really think you're—"

SHALL I ASK YOU AGAIN?

She fled from the room, white-faced.

Albert squinted at Mort along the length of the sword, and smiled a lopsided, humorless smile.

"You won't be able to control it forever," he said.

"I don't want to. I just want to control it for long enough."

"You're receptive now, see? The longer the master is away, the more you'll become just like him. Only it'll be worse, because you'll remember all about being human and—"

"What about you, then?" snapped Mort. "What can you remember about being human? If you went back, how much life have you got left?"

"Ninety-one days, three hours and five minutes," said Albert promptly. "I knew he was on my trail, see? But I'm safe here and he's not such a bad master. Sometimes I don't know what he'd do without me."

"Yes, no one dies in Death's own kingdom. And you're pleased with that?" said Mort.

"I'm more than two thousand years old, I am. I've lived longer than anyone in the world."

Mort shook his head.

"You haven't, you know," he said. "You've just stretched things out more. No one really lives here. The time in this place is just a sham. It's not real. Nothing changes. I'd rather die and see what happens next than spend eternity here."

Albert pinched his nose reflectively. "Yes, well, you might," he conceded, "but I was a wizard, you know. I was pretty good at it. They put up a statue to me, you know. But you don't live a long life as a wizard without making a few enemies, see, ones who'll . . . wait on the Other Side."

He sniffed. "They ain't all got two legs, either. Some of them ain't got legs at all. Or faces. Death don't frighten me. It's what comes after."

"Help me, then."

"What good will that do me?"

"One day you might need some friends on the Other Side," said Mort. He thought for a few seconds and added, "If I were you, it wouldn't do any harm to give my soul a bit of a last-minute polish. Some of those waiting for you might not like the taste of that."

Albert shuddered and shut his eyes.

"You don't know about that what you talk about," he added, with more feeling than grammar, "else you wouldn't say that. What do you want from me?"

Mort told him.

Albert cackled.

"Just that? Just change Reality? You can't. There isn't any magic strong enough any more. The Great Spells could of done it. Nothing else. And that's it, so you might as well do as you please and the best of luck to you."

Ysabell came back, a little out of breath, clutching the latest volume of Albert's life. Albert sniffed again. The tiny drip on the end of his nose fascinated Mort. It was always on the point of dropping off but never had the courage. Just like him, he thought.

"You can't do anything to me with the book," said the old wizard warily.

"I don't intend to. But it strikes me that you don't get to be a powerful wizard by telling the truth all the time. Ysabell, read out what's being written."

" 'Albert looked at him uncertainly,' " Ysabell read.

"You can't believe everything writ down there—"

"—'he burst out, knowing in the flinty pit of his heart that Mort certainly could,' " Ysabell read.

"Stop it!"

" 'he shouted, trying to put at the back of his mind the knowledge that even if Reality could not be stopped it might be possible to slow it down a little.' "

How?

" 'intoned Mort in the leaden tones of Death,' " began Ysabell dutifully.

"Yes, yes, all right, you needn't bother with my bit," snapped Mort irritably.

"Pardon me for living, I'm sure."

NO ONE GETS PARDONED FOR LIVING.

"And don't talk like that to me, thank you. It doesn't frighten me," she said. She glanced down at the book, where the moving line of writing was calling her a liar.

"Tell me how, wizard," said Mort.

"My magic's all I've got left!" wailed Albert.

"You don't need it, you old miser."

"You don't frighten me, boy—"

LOOK INTO MY FACE AND TELL ME THAT.

Mort snapped his fingers imperiously. Ysabell bent her head over the book again.

" 'Albert looked into the blue glow of those eyes and the last of his defiance drained away,' " she read, " 'for he saw not just Death but Death with all the human seasonings of vengeance and cruelty and distaste, and with a terrible certainty he knew that this was the last chance and Mort would send him back into Time and hunt him down and take him and deliver him bodily into the dark Dungeon Dimensions where creatures of horror would dot dot dot dot dot,' " she finished. "It's just dots for half a page."

"That's because the book daren't even mention them,"

whispered Albert. He tried to shut his eyes but the pictures in the darkness behind his eyelids were so vivid that he opened them again. Even Mort was better than that.

"All right," he said. "There is one spell. It slows down time over a little area. I'll write it down, but you'll have to find a wizard to say it."

"I can do that."

Albert ran a tongue like an old loofah over his dry lips.

"There is a price, though," he added. "You must complete the Duty first."

"Ysabell?" said Mort. She looked at the page in front of her.

"He means it," she said. "If you don't then everything will go wrong and he'll drop back into Time anyway."

All three of them turned to look at the great clock that dominated the hallway. Its pendulum blade sawed slowly through the air, cutting time into little pieces.

Mort groaned.

"There isn't enough time!" he groaned. "I can't do both of them in time!" he groaned. "I can't do both of them in time!"

"The master would have found time," observed Albert.

Mort wrenched the blade from the doorway and shook it furiously but ineffectually towards Albert, who flinched.

"Write down the spell, then," he shouted. "And do it fast!"

He turned on his heel and stalked back into Death's study. There was a large disc of the world in one corner, complete down to solid silver elephants standing on the back of a Great A'Tuin cast in bronze and more than a meter long. The great rivers were represented by veins of jade, the deserts by powdered diamond and the most notable cities were picked out in precious stones; Ankh-Morpork, for instance, was a carbuncle.

He plonked the two glasses down at the approximate locations of their owners and flopped down in Death's chair, glaring at them, willing them to be closer together. The chair squeaked gently as he swivelled from side to side, glowering at the little disc.

After a while Ysabell came in, treading softly.

"Albert's written it down," she said quietly. "I've checked the book. It isn't a trick. He's gone and locked himself in his room now and—"

"Look at these two! I mean, will you look at them!"

"I think you should calm down a bit, Mort."

"How can I calm down with, look, this one over here almost in the Great Nef, and *this* one right in Bes Pelargic and then I've got to get back to Sto Lat. That's a ten thousand mile round trip however you look at it. It can't be done."

"I'm sure you'll find a way. And I'll help."

He looked at her for the first time and saw she was wearing her outdoor coat, the unsuitable one with the big fur collar.

"You? What could you do?"

"Binky can easily carry two," said Ysabell meekly. She waved a paper package vaguely. "I've packed us something to eat. I could—hold open doors and things."

Mort laughed mirthlessly. THAT WON'T BE NECESSARY.

"I wish you'd stop talking like that."

"I can't take passengers. You'll slow me down."

Ysabell sighed. "Look, how about this? Let's pretend we've had the row and I've won. See? It saves a lot of effort. I actually think you might find Binky rather reluctant to go if I'm not there. I've fed him an awful lot of sugar lumps over the years. Now—are we going?"

Albert sat on his narrow bed, glowering at the wall. He heard the sound of hoofbeats, abruptly cut off as Binky got airborne, and muttered under his breath.

Twenty minutes passed. Expressions flitted across the old wizard's face like cloud shadows across a hillside. Occasionally he'd whisper something to himself, like "I told 'em" or "Never would of stood for it" or "The master ought to be tole."

Eventually he seemed to reach an agreement with himself, knelt down gingerly and pulled a battered trunk from under his bed. He opened it with difficulty and unfolded a dusty gray robe that scattered mothballs and tarnished sequins across the floor. He pulled it on, brushed off the worst of the dust, and crawled under the bed again. There was a lot of muffled cursing and the occasional clink of china and finally Albert emerged holding a staff taller than he was.

It was thicker than any normal staff, mainly because of the carvings that covered it from top to bottom. They were actually quite indistinct, but gave the impression that if you could see them better you would regret it.

Albert brushed himself down again and examined himself critically in the washstand mirror.

Then he said, "Hat. No hat. Got to have a hat for the wizarding. Damn."

He stamped out of the room and returned after a busy fifteen minutes which included a circular hole cut out of the carpet in Mort's bedroom, the silver paper taken out from behind the mirror in Ysabell's room, a needle and thread from the box under the sink in the kitchen and a few loose sequins scraped up from the bottom of the robe chest. The end result was not as good as he would have liked and tended to slip rakishly over one eye, but it was black and had stars and moons on it and proclaimed its owner to be, without any doubt, a wizard, although possibly a desperate one.

He felt properly dressed for the first time in two thousand years. It was a disconcerting feeling and caused him a second's reflection before he kicked aside the rag rug beside the bed and used the staff to draw a circle on the floor.

When the tip of the staff passed it left a line of glowing octarine, the eighth color of the spectrum, the color of magic, the pigment of the imagination.

He marked eight points on its circumference and joined them up to form an octogram. A low throbbing began to fill the room.

Alberto Malich stepped into the center and held the staff above his head. He felt it wake to his grip, felt the tingle of the sleeping power unfold itself slowly and deliberately, like a waking tiger. It triggered old memories of power and magic that buzzed through the cobwebbed attics of his mind. He felt alive for the first time in centuries.

He licked his lips. The throbbing had died away, leaving a strange, waiting kind of silence.

Malich raised his head and shouted one single syllable.

Blue-green fire flashed from both ends of the staff. Streams of octarine flame spouted from the eight points of the octogram and enveloped the wizard. All this wasn't actually necessary to accomplish the spell, but wizards consider appearances are very important. . . .

So are disappearances. He vanished.

Stratohemispheric winds whipped at Mort's cloak.

"Where are we going first?" yelled Ysabell in his ear.

"Bes Pelargic!" shouted Mort, the gale whirling his words away.

"Where's that?"

"Agatean Empire! Counterweight Continent!"

He pointed downward.

He wasn't forcing Binky at the moment, knowing the miles that lay ahead, and the big white horse was currently running at an easy gallop out over the ocean. Ysabell looked down at roaring green waves topped with white foam, and clung tighter to Mort.

Mort peered ahead at the cloudbank that marked the distant continent and resisted the urge to hurry Binky along with the flat of his sword. He'd never struck the horse and wasn't at all confident about what would happen if he did. All he could do was wait.

A hand appeared under his arm, holding a sandwich.

"There's ham or cheese and chutney," she said. "You might as well eat, there's nothing else to do."

Mort looked down at the soggy triangle and tried to remember when he last had a meal. Some time beyond the reach of a clock, anyway—he'd need a calendar to calculate it. He took the sandwich.

"Thanks," he said, as graciously as he could manage.

The tiny sun rolled down towards the horizon, towing its lazy daylight behind it. The clouds ahead grew, and became outlined in pink and orange. After a while he could make out the darker blur of land below them, with here and there the lights of a city.

Half an hour later he was sure he could see individual buildings. Agatean architecture inclined towards squat pyramids.

Binky lost height until his hooves were barely a few feet above the sea. Mort examined the hourglass again, and gently tugged on the reins to direct the horse towards a seaport a little Rimwards of their present course.

There were a few ships at anchor, mostly single-sailed coastal traders. The Empire didn't encourage its subjects to go far away, in case they saw things that might disturb them. For the same reason it had built a wall around the entire country, patrolled by the Heavenly Guard whose main function was to tread heavily on the fingers of any inhabitants who felt they might like to step outside for five minutes for a breath of fresh air.

This didn't happen often, because most of the subjects of the Sun Emperor were quite happy to live inside the Wall. It's a fact of life that everyone is on one side or other of a wall, so the only thing to do is forget about it or evolve stronger fingers.

"Who runs this place?" said Ysabell, as they passed over the harbor.

"There's some kind of boy emperor," said Mort. "But the top man is really the Grand Vizier, I think."

"Never trust a Grand Vizier," said Ysabell wisely.

In fact the Sun Emperor didn't. The Vizier, whose name was Nine Turning Mirrors, had some very clear views about who should run the country, e.g., that it should be him, and now the boy was getting big enough to ask questions like

"Don't you think the wall would look better with a few gates in it?" and "Yes, but what is it like on the other side?" He had decided that in the Emperor's own best interests he should be painfully poisoned and buried in quicklime.

Binky landed on the raked gravel outside the low, many-roomed palace, severely rearranging the harmony of the universe.* Mort slid off his back and helped Ysabell down.

"Just don't get in the way, will you?" he said urgently. "And don't ask questions either."

He ran up some lacquered steps and hurried through the silent rooms, pausing occasionally to take his bearings from the hourglass. At last he sidled down a corridor and peered through an ornate lattice into a long low room where the Court was at its evening meal.

The young Sun Emperor was sitting crosslegged at the head of the mat with his cloak of vermine and feathers spread out behind him. He looked as though he was outgrowing it. The rest of the Court was sitting around the mat in strict and complicated order of precedence, but there was no mistaking the Vizier, who was tucking into his bowl of *squishi* and boiled seaweed in a highly suspicious fashion. No one seemed to be about to die.

Mort padded along the passage, turned the corner and nearly walked into several large members of the Heavenly Guard, who were clustered around a spyhole in the paper wall and passing a cigarette from hand to hand in that palm-cupped way of soldiers on duty.

He tiptoed back to the lattice and overheard the conversation thus:

---

*The stone garden of Universal Peace and Simplicity, laid out to the orders of the old Emperor One Sun Mirror**, used economy of position and shadow to symbolize the basic unity of soul and matter and the harmony of all things. It was said the secrets at the very heart of reality lay hidden in the precise ordering of its stones.

**Whose other claim to fame was his habit of cutting off his enemies' lips and legs and then promising them their freedom if they could run through the city playing a trumpet.

"I am the most unfortunate of mortals, O Immanent Presence, to find such as this in my otherwise satisfactory *squishi*," said the Vizier, extending his chopsticks.

The Court craned to see. So did Mort. Mort couldn't help agreeing with the statement, though—the thing was a sort of blue-green lump with rubbery tubes dangling from it.

"The preparer of food will be disciplined, Noble Personage of Scholarship," said the Emperor. "Who got the spare ribs?"

"No, O Perceptive Father of Your People, I was rather referring to the fact that this is, I believe, the bladder and spleen of the deepwater puff eel, allegedly the most tasty of morsels to the extent that it may be eaten only by those beloved of the gods themselves or so it is written, among such company of course I do not include my miserable self."

With a deft flick he transported it to the bowl of the Emperor, where it wobbled to a standstill. The boy looked at it for some time, and then skewered it on a chopstick.

"Ah," he said, "but is it not also written by none other than the great philosopher Ly Tin Wheedle that a scholar may be ranked above princes? I seem to remember you giving me the passage to read once, O Faithful and Assiduous Seeker of Knowledge."

The thing followed another brief arc through the air and flopped apologetically into the Vizier's bowl. He scooped it up in a quick movement and poised it for a second service. His eyes narrowed.

"Such may be generally the case, O Jade River of Wisdom, but specifically I cannot be ranked above the Emperor whom I love as my own son and have done ever since his late father's unfortunate death, and thus I lay this small offering at your feet."

The eyes of the court followed the wretched organ on its third flight across the mat, but the Emperor snatched up his fan and brought off a magnificent volley that ended back in the Vizier's bowl with such force that it sent up a spray of seaweed.

"*Somebody* eat it, for heaven's sake," shouted Mort, totally unheard. "I'm in a hurry!"

"Thou art indeed the most thoughtful of servants, O Devoted and Indeed Only Companion of My Late Father and Grandfather When They Passed Over, and therefore I decree that your reward shall be this most rare and exquisite of morsels."

The Vizier prodded the thing uncertainly, and looked into the Emperor's smile. It was bright and terrible. He fumbled for an excuse.

"Alas, it would seem that I have already eaten far too much—" he began, but the Emperor waved him into silence.

"Doubtless it requires a suitable seasoning," he said, and clapped his hands. The wall behind him ripped from top to bottom and four Heavenly Guards stepped through, three of them brandishing *cando* swords and the fourth trying hurriedly to swallow a lighted dog-end.

The Vizier's bowl dropped from his hands.

"My most faithful of servants believes he has no space left for this final mouthful," said the Emperor. "Doubtless you can investigate his stomach to see if this is true. Why has that man got smoke coming out of his ears?"

"Anxious for action, O Sky Eminence," said the sergeant quickly. "No stopping him, I'm afraid."

"Then let him take his knife and—oh, the Vizier seems to be hungry after all. Well done."

There was absolute silence while the Vizier's cheeks bulged rhythmically. Then he gulped.

"Delicious," he said. "Superb. Truly the food of the gods, and now, if you will excuse me—" He unfolded his legs and made as if to stand up. Little beads of sweat had appeared on his forehead.

"You wish to depart?" said the Emperor, raising his eyebrows.

"Pressing matters of state, O Perspicacious Personage of—"

"Be seated. Rising so soon after meals can be bad for the digestion," said the Emperor, and the guards nodded agreement. "Besides, there are no urgent matters of state unless you refer to those in the small red bottle marked 'Antidote' in the black lacquered cabinet on the bamboo rug in your quarters, O Lamp of Midnight Oil."

There was a ringing in the Vizier's ears. His face began to go blue.

"You see?" said the Emperor. "Untimely activity on a heavy stomach is conducive to ill humors. May this message go swiftly to all corners of my country, that all men may know of your unfortunate condition and derive instruction thereby."

"I . . . must . . . congratulate your . . . Personage on such . . . consideration," said the Vizier, and fell forward into a dish of boiled soft-shelled crabs.

"I had an *excellent* teacher," said the Emperor.

ABOUT TIME, TOO, said Mort, and swung the sword.

A moment later the soul of the Vizier got up from the mat and looked Mort up and down.

"Who are you, barbarian?" he snapped.

DEATH.

"Not my Death," said the Vizier firmly. "Where's the Black Celestial Dragon of Fire?"

HE COULDN'T COME, said Mort. There were shadows forming in the air behind the Vizier's soul. Several of them wore emperor's robes, but there were plenty of others jostling them, and they all looked most anxious to welcome the newcomer to the lands of the dead.

"I think there's some people here to see you," said Mort, and hurried away. As he reached the passageway the Vizier's soul started to scream. . . .

Ysabell was standing patiently by Binky, who was making a late lunch of a five-hundred-year-old bonsai tree.

"One down," said Mort, climbing into the saddle. "Come

on. I've got a bad feeling about the next one, and we haven't
much time."

Albert materialized in the center of Unseen University, in
the same place, in fact, from which he had departed the
world some two thousand years before.

He grunted with satisfaction and brushed a few specks of
dust off his robe.

He became aware that he was being watched; on looking
up, he discovered that he had flashed into existence under
the stern marble gaze of himself.

He adjusted his spectacles and peered disapprovingly at
the bronze plaque screwed to his pedestal. It said:

"Alberto Malich, Founder of This University. AM
1,222–1,289. 'We Will Not See His Like Again.' "

So much for prediction, he thought. And if they thought
so much of him they could at least have hired a decent sculp-
tor. It was disgraceful. The nose was all wrong. Call that a
leg? People had been carving their names on it, too. He
wouldn't be seen dead in a hat like that, either. Of course, if
he could help it, he wouldn't be seen dead at all.

Albert aimed an octarine thunderbolt at the ghastly thing
and grinned evilly as it exploded into dust.

"Right," he said to the Disc at large, "I'm back." The tingle
from the magic coursed all the way up his arm and started a
warm glow in his mind. How he'd missed it, all these years.

Wizards came hurrying through the big double doors at
the sound of the explosion and cleared the wrong conclusion
from a standing start.

There was the pedestal, empty. There was a cloud of marble dust over everything. And striding out of it, muttering to
himself, was Albert.

The wizards at the back of the crowd started to have it
away as quickly and quietly as possible. There wasn't one of
them that hadn't, at some time in his jolly youth, put a com-

mon bedroom utensil on old Albert's head or carved his name somewhere on the statue's chilly anatomy, or spilled beer on the pedestal. Worse than that, too, during Rag Week when the drink flowed quickly and the privy seemed too far to stagger. These had all seemed hilarious ideas at the time. They suddenly didn't, now.

Only two figures remained to face the statue's wrath, one because he had got his robe caught in the door and the other because he was, in fact, an ape and could therefore take a relaxed attitude to human affairs.

Albert grabbed the wizard, who was trying desperately to walk into the wall. The man squealed.

"All right, all right, I admit it! I was drunk at the time, believe me, didn't mean it, gosh, I'm sorry, I'm so sorry—"

"What are you bleating about, man?" said Albert, genuinely puzzled.

"—so sorry, if I tried to tell you how sorry I am we'd—"

"Stop this bloody nonsense!" Albert glanced down at the little ape, who gave him a warm friendly smile. "What's your name, man?"

"Yes, sir, I'll stop, sir, right away, no more nonsense, sir . . . Rincewind, sir. Assistant librarian, if it's all right by you."

Albert looked him up and down. The man had a desperate scuffed look, like something left out for the laundry. He decided that if this was what wizarding had come to, someone ought to do something about it.

"What sort of librarian would have you for assistant?" he demanded irritably.

"Oook."

Something like a warm soft leather glove tried to hold his hand.

"A monkey! In *my* university!"

"Orangoutang, sir. He used to be a wizard but got caught in some magic, sir, now he won't let us turn him back, and he's the only one who knows where all the books are," said

Rincewind urgently. "I look after his bananas," he added, feeling some additional explanation was called for.

Albert glared at him. "Shut up."

"Shutting up right away, sir."

"And tell me where Death is."

"Death, sir?" said Rincewind, backing against the wall.

"Tall, skeletal, blue eyes, stalks, TALKS LIKE THIS . . . Death. Seen him lately?"

Rincewind swallowed. "Not lately, sir."

"Well, I want him. This nonsense has got to stop. I'm going to stop it *now*, see? I want the eight most senior wizards assembled here, right, in half an hour with all the necessary equipment to perform the Rite of AshkEnte, is that understood? Not that the sight of you lot gives me any confidence. Bunch of pantywaisters the lot of you, and stop trying to hold my hand!"

"Oook."

"And now I'm going to the pub," snapped Albert. "Do they sell any halfway decent cat's piss anywhere these days?"

"There's the Drum, sir," said Rincewind.

"The Broken Drum? In Filigree Street? Still there?"

"Well, they change the name sometimes and rebuild it completely but the site has been, er, on the site for years. I expect you're pretty dry, eh, sir?" Rincewind said, with an air of ghastly camaraderie.

"What would you know about it?" said Albert sharply.

"Absolutely nothing, sir," said Rincewind promptly.

"I'm going to the Drum, then. Half an hour, mind. And if they're not waiting for me when I come back, then well, they'd just better be!"

He stormed out of the hall in a cloud of marble dust.

Rincewind watched him go. The librarian held his hand.

"You know the worst of it?" said Rincewind.

"Oook?"

"I don't even *remember* walking under a mirror."

* * *

At about the time Albert was in The Mended Drum arguing
with the landlord over a yellowing bar tab that had been
handed down carefully from father to son through one regi-
cide, three civil wars, sixty-one major fires, four hundred
and ninety robberies and more than fifteen thousand bar-
room brawls to record the fact that Alberto Malich still owed
the management three copper pieces plus interest currently
standing at the contents of most of the Disc's larger stron-
grooms, which proved once again that an Ankhian merchant
with an unpaid bill has the kind of memory that would make
an elephant blink . . . at about this time, Binky was leaving a
vapor trail in skies above the great mysterious continent of
Klatch.

Far below drums sounded in the scented, shadowy jungles
and columns of curling mist rose from hidden rivers where
nameless beasts lurked under the surface and waited for supper to walk past.

"There's no more cheese, you'll have to have the ham,"
said Ysabell. "What's that light over there?"

"The Light Dams," said Mort. "We're getting closer." He
pulled the hourglass out of his pocket and checked the level
of the sand.

"But not close enough, dammit!"

The Light Dams lay like pools of light hubwards of their
course, which is exactly what they were; some of the tribes
constructed mirror walls in the desert mountains to collect
the Disc sunlight, which is slow and slightly heavy. It was
used as currency.

Binky glided over the campfires of the nomads and the
silent marshes of the Tsort river. Ahead of them dark, familiar shapes began to reveal themselves in the moonlight.

"The Pyramids of Tsort by moonlight!" breathed Ysabell.
"How romantic!"

MORTARED WITH THE BLOOD OF THOUSANDS OF SLAVES,
observed Mort.

"Please don't."

"I'm sorry, but the practical fact of the matter is that these—"

"All right, all right, you've made your point," said Ysabell irritably.

"It's a lot of effort to go to to bury a dead king," said Mort, as they circled above one of the smaller pyramids. "They fill them full of preservative, you know, so they'll survive into the next world."

"Does it work?"

"Not noticeably." Mort leaned over Binky's neck. "Torches down there," he said. "Hang On."

A procession was winding away from the avenue of pyramids, led by a giant statue of Offler the Crocodile God borne by a hundred sweating slaves. Binky cantered above it, entirely unnoticed, and performed a perfect four-point landing on the hard-packed sand outside the pyramid's entrance.

"They've pickled another king," said Mort. He examined the glass again in the moonlight. It was quite plain, not the sort normally associated with royalty.

"That can't be him," said Ysabell. "They don't pickle them when they're still alive, do they?"

"I hope not, because I read where, before they do the preserving, they, um, cut them open and remove—"

"I don't want to hear it—"

"—all the soft bits," Mort concluded lamely. "It's just as well the pickling doesn't work, really, just imagine having to walk around with no—"

"So it isn't the king you've come to take," said Ysabell loudly. "Who is it, then?"

Mort turned towards the dark entrance. It wouldn't be sealed until dawn, to give time for the dead king's soul to leave. It looked deep and foreboding, hinting at purposes considerably more dire than, say, keeping a razor blade nice and sharp.

"Let's find out," he said.

*  *  *

"Look out! He's coming back!"

The University's eight most senior wizards shuffled into line, tried to smooth out their beards and in general made an unsuccessful effort to look presentable. It wasn't easy. They had been snatched from their workrooms, or a postprandial brandy in front of a roaring fire, or quiet contemplation under a handkerchief in a comfy chair somewhere, and all of them were feeling extremely apprehensive and rather bewildered. They kept glancing at the empty pedestal.

Only one creature could have duplicated the expressions on their faces, and that would be a pigeon who has heard not only that Lord Nelson has got down off his column but has also been seen buying a 12-bore repeater and a box of cartridges.

"He's coming up the corridor!" shouted Rincewind, and dived behind a pillar.

The assembled mages watched the big double doors as if they were about to explode, which shows how prescient they were, because they exploded. Matchstick-sized bits of oak rained down among them and a small thin figure stood outlined against the light. It held a smoking staff in one hand. The other held a small yellow toad.

"Rincewind!" bawled Albert.

"Sir!"

"Take this thing away and dispose of it."

The toad crawled into Rincewind's hand and gave him an apologetic look.

"That's the last time that bloody landlord gives any lip to a wizard," said Albert with smug satisfaction. "It seems I turn my back for a few hundred years and suddenly people in this town are encouraged to think they can talk back to wizards, eh?"

One of the senior wizards mumbled something.

"What was that? Speak up, man!"

"As the bursar of this university I must say that we've

always encouraged a good neighbor policy with respect to the community," mumbled the wizard, trying to avoid Albert's gimlet stare. He had an upturned chamber pot on his conscience, with three cases of obscene graffiti to be taken into consideration.

Albert let his mouth drop open. "Why?" he said.

"Well, er, a sense of civic duty, we feel it's vitally important that we show an examp—arrgh!"

The wizard tried desperately to beat out the flames in his beard. Albert lowered his staff and looked slowly along the row of mages. They swayed away from his stare like grass in a gale.

"Anyone else want to show a sense of civic duty?" he said. "Good neighbors, anybody?" He drew himself up to his full height. "You spineless maggots! I didn't found this University so you could lend people the bloody lawnmower! What's the use of having the power if you don't wield it? Man doesn't show you respect, you don't leave enough of his damn inn to roast chestnuts on, understand?"

Something like a soft sigh went up from the assembled wizards. They stared sadly at the toad in Rincewind's hand. Most of them, in the days of their youth, had mastered the art of getting rascally drunk at the Drum. Of course, all that was behind them now, but the Guild of Merchants' annual knife-and-fork supper would have been held in the Drum's upstairs room the following evening, and all the Eighth Level wizards had been sent complimentary tickets; there would have been roast swan and two kinds of trifle and lots of fraternal toasts to "Our esteemed, nay, distinguished guests" until it was time for the college porters to turn up with the wheelbarrows.

Albert strutted along the row, poking the occasional paunch with his staff. His mind danced and sang. Go back? Never! This was power, this was living; he'd challenge old boniface and spit in his empty eye.

"By the Smoking Mirror of Grism, there's going to be a few changes around here!"

Those wizards who had studied history nodded uncomfortably. It would be back to the stone floors and getting up when it was still dark and no alcohol under any circumstances and memorizing the true names of everything until the brain squeaked.

*"What's that man doing!"*

A wizard who had absent-mindedly reached for his tobacco pouch let the half-formed cigarette fall from his trembling fingers. It bounced when it hit the floor and all the wizards watched it roll with longing eyes until Albert stepped forward smartly and squashed it.

Albert spun round. Rincewind, who had been following him as a sort of unofficial adjutant, nearly walked into him.

"You! Rincething! D'yer smoke?"

"No, sir! Filthy habit!" Rincewind avoided the gaze of his superiors. He was suddenly aware that he had made some lifelong enemies, and it was no consolation to know that he probably wouldn't have them for very long.

"Right! Hold my staff. Now, you bunch of miserable back-sliders, this is going to stop, d'yer hear? First thing tomorrow, up at dawn, three times round the quadrangle and back here for physical jerks! Balanced meals! Study! Healthy exercise! And that bloody monkey goes to a circus, first thing!"

"Oook?"

Several of the older wizards shut their eyes.

"But first," said Albert, lowering his voice, "you'll oblige me by setting up the Rite of AshkEnte."

"I have some unfinished business," he added.

Mort strode through the cat-black corridors of the pyramid, with Ysabell hurrying along behind him. The faint glow from his sword illuminated unpleasant things; Offler the Crocodile God was a cosmetics advert compared to some of the things the people of Tsort worshipped. In alcoves along the way were statues of creatures apparently built of all the bits God had left over.

"What are they here for?" whispered Ysabell.

"The Tsortean priests say they come alive when the pyramid is sealed and prowl the corridors to protect the body of the king from tomb robbers," said Mort.

"What a horrible superstition."

"Who said anything about superstition?" said Mort absently.

"They really come alive?"

"All I'll say is that when the Tsorteans put a curse on a place, they don't mess about."

Mort turned a corner and Ysabell lost sight of him for a heart-stopping moment. She scurried through the darkness and cannoned into him. He was examining a dog-headed bird.

"Urgh," she said. "Doesn't it send shivers up your spine?"

"No," said Mort flatly.

"Why not?"

BECAUSE I AM MORT. He turned, and she saw his eyes glow like blue pinpoints.

"Stop it!"

I—CAN'T.

She tried to laugh. It didn't work. "You're not Death," she said. "You're only doing his job."

DEATH IS WHOEVER DOES DEATH'S JOB.

The shocked pause that followed this was broken by a groan from further along the dark passage. Mort turned on his heel and hurried towards it.

He's right, thought Ysabell. Even the way he moves. . . .

But the fear of the darkness that the light was dragging towards her overcame any other doubts and she crept after him, around another corner and into what appeared, in the fitful glow from the sword, to be a cross between a treasury and a very cluttered attic.

"What's this place?" she whispered. "I've never seen so much stuff!"

THE KING TAKES IT WITH HIM INTO THE NEXT WORLD, said Mort.

"He certainly doesn't believe in traveling light. Look, there's a whole boat. And a gold bathtub!"

DOUBTLESS HE WILL WISH TO KEEP CLEAN WHEN HE GETS THERE.

"And all those statues!"

THOSE STATUES, I'M SORRY TO SAY, WERE PEOPLE. SERVANTS FOR THE KING, YOU UNDERSTAND.

Ysabell's face set grimly.

THE PRIESTS GIVE THEM POISON.

There was another groan, from the other side of the cluttered room. Mort followed it to its source, stepping awkwardly over rolls of carpet, bunches of dates, crates of crockery and piles of gems. The king obviously hadn't been able to decide what he was going to leave behind on his journey, so had decided to play safe and take everything.

ONLY IT DOESN'T ALWAYS WORK QUICKLY, Mort added somberly.

Ysabell clambered gamely after him, and peered over a canoe at a young girl sprawled across a pile of rugs. She was wearing gauze trousers, a waistcoat cut from not enough material, and enough bangles to moor a decent-sized ship. There was a green stain around her mouth.

"Does it hurt?" said Ysabell quietly.

NO. THEY THINK IT TAKES THEM TO PARADISE.

"Does it?"

MAYBE. WHO KNOWS? Mort took the hourglass out of an inner pocket and inspected it by the gleam of the sword. He seemed to be counting to himself, and then with a sudden movement tossed the glass over his shoulder and brought the sword down with his other hand.

The girl's shade sat up and stretched, with a clink of

ghostly jewelry. She caught sight of Mort, and bowed her head.

"My lord!"

NO ONE'S LORD, said Mort. NOW RUN ALONG TO WHEREVER YOU BELIEVE YOU'RE GOING.

"I shall be a concubine at the heavenly court of King Zetesphut, who will dwell among the stars forever," she said firmly.

"You don't have to be," said Ysabell sharply. The girl turned to her, wide-eyed.

"Oh, but I must. I've been training for it," she said, as she faded from view. "I've only managed to be a handmaiden up till now."

She vanished. Ysabell stared with dark disapproval at the space she had occupied.

"Well!" she said, and, "Did you see what she had on?"

LET'S GET OUT OF HERE.

"But it can't be true about King Whosis dwelling among the stars," she grumbled as they found their way out of the crowded room. "There's nothing but empty space up there."

IT'S HARD TO EXPLAIN, said Mort. HE'LL DWELL AMONG THE STARS IN HIS OWN MIND.

"With slaves?"

IF THAT'S WHAT THEY THINK THEY ARE.

"That's not very fair."

THERE'S NO JUSTICE, said Mort. JUST US.

They hurried back along the avenues of waiting ghouls and were nearly running when they burst out into the desert night air. Ysabell leaned against the rough stonework and panted for breath.

Mort wasn't out of breath.

He wasn't breathing.

I WILL TAKE YOU WHEREVER YOU WANT, he said, AND THEN I MUST LEAVE YOU.

"But I thought you wanted to rescue the princess!"

Mort shook his head.

I HAVE NO CHOICE. THERE ARE NO CHOICES.

She ran forward and grabbed his arm as he turned towards the waiting Binky. He removed her hand gently.

I HAVE FINISHED MY APPRENTICESHIP.

"It's all in your own mind!" yelled Ysabell. "You're whatever you think you are!"

She stopped and looked down. The sand around Mort's feet was beginning to whip up in little spurts and twirling dust devils.

There was a crackle in the air, and a greasy feel. Mort looked uneasy.

SOMEONE IS PERFORMING THE RITE OF ASH—

It hit like a hammer, a force from out of the sky that blew the sand into a crater. There was a low buzzing and the smell of hot tin.

Mort looked around himself in the gale of rushing sand, turning as if in a dream, alone in the calm center of the gale. Lightning flashed in the whirling cloud. Deep inside his own mind he struggled to break free, but something had him in its grip and he could no more resist than a compass needle can ignore the compulsion to point towards the Hub.

At last he found what he was searching for. It was a doorway edged in octarine light, leading to a short tunnel. There were figures at the other end, beckoning to him.

I COME, he said, and then turned as he heard the sudden noise behind him. Eleven stone of young womanhood hit him squarely in the chest, lifting him off the ground.

Mort landed with Ysabell kneeling on him, holding on grimly to his arms.

LET ME GO, he intoned. I HAVE BEEN SUMMONED.

"Not you, idiot!"

She stared into the blue, pupil-less pools of his eyes. It was like looking down a rushing tunnel.

Mort arched his back and screamed a curse so ancient and virulent that in the strong magical field it actually took on a form, flapped its leathery wings and slunk away. A private thunderstorm crashed around the sand dunes.

His eyes drew her again. She looked away before she dropped like a stone down a well made of blue light.

I COMMAND YOU. Mort's voice could have cut holes in rock.

"Father tried that tone on me for years," she said calmly. "Generally when he wanted me to clean my bedroom. It didn't work then, either."

Mort screamed another curse, which flopped out of the air and tried to bury itself in the sand.

THE PAIN—

"It's all in your head," she said, bracing herself against the force that wanted to drag them towards that flickering doorway. "You're not Death. You're just Mort. You're whatever I think you are."

In the center of the blurred blueness of his eyes were two tiny brown dots, rising at the speed of sight.

The storm around them rose and wailed. Mort screamed.


The Rite of AshkEnte, quite simply, summons and binds Death. Students of the occult will be aware that it can be performed with a simple incantation, three small bits of wood and 4cc of mouse blood, but no wizard worth his pointy hat would dream of doing anything so unimpressive; they knew in their hearts that if a spell didn't involve big yellow candles, lots of rare incense, circles drawn on the floor with eight different colors of chalk and a few cauldrons around the place then it simply wasn't worth contemplating.

The eight wizards at their stations on the points of the great ceremonial octogram swayed and chanted, their arms held out sideways so they were just touching the fingertips of the mages on either side.

But something was going wrong. True, a mist had formed in the very center of the living octogram, but it was writhing and turning in on itself, refusing to focus.

"More power!" shouted Albert. "Give it more power!"

A figure appeared momentarily in the smoke, black-robed and holding a glittering sword. Albert swore as he caught a glimpse of the pale face under the cowl; it wasn't pale enough.

"No!" Albert yelled, ducking into the octogram and flailing at the flickering shape with his hands. "Not you, not you. . . ."

And, in faraway Tsort, Ysabell forgot she was a lady, bunched her fist, narrowed her eyes and caught Mort squarely on the jaw. The world around her exploded. . . .

In the kitchen of Harga's House of Ribs the frying pan crashed to the floor, sending the cats scurrying out of the door. . . .

In the great hall of the Unseen University everything happened at once.*

The tremendous force the wizards had been exerting on the shadow realm suddenly had one focus. Like a reluctant cork from a bottle, like a dollop of fiery ketchup from the upturned sauce bottle of Infinity, Death landed in the octogram and swore.

Albert realized just too late that he was inside the charmed ring and made a dive for the edge. But skeletal fingers caught him by the hem of his robe.

The wizards, such of them who were still on their feet and conscious, were rather surprised to see that Death was wearing an apron and holding a small kitten.

"Why did you have" TO SPOIL IT ALL?

"Spoil it all? Have you seen what the lad has done?" snapped Albert, still trying to reach the edge of the ring.

Death raised his skull and sniffed the air.

The sound cut through all the other noises in the hall and forced them into silence.

---

*This is not precisely true. It is generally agreed by philosophers that the shortest time in which everything can happen is one thousand billion years.

It was the kind of noise that is heard on the twilight edges of dreams, the sort that you wake from in a cold sweat of mortal horror. It was the snuffling under the door of dread. It was like the snuffling of a hedgehog, but if so then it was the kind of hedgehog that crashes out of the verges and flattens lorries. It was the kind of noise you wouldn't want to hear twice; you wouldn't want to hear it once.

Death straightened up slowly.

IS THIS HOW HE REPAYS MY KINDNESS? TO STEAL MY DAUGHTER, INSULT MY SERVANTS, AND RISK THE FABRIC OF REALITY ON A PERSONAL WHIM? OH, FOOLISH, FOOLISH, I HAVE BEEN FOOLISH TOO LONG!

"Master, if you would just be so good as to let go of my robe—" began Albert, and the wizard noticed a pleading edge to his voice that hadn't been there before.

Death ignored him. He snapped his fingers like a castanet and the apron around his waist exploded into brief flames. The kitten, however, he put down very carefully and gently pushed away with his foot.

DID I NOT GIVE HIM THE GREATEST OPPORTUNITY?

"Exactly, master, and now if you could see your way clear—"

SKILLS? A CAREER STRUCTURE? PROSPECTS? A JOB FOR LIFE?

"Indeed, and if you would but let go—"

The change in Albert's voice was complete. The trumpets of command had become the piccolos of supplication. He sounded terrified, in fact, but he managed to catch Rincewind's eye and hiss:

"My staff! Throw me my staff! While he is in the circle he is not invincible! Let me have my staff and I can break free!"

Rincewind said: "Pardon?"

OH, MINE IS THE FAULT FOR GIVING IN TO THESE WEAK-NESSES OF WHAT FOR WANT OF A BETTER WORD I SHALL CALL THE FLESH!

"My staff, you idiot, my staff!" gibbered Albert.

"Sorry?"

WELL DONE, MY SERVANT, FOR CALLING ME TO MY SENSES, said Death. LET US LOSE NO TIME.

"My sta—!"

There was an implosion and an inrush of air. The candle flames stretched out like lines of fire for a moment, and then went out.

Some time passed.

Then the bursar's voice from somewhere near the floor said, "That was very unkind, Rincewind, losing his staff like that. Remind me to discipline you severely one of these days. Anyone got a light?"

"I don't know what happened to it! I just leaned it against the pillar here and now it's—"

"Oook."

"Oh," said Rincewind.

"Extra banana ration, that ape," said the bursar levelly. A match flared and someone managed to get a candle alight. Wizards started to pick themselves off the floor.

"Well, that was a lesson to all of us," the bursar continued, brushing dust and candlewax off his robe. He looked up, expecting to see the statue of Alberto Malich back on its pedestal.

"Clearly even statues have feelings," he said. "I myself recall, when I was but a first-year student, writing my name on his well, never mind. The point is, I propose here and now we replace the statue."

Dead silence greeted this suggestion.

"With, say, an exact likeness cast in gold. Suitably embellished with jewels, as befits our great founder," he went on brightly.

"And to make sure no students deface it in any way I suggest we then erect it in the deepest cellar," he continued.

"And then lock the door," he added. Several wizards began to cheer up.

"And throw away the key?" said Rincewind.

"And weld the door," the bursar said. He had just remembered about The Mended Drum. He thought for a while and remembered about the physical fitness regime as well.

"And then brick up the doorway," he said. There was a round of applause.

"And throw away the bricklayer!" chortled Rincewind, who felt he was getting the hang of this.

The bursar scowled at him. "No need to get carried away," he said.

In the silence a larger than usual sand dune humped up awkwardly and then fell away to reveal Binky, blowing the sand out of his nostrils and shaking his mane.

Mort opened his eyes.

There should be a word for that brief period just after waking when the mind is full of warm pink nothing. You lie there entirely empty of thought, except for a growing suspicion that heading towards you, like a sockful of damp sand in a nocturnal alleyway, are all the recollections you'd really rather do without, and which amount to the fact that the only mitigating factor in your horrible future is the certainty that it will be quite short.

Mort sat up and put his hands on top of his head to stop it unscrewing.

The sand beside him heaved and Ysabell pushed herself into a sitting position. Her hair was full of sand and her face was grimy with pyramid dust. Some of her hair had frizzled at the tips. She stared listlessly at him.

"Did you hit me?" he said, gently testing his jaw.

"Yes."

"Oh."

He looked at the sky, as though it could remind him about things. He had to be somewhere, soon, he recalled. Then he remembered something else.

"Thank you," he said.

"Any time, I assure you." Ysabell made it to her feet and tried to brush the dirt and cobwebs off her dress.

"Are we going to rescue this princess of yours?" she said diffidently.

Mort's own personal, internal reality caught up with him. He shot to his feet with a strangled cry, watched blue fireworks explode in front of his eyes, and collapsed again. Ysabell caught him under the shoulders and hauled him back on his feet.

"Let's go down to the river," she said. "I think we could all do with a drink."

"What happened to me?"

She shrugged as best she could while supporting his weight.

"Someone used the Rite of AshkEnte. Father hates it, he says they always summon him at inconvenient moments. The part of you that was Death went and you stayed behind. I think. At least you've got your own voice back."

"What time is it?"

"What time did you say the priests close up the pyramid?"

Mort squinted through streaming eyes back towards the tomb of the king. Sure enough, torchlit fingers were working on the door. Soon, according to the legend, the guardians would come to life and begin their endless patrol.

He knew they would. He remembered the knowledge. He remembered his mind feeling as cold as ice and limitless as the night sky. He remembered being summoned into reluctant existence at the moment the first creature lived, in the certain knowledge that he would outlive life until the last being in the universe passed to its reward, when it would then be his job, figuratively speaking, to put the chairs on the tables and turn all the lights off.

He remembered the loneliness.

"Don't leave me," he said urgently.

"I'm here," she said. "For as long as you need me."

"It's midnight," he said dully, sinking down by the Tsort and lowering his aching head to the water. Beside him there was a noise like a bath emptying as Binky also took a drink.

"Does that mean we're too late?"

"Yes."

"I'm sorry. I wish there was something I could do."

"There isn't."

"At least you kept your promise to Albert."

"Yes," said Mort, bitterly. "At least I did that."

Nearly all the way from one side of the Disc to the other. . . .

There should be a word for the microscopic spark of hope that you dare not entertain in case the mere act of acknowledging it will cause it to vanish, like trying to look at a photon. You can only sidle up to it, looking past it, *walking* past it, waiting for it to get big enough to face the world.

He raised his dripping head and looked towards the sunset horizon, trying to remember the big model of the Disc in Death's study without actually letting the universe know what he was entertaining.

At times like this it can seem that eventuality is so finely balanced that merely thinking too loud can spoil everything.

He oriented himself by the thin streamers of Hublight dancing against the stars, and made an inspired guess that Sto Lat was . . . over there. . . .

"Midnight," he said aloud.

"Gone midnight now," said Ysabell.

Mort stood up, trying not to let the delight radiate out from him like a beacon, and grabbed Binky's harness.

"Come on," he said. "We haven't got much time."

"What are you talking about?"

Mort reached down to swing her up behind him. It was a nice idea, but merely meant that he nearly pulled himself out of the saddle. She pushed him back gently and climbed up by herself. Binky skittered sideways, sensing Mort's feverish excitement, and snorted and pawed at the sand.

"I said, what are you talking about?"

Mort turned the horse to face the distant glow of the sunset.

"The speed of night," he said.

Cutwell poked his head over the palace battlements and groaned. The interface was only a street away, clearly visible in the octarine, and he didn't have to imagine the sizzling. He could hear it—a nasty, saw-toothed buzz as random particles of possibility hit the interface and gave up their energy as noise. As it ground its way up the street the pearly wall swallowed the bunting, the torches and the waiting crowds, leaving only dark streets. Somewhere out there, Cutwell thought, I'm fast asleep in my bed and none of this has happened. Lucky me.

He ducked down, skidded down the ladder to the cobbles and legged it back to the main hall with the skirts of his robe flapping around his ankles. He slipped in through the small postern in the great door and ordered the guards to lock it, then grabbed his skirts again and pounded along a side passage so that the guests wouldn't notice him.

The hall was lit with thousands of candles and crowded with Sto Plain dignitaries, nearly all of them slightly unsure why they were there. And, of course, there was the elephant.

It was the elephant that had convinced Cutwell that he had gone off the rails of sanity, but it seemed like a good idea a few hours ago, when his exasperation at the High Priest's poor eyesight had run into the recollection that a lumber mill on the edge of town possessed said beast for the purposes of heavy haulage. It was elderly, arthritic and had an uncertain temper, but it had one important advantage as a sacrificial victim. The High Priest should be able to see it.

Half a dozen guards were gingerly trying to restrain the creature, in whose slow brain the realization had dawned that it should be in its familiar stable, with plenty of hay and water and time to dream of the hot days on the great khaki plains of Klatch. It was getting restless.

It will shortly become apparent that another reason for its growing friskiness is the fact that, in the pre-ceremony confusion, its trunk found the ceremonial chalice containing a gallon of strong wine and drained the lot. Strange hot ideas are beginning to bubble in front of its crusted eyes, of uprooted baobabs, mating fights with other bulls, glorious stampedes through native villages and other half-remembered pleasures. Soon it will start to see pink people.

Fortunately this was unknown to Cutwell, who caught the eye of the High Priest's assistant—a forward-looking young man who had the foresight to provide himself with a long rubber apron and waders—and signaled that the ceremony should begin.

He darted back into the priest's robing room and struggled into the special ceremonial robe the palace seamstress had made up for him, digging deep into her workbasket for scraps of lace, sequins and gold thread to produce a garment of such dazzling tastelessness that even the ArchChancellor of Unseen University wouldn't have been ashamed to wear it. Cutwell allowed himself five seconds to admire himself in the mirror before ramming the pointy hat on his head and running back to the door, stopping just in time to emerge at a sedate pace as befitted a person of substance.

He reached the High Priest as Keli started her advance up the central aisle, flanked by maidservants who fussed around her like tugs around a liner.

Despite the drawbacks of the hereditary dress, Cutwell thought she looked beautiful. There was something about her that made him—

He gritted his teeth and tried to concentrate on the security arrangements. He had put guards at various vantage points in the hall in case the Duke of Sto Helit tried any last-minute rearrangement of the royal succession, and reminded himself to keep a special eye on the duke himself, who was sitting in the front row of seats with a strange quiet smile on his face. The duke caught Cutwell's eye, and the wizard hastily looked away.

The High Priest held up his hands for silence. Cutwell sidled towards him as the old man turned towards the Hub and in a cracked voice began the invocation to the gods.

Cutwell let his eyes slip back towards the duke.

"Hear me, mm, O gods—"

Was Sto Helit looking up into the bat-haunted darkness of the rafters?

"—hear me, O Blind Io of the Hundred Eyes; hear me, O Great Offler of the Bird-Haunted Mouth; hear me, O Merciful Fate; hear me, O Cold, mm, Destiny; hear me, O Seven-handed Sek; hear me, O Hoki of the Woods; hear me, O—"

With dull horror Cutwell realized that the daft old fool, against all instruction, was going to mention the whole lot. There were more than nine hundred known gods on the Disc, and research theologians were discovering more every year. It could take hours. The congregation was already beginning to shuffle its feet.

Keli was standing in front of the altar with a look of fury on her face. Cutwell nudged the High Priest in the ribs, which had no noticeable effect, and then waggled his eyebrows ferociously at the young acolyte.

"Stop him!" he hissed. "We haven't got time!"

"The gods would be displeased—"

"Not as displeased as me, and I'm *here*."

The acolyte looked at Cutwell's expression for a moment and decided that he'd better explain to the gods later. He tapped the High Priest on the shoulder and whispered something in his ear.

"—O Steikhegel, god of, mm, isolated cow byres; hear me, O—hello? What?"

Murmur, murmur.

"This is, mm, very irregular. Very well, we shall go straight to the, mm, Recitation of the Lineage."

Murmur, murmur.

The High Priest scowled at Cutwell, or at least where he believed Cutwell to be.

"Oh, all right. Mm, prepare the incense and fragrances for the Shriving of the Fourfold-Path."

Murmur, murmur.

The High Priest's face darkened.

"I suppose, mm, a short prayer, mm, is totally out of the question?" he said acidly.

"If some people don't get a move on," said Keli demurely, "there is going to be trouble."

Murmur.

"I don't know, I'm sure," said the High Priest. "People might as well not bother with a religious, mm, ceremony at all. Fetch the bloody elephant, then."

The acolyte gave Cutwell a frantic look and waved at the guards. As they urged their gently-swaying charge forward with shouts and pointed sticks the young priest sidled towards Cutwell and pushed something into his hand.

He looked down. It was a waterproof hat.

"Is this necessary?"

"He's very devout," said the acolyte. "We may need a snorkel."

The elephant reached the altar and was forced, without too much difficulty, to kneel. It hiccupped.

"Well, where is it, then?" snapped the High Priest. "Let's get this, mm, *farce* over with!"

Murmur went the acolyte. The High Priest listened, nodded gravely, picked up his white-handled sacrificial knife and raised it double-handed over his head. The whole hall watched, holding its breath. Then he lowered it again.

"*Where* in front of me?"

Murmur.

"I certainly don't need your help, my lad! I've been sacri-
ficing man and boy—and, mm, women and animals—for
seventy years, and when I can't use the, mm, knife you can
put me to bed with a shovel!"

And he brought the blade down in a wild sweep which, by
sheer luck, gave the elephant a mild flesh wound on the
trunk.

The creature awoke from its pleasant reflective stupor and
squealed. The acolyte turned in horror to look at two tiny
bloodshot eyes squinting down the length of an enraged
trunk, and cleared the altar in one standing jump.

The elephant was enraged. Vague confusing recollections
flooded its aching head, of fires and shouts and men with
nets and cages and spears and too many years hauling heavy
tree trunks. It brought its trunk down across the altar stone
and somewhat to its own surprise smashed it in two, levered
the two parts into the air with its tusks, tried unsuccessfully
to uproot a stone pillar and then, feeling the sudden need for
a breath of fresh air, started to charge arthritically down the
length of the hall.

It hit the door at a dead run, its blood loud with the call of
the herd and fizzing with alcohol, and took it off at the
hinges. Still wearing the frame on its shoulders it careened
across the courtyard, smashed the outer gates, burped, thun-
dered through the sleeping city and was still slowly acceler-
ating when it sniffed the distant dark continent of Klatch on
the night breeze and, tail raised, followed the ancient call of
home.

Back in the hall there was dust and shouts and confusion.
Cutwell pushed his hat out of his eyes and got to his hands
and knees.

"Thank you," said Keli, who had been lying underneath
him. "And why did you jump on top of me?"

"My first instinct was to protect you, your Majesty."

"Yes, instinct it may have been, but—" She started to say

that maybe the elephant would have weighed less, but the sight of his big, serious and rather flushed face stopped her.

"We will talk about this later," she said, sitting up and brushing the dust off her. "In the meantime, I think we will dispense with the sacrifice. I'm not your Majesty yet, just your Highness, and now if someone will fetch the crown—"

There was the snick of a safety catch behind them.

"The wizard will put his hands where I can see them," said the duke.

Cutwell stood up slowly, and turned around. The duke was backed by half a dozen large serious men, the type of men whose only function in life is to loom behind people like the duke. They had a dozen large serious crossbows, whose main purpose was to appear to be on the point of going off.

The princess sprang to her feet and launched herself at her uncle, but Cutwell grabbed her.

"No," he said, quietly. "This isn't the kind of man who ties you up in a cellar with just enough time for the mice to eat your ropes before the flood waters rise. This is the kind of man who just kills you here and now."

The duke bowed.

"I think it can be truly said that the gods have spoken," he said. "Clearly the princess was tragically crushed by the rogue elephant. The people will be upset. I will personally decree a week of mourning."

"You can't do that, all the guests have seen—!" the princess began, nearly in tears.

Cutwell shook his head. He could see the guards moving through the crowds of bewildered guests.

"They haven't," he said. "You'll be amazed at what they haven't seen. Especially when they learn that being tragically crushed to death by rogue elephants can be catching. You can even die of it in bed."

The duke laughed pleasantly.

"You really are quite intelligent for a wizard," he said. "Now, I am merely proposing banishment—"

"You won't get away with this," said Cutwell. He thought for a bit, and added, "Well, you will probably get away with it, but you'll feel bad about it on your deathbed and you'll wish—"

He stopped talking. His jaw dropped.

The duke half turned to follow his gaze.

"Well, wizard? What have you seen?"

"You won't get away with it," said Cutwell hysterically. "You won't even *be* here. This is going to have never happened, do you realize?"

"Watch his hands," said the duke. "If he even moves his fingers, shoot them."

He looked around again, puzzled. The wizard had sounded genuine. Of course, it was said wizards could see things that weren't there. . . .

"It doesn't even matter if you kill me," Cutwell babbled, "because tomorrow I'll wake up in my own bed and this won't have happened anyway. It's come through the wall!"

Night rolled onwards across the Disc. It was always there, of course, lurking in shadows and holes and cellars, but as the slow light of day drifted after the sun the pools and lakes of night spread out, met and merged. Light on the Discworld moves slowly because of the vast magical field.

Light on the Discworld isn't like light elsewhere. It's grown up a bit, it's been around, it doesn't feel the need to rush everywhere. It knows that however fast it goes darkness always gets there first, so it takes it easy.

Midnight glided across the landscape like a velvet bat. And faster than midnight, a tiny spark against the dark world of the Disc, Binky pounded after it. Flames roared back from his hooves. Muscles moved under his glistening skin like snakes in oil.

They moved in silence. Ysabell took one arm from around

Mort's waist and watched sparks glitter around her fingers in all eight colors of the rainbow. Little crackling serpents of light flowed down her arm and flashed off the tips of her hair.

Mort took the horse down lower, leaving a boiling wake of cloud that extended for miles behind them.

"Now I know I'm going mad," he muttered.

"Why?"

"I just saw an elephant down there. Whoa, boy. Look, you can see Sto Lat up ahead."

Ysabell peered over his shoulder at the distant gleam of light.

"How long have we got?" she said nervously.

"I don't know. A few minutes, perhaps."

"Mort, I hadn't asked you before—"

"Well?"

"What are you going to *do* when we get there?"

"I don't know," he said. "I was sort of hoping something would suggest itself at the time."

"Has it?"

"No. But it isn't time yet. Albert's spell may help. And I—"

The dome of reality squatted over the palace like a collapsing jellyfish. Mort's voice trailed into horrified silence. Then Ysabell said, "Well, I think it's *nearly* time. What are we going to do?"

"Hold tight!"

Binky glided through the smashed gates of the outer courtyard, slid across the cobbles in a trail of sparks and leapt through the ravaged doorway of the hall. The pearly wall of the interface loomed up and passed like a shock of cold spray.

Mort had a confused vision of Keli and Cutwell and a group of large men diving for their lives. He recognized the features of the duke and drew his sword, vaulting from the saddle as soon as the steaming horse skidded to a halt.

"Don't you lay a finger on her!" he screamed. "I'll have your head off!"

"This is certainly most impressive," said the duke, drawing his own sword. "And also very foolish. I—"

He stopped. His eyes glazed over. He toppled forward. Cutwell put down the big silver candlestick he'd wielded and gave Mort an apologetic smile.

Mort turned towards the guards, the blue flame of Death's sword humming through the air.

"Anyone else want some?" he snarled. They backed away, and then turned and ran. As they passed through the interface they vanished. There were no guests outside there, either. In the real reality the hall was dark and empty.

The four of them were left in a hemisphere that was rapidly growing smaller.

Mort sidled over to Cutwell.

"Any ideas?" he said. "I've got a magic spell here somewhere—"

"Forget it. If I try any magic in here now it'll blow our heads off. This little reality is too small to contain it."

Mort sagged against the remains of the altar. He felt empty, drained. For a moment he watched the sizzling wall of the interface drifting nearer. He'd survive it, he hoped, and so would Ysabell. Cutwell wouldn't, but *a* Cutwell would. Only Keli—

"Am I going to be crowned or not?" she said icily. "I've got to die a queen! It'd be terrible to be dead *and* common!"

Mort gave her an unfocused look, trying to remember what on earth she was talking about. Ysabell fished around in the wreckage behind the altar, and came up with a rather battered gold circlet set with small diamonds.

"Is this it?" she said.

"That's the crown," said Keli, nearly in tears. "But there's no priest or anything."

Mort sighed deeply.

"Cutwell, if this is our own reality we can rearrange it the way we want, can't we?"

"What had you in mind?"

"You're now a priest. Name your own god."

Cutwell curtsied, and took the crown from Ysabell.

"You're all making fun of me!" snapped Keli.

"Sorry," said Mort, wearily. "It's been rather a long day."

"I hope I can do this right," said Cutwell solemnly. "I've never crowned anyone before."

"I've never been crowned before!"

"Good," said Cutwell soothingly. "We can learn together." He started to mutter some impressive words in a strange tongue. It was in fact a simple spell for ridding the clothing of fleas, but he thought, what the hell. And then he thought, gosh, in this reality I'm the most powerful wizard there ever was, that'd be something to tell my grandch . . . He gritted his teeth. There'd be some rules changed in this reality, that was for sure.

Ysabell sat down beside Mort and slipped her hand in his.

"Well?" she said quietly. "This is the time. Has anything suggested itself?"

"No."

The interface was more than halfway down the hall, slowing slightly as it relentlessly ground down the pressure of the intruding reality.

Something wet and warm blew in Mort's ear. He reached up and touched Binky's muzzle.

"Dear old horse," he said. "And I'm right out of sugar lumps. You'll have to find your way home by yourself—"

His hand stopped in mid-pat.

"We can all go home," he said.

"I don't think father would like that very much," said Ysabell, but Mort ignored her.

"Cutwell!"

"Yes?"

"We're leaving. Are you coming? You'll still exist when the interface closes."

"Part of me will," said the wizard.

"That's what I meant," said Mort, swinging himself up on to Binky's back.

"But speaking as the part that won't, I'd like to join you," said Cutwell quickly.

"I intend to stay here to die in my own kingdom," said Keli.

"What you intend doesn't signify," said Mort. "I've come all the way across the Disc to rescue you, d'you see, and you're going to be rescued."

"But I'm the queen!" said Keli. Uncertainty welled up in her eyes, and she spun round to Cutwell, who lowered his candle-stick guiltily. "I heard you say the words! I am queen, aren't I?"

"Oh, yes," said Cutwell instantly; and then, because a wizard's word is supposed to be harder than cast iron, added virtuously, "And totally free from infestation, too."

"Cutwell!" snapped Mort. The wizard nodded, caught Keli around the waist and bodily hoisted her on to Binky's back. Hoisting his skirts around his waist he clambered up behind Mort and reached down and swung Ysabell up behind him. The horse jigged across the floor, complaining about the overloading, but Mort turned him towards the broken doorway and urged him forward.

The interface followed them as they clattered down the hall and into the courtyard, rising slowly. Its pearly fog was only yards away, tightening by inches.

"Excuse me," said Cutwell to Ysabell, raising his hat. "Igneous Cutwell, Wizard 1st Grade (UU), former Royal Recognizer and soon to be beheaded probably. Would you happen to know where we are going?"

"To my father's country," shouted Ysabell, above the wind of their passage.

"Have I ever met him?"

"I don't think so. You'd have remembered."

The top of the palace wall scraped Binky's hooves as, muscles straining, he sought for more height. Cutwell leaned backward again, holding on to his hat.

"Who is this gentleman of which we speak?" he yelled.

"Death," said Ysabell.

"Not—"

"Yes."

"Oh." Cutwell peered down at the distant rooftops, and gave her a lopsided smile. "Would it save time if I just jumped off now?"

"He's quite nice if you get to know him," said Ysabell defensively.

"Is he? Do you think we'll get the chance?"

"Hold on!" said Mort. "We should be going across just about—"

A hole full of blackness rushed out of the sky and caught them.

The interface bobbed uncertainly, empty as a pauper's pocket, and carried on shrinking.


The front door opened. Ysabell poked her head out.

"There's no one at home," she said. "You'd better come in."

The other three filed into the hallway. Cutwell conscientiously wiped his feet.

"It's a bit small," said Keli, critically.

"It's a lot bigger inside," said Mort, and turned to Ysabell. "Have you looked everywhere?"

"I can't even find Albert," she said. "I can't remember him ever not being here."

She coughed, remembering her duties as hostess.

"Would anyone like a drink?" she said. Keli ignored her.

"I was expecting a castle at least," she said. "Big and black, with great dark towers. Not an umbrella stand."

"It has got a scythe in it," Cutwell pointed out.

"Let's all go into the study and sit down and I'm sure we'll all feel better," said Ysabell hurriedly, and pushed open the black baize door.

Cutwell and Keli stepped through, bickering. Ysabell took Mort's arm.

"What are we going to do now?" she said. "Father will be very angry if he finds them here."

"I'll think of something," said Mort. "I'll rewrite the autobiographies or something." He smiled weakly. "Don't worry. I'll think of something."

The door slammed behind him. Mort turned to look into Albert's grinning face.

The big leather armchair behind the desk revolved slowly. Death looked at Mort over steepled fingers. When he was quite certain he had their full, horrified attention, he said:

YOU HAD BETTER START NOW.

He stood up, appearing to grow larger as the room darkened.

DON'T BOTHER TO APOLOGIZE, he added.

Keli buried her head in Cutwell's ample chest.

I AM *BACK*. AND I AM *ANGRY*.

"Master, I—" Mort began.

SHUT UP, said Death. He beckoned Keli with a calcareous forefinger. She turned to look at him, her body not daring to disobey.

Death reached out and touched her chin. Mort's hand went to his sword.

IS THIS THE FACE THAT LAUNCHED A THOUSAND SHIPS, AND BURNED THE TOPLESS TOWERS OF PSEUDOPOLIS? wondered Death. Keli stared hypnotized at the red pinpoints miles deep in those dark sockets.

"Er, excuse me," said Cutwell, holding his hat respectfully, Mexican fashion.

WELL? said Death, distracted.

"It isn't, sir. You must be thinking about another face."

WHAT IS YOUR NAME?

"Cutwell, sir. I'm a wizard, sir."

I'M A WIZARD, SIR, Death sneered. BE SILENT, WIZARD.

"Sir." Cutwell stepped back.

Death turned to Ysabell.

DAUGHTER, EXPLAIN YOURSELF. WHY DID YOU AID THIS FOOL?

Ysabell curtsied nervously.

"I—love him, Father. I think."

"You do?" said Mort, astonished. "You never said!"

"There didn't seem to be time," said Ysabell. "Father, he didn't mean—"

BE SILENT.

Ysabell dropped her gaze. "Yes, Father."

Death stalked around the desk until he was standing directly in front of Mort. He stared at him for a long time.

Then in one blurred movement his hand struck Mort across the face, knocking him off his feet.

I INVITE YOU INTO MY HOME, he said, I TRAIN YOU, I FEED YOU, I CLOTHE YOU, I GIVE YOU OPPORTUNITIES YOU COULD NOT DREAM OF, AND THUS YOU REPAY ME. YOU SEDUCE MY DAUGHTER FROM ME, YOU NEGLECT THE DUTY, YOU MAKE RIPPLES IN REALITY THAT WILL TAKE A CENTURY TO HEAL. YOUR ILL-TIMED ACTIONS HAVE DOOMED YOUR COMRADES TO OBLIVION. THE GODS WILL DEMAND NOTHING LESS.

ALL IN ALL, BOY, NOT A GOOD START TO YOUR FIRST JOB.

Mort struggled into a sitting position, holding his cheek. It burned coldly, like comet ice.

"Mort," he said.

IT SPEAKS! WHAT DOES IT SAY?

"You could let them go," said Mort. "They just got involved. It wasn't their fault. You could rearrange this so—"

WHY SHOULD I DO THAT? THEY BELONG TO ME NOW.

"I'll fight you for them," said Mort.

VERY NOBLE. MORTALS FIGHT ME ALL THE TIME. YOU ARE DISMISSED.

Mort got to his feet. He remembered what being Death had been like. He caught hold of the feeling, let it surface. . . .

No, he said.

AH. YOU CHALLENGE ME AS BETWEEN EQUALS, THEN?

Mort swallowed. But at least the way was clear now. When you step off a cliff, your life takes a very definite direction.

"If necessary," he said. "And if I win—"

IF YOU WIN, YOU WILL BE IN A POSITION TO DO WHATEVER YOU PLEASE, said Death. FOLLOW ME.

He stalked past Mort and out into the hall.

The other four looked at Mort.

"Are you sure you know what you're doing?" said Cutwell.

"No."

"You can't beat the master," said Albert. He sighed. "Take it from me."

"What will happen if you lose?" said Keli.

"I won't lose," said Mort. "That's the trouble."

"Father wants him to win," said Ysabell bitterly.

"You mean he'll let Mort win?" said Cutwell.

"Oh, no, he won't *let* him win. He just wants him to win."

Mort nodded. As they followed Death's dark shape he reflected on an endless future, serving whatever mysterious purpose the Creator had in mind, living outside Time. He couldn't blame Death for wanting to quit the job. Death had said the bones were not compulsory, but perhaps that wouldn't matter. Would eternity feel like a long time, or were all lives—from a personal viewpoint—entirely the same length?

Hi, said a voice in his head. Remember me? I'm you. I got you into this.

"Thanks," he said bitterly. The others glanced at him.

You could come through this, the voice said. You've got a big advantage. You've been him, and he's never been you.

Death swept through the hall and into the Long Room, the candles obediently flicking into flame as he entered.

ALBERT.

"Master?"

FETCH THE GLASSES.

"Master."

Cutwell grabbed the old man's arm.

"You're a wizard," he hissed. "You don't have to do what he says!"

"How old are you, lad?" said Albert, kindly.

"Twenty."

"When you're my age you'll see your choices differently." He turned to Mort. "Sorry."

Mort drew his sword, its blade almost invisible in the light from the candles. Death turned and stood facing him, a thin silhouette against a towering rack of hourglasses.

He held out his arms. The scythe appeared in them with a tiny thunderclap.

Albert came back down one of the glass-lined alleys with two hourglasses, and set them down wordlessly on a ledge on one of the pillars.

One was several times the size of the ordinary glasses— black, thin and decorated with a complicated skull-and-bones motif.

That wasn't the most unpleasant thing about it.

Mort groaned inwardly. He couldn't see any sand in there.

The smaller glass beside it was quite plain and unadorned. Mort reached for it.

"May I?" he said.

BE MY GUEST.

The name Mort was engraved on the top bulb. He held it up to the light, noting without any real surprise that there was hardly any sand left. When he held it to his ear he thought he could hear, even above the ever-present roar of the millions of lifetimers around him, the sound of his own life pouring away.

He put it down very carefully.

Death turned to Cutwell.

MR. WIZARD, SIR, YOU WILL BE GOOD ENOUGH TO GIVE US A COUNT OF THREE.

Cutwell nodded glumly.

"Are you sure this couldn't all be sorted out by getting around a table—" he began.

NO.

"No."

Mort and Death circled one another warily, their reflections flickering across the banks of hourglasses.

"One," said Cutwell.

Death spun his scythe menacingly.

"Two."

The blades met in mid-air with a noise like a cat sliding down a pane of glass.

"They both cheated!" said Keli. Ysabell nodded. "Of course," she said.

Mort jumped back, bringing the sword round in a too-slow arc that Death easily deflected, turning the parry into a wicked low sweep that Mort avoided only by a clumsy standing jump.

Although the scythe isn't preeminent among weapons of war, anyone who has been on the wrong end of, say, a peasants' revolt will know that in skilled hands it is fearsome. Once its owner gets it weaving and spinning no one—including the wielder—is quite certain where the blade is now and where it will be next.

Death advanced, grinning. Mort ducked a cut at head height and dived sideways, hearing a tinkle behind him as the tip of the scythe caught a glass on the nearest shelf. . . .

. . . in a dark alley in Morpork a night soil entrepreneur clutched at his chest and pitched forward over his cart. . . .

Mort rolled and came up swinging the sword double-handed over his head, feeling a twang of dark exhilaration as Death darted backwards across the checkered tiles. The wild swing cut through a shelf; one after another its burden of glasses started to slide towards the floor. Mort was dimly aware of Ysabell scurrying past him to catch them one by one. . . .

. . . across the Disc four people miraculously escaped death by falling. . . .

. . . and then he ran forward, pressing home his advantage. Death's hands moved in a blur as he blocked every chop and thrust, and then changed grip on the scythe and brought the blade swinging up in an arc that Mort sidestepped awkwardly, nicking the frame of an hourglass with the hilt of his sword and sending it flying across the room. . . .

. . . in the Ramtop mountains a tharga-herder, searching by lamplight in the high meadows for a lost cow, missed his footing and plunged over a thousand foot drop. . . .

. . . Cutwell dived forward and caught the tumbling glass in one desperately outstretched hand, hit the floor and slid along on his stomach. . . .

. . . a gnarled sycamore mysteriously loomed under the screaming herder and broke his fall, removing his major problems—death, the judgement of the gods, the uncertainty of Paradise and so on—and replacing them with the comparatively simple one of climbing back up about one hundred feet of sheer, icy cliff in pitch darkness.

There was a pause as the combatants backed away from each other and circled again, looking for an opening.

"Surely there's something we can do?" said Keli.

"Mort will lose either way," said Ysabell, shaking her head. Cutwell shook the silver candlestick out of his baggy sleeve and tossed it thoughtfully from hand to hand.

Death hefted the scythe threateningly, incidentally smashing an hourglass by his shoulder. . . .

. . . in Bes Pelargic the Emperor's chief torturer slumped backwards into his own acid pit. . . .

. . . and took another swing which Mort dodged by sheer luck. But only just. He could feel the hot ache in his muscles and the numbing grayness of fatigue poisons in his brain, two disadvantages that Death did not have to consider.

Death noticed.

YIELD, he said. I MAY BE MERCIFUL.

To illustrate the point he made a roundarm slash that Mort caught, clumsily, on the edge of his sword. The scythe blade bounced up, splintered a glass into a thousand shards. . . .

. . . the Duke of Sto Helit clutched at his heart, felt the icy stab of pain, screamed soundlessly and tumbled from his horse. . . .

Mort backed away until he felt the roughness of a stone pillar on his neck. Death's glass with its dauntingly empty bulbs was a few inches from his head.

Death himself wasn't paying much attention. He was looking down thoughtfully at the jagged remains of the Duke's life.

Mort yelled and swung his sword up, to the faint cheers of the crowd that had been waiting for him to do this for some time. Even Albert clapped his wrinkled hands.

But instead of the tinkle of glass that Mort had expected there was—nothing.

He turned and tried again. The blade passed right through the glass without breaking it.

The change in the texture of the air made him bring the sword around and back in time to deflect a vicious downward sweep. Death sprang away in time to dodge Mort's counter thrust, which was slow and weak.

THUS IT ENDS, BOY.

"Mort," said Mort. He looked up.

"Mort," he repeated, and brought the sword up in a stroke that cut the scythe's handle in two. Anger bubbled up inside him. If he was going to die, then at least he'd die with the right name.

"Mort, you bastard!" he screamed, and propelled himself straight towards the grinning skull with the sword whirring in a complicated dance of blue light. Death staggered backwards, laughing, crouching under the rain of furious strokes that sliced the scythe handle into more pieces.

Mort circled him, chopping and thrusting and dully aware, even through the red mists of fury, that Death was following his every move, holding the orphaned scythe-blade like a sword. There was no opening, and the motor of his anger wouldn't last. You'll never beat him, he told himself. The best we can do is hold him off for a while. And losing is probably better than winning. Who needs eternity, anyway?

Through the curtain of his fatigue he saw Death unfold the length of his bones and bring his blade around in a slow, leisurely arc as though it was moving through treacle.

"Father!" screamed Ysabell.

Death turned his head.

Perhaps Mort's mind welcomed the prospect of the life to come but his body, which maybe felt it had most to lose in the deal, objected. It brought his sword arm up in one unstoppable stroke that flicked Death's blade from his hand, and then pinned him against the nearest pillar.

In the sudden hush Mort realized he could no longer hear an intrusive little noise that had been just at his threshold of hearing for the last ten minutes. His eyes darted sideways.

The last of his sand was running out.

STRIKE.

Mort raised the sword, and looked into the twin blue fires.

He lowered the sword.

"No."

Death's foot lashed out at groin height with a speed that even made Cutwell wince.

Mort silently curled into a ball and rolled across the floor. Through his tears he saw Death advancing, scytheblade in one hand and Mort's own hourglass in the other. He saw Keli and Ysabell swept disdainfully aside as they made a grab for the robe. He saw Cutwell elbowed in the ribs, his candle-stick clattering across the tiles.

Death stood over him. The tip of the blade hovered in front of Mort's eyes for a moment, and then swept upwards.

"You're right. There's no justice. There's just you."

Death hesitated, and then slowly lowered the blade. He turned and looked down into Ysabell's face. She was shaking with anger.

YOUR MEANING?

She glowered up at Death's face and then her hand swung back and swung around and swung forward and connected with a sound like a dice box.

It was nothing like as loud as the silence that followed it.

Keli shut her eyes. Cutwell turned away and put his arms over his head.

Death raised a hand to his skull, very slowly.

Ysabell's chest rose and fell in a manner that should have made Cutwell give up magic for life.

Finally, in a voice even more hollow than usual, Death said: WHY?

"You said that to tinker with the fate of one individual could destroy the whole world," said Ysabell.

YES?

"You meddled with his. And mine." She pointed a trembling finger at the splinters of glass on the floor. "And those, too."

WELL?

"What will the gods demand for *that*?"

FROM ME?

"Yes!"

Death looked surprised. THE GODS CAN DEMAND NOTHING OF ME. EVEN GODS ANSWER TO ME, EVENTUALLY.

"Doesn't seem very fair, does it? Don't the gods bother about justice and mercy?" snapped Ysabell. Without anyone quite noticing she had picked up the sword.

Death grinned. I APPLAUD YOUR EFFORTS, he said, BUT THEY AVAIL YOU NAUGHT. STAND ASIDE.

"No."

YOU MUST BE AWARE THAT EVEN LOVE IS NO DEFENSE
AGAINST ME. I AM SORRY.

Ysabell raised the sword. "You're sorry?"

STAND ASIDE, I SAY.

"No. You're just being vindictive. It's not fair!"

Death bowed his skull for a moment, then looked up with
his eyes blazing.

*YOU WILL DO AS YOU ARE TOLD.*

"I will not."

YOU'RE MAKING THIS VERY DIFFICULT.

"Good."

Death's fingers drummed impatiently on the scytheblade,
like a mouse tapdancing on a tin. He seemed to be thinking.
He looked at Ysabell standing over Mort, and then turned
and looked at the others crouching against a shelf.

No, he said eventually. NO. I CANNOT BE BIDDEN. I CANNOT
BE FORCED. I WILL DO ONLY THAT WHICH I KNOW TO BE RIGHT.

He waved a hand, and the sword whirred out of Ysabell's
grasp. He made another complicated gesture and the girl
herself was picked up and pressed gently but firmly against
the nearest pillar.

Mort saw the dark reaper advance on him again, blade
swinging back for the final stroke. He stood over the boy.

YOU DON'T KNOW HOW SORRY THIS MAKES ME, he said.

Mort pulled himself on to his elbows.

"I might," he said.

Death gave him a surprised look for several seconds, and
then started to laugh. The sound bounced eerily around the
room, ringing off the shelves as Death, still laughing like an
earthquake in a graveyard, held Mort's own glass in front of
its owner's eyes.

Mort tried to focus. He saw the last grain of sand skid
down the glossy surface, teeter on the edge and then drop,
tumbling in slow motion, towards the bottom. Candlelight
flickered off its tiny silica facets as it spun gently downward.
It landed soundlessly, throwing up a tiny crater.

The light in Death's eyes flared until it filled Mort's vision and the sound of his laughter rattled the universe.

And then Death turned the hourglass over.

Once again the great hall of Sto Lat was brilliant with candlelight and loud with music.

As the guests flocked down the steps and descended on the cold buffet the Master of Ceremonies was in non-stop voice, introducing those who, by reason of importance or simple absent-mindedness, had turned up late. As for example:

"The Royal Recognizer, Master of the Queen's Bedchamber, His Ipississumussness Igneous Cutwell, Wizard 1st Grade (UU)."

Cutwell advanced on the royal couple, grinning, a large cigar in one hand.

"May I kiss the bride?" he said.

"If it's allowed for wizards," said Ysabell, offering a cheek.

"We thought the fireworks were marvelous," said Mort. "And I expect they'll soon be able to rebuild the outer wall. No doubt you'll be able to find your way to the food."

"He's looking a lot better these days," said Ysabell behind her fixed grin, as Cutwell disappeared into the throng.

"Certainly there's a lot to be said for being the only person who doesn't bother to obey the queen," said Mort, exchanging nods with a passing nobleman.

"They say he's the real power behind the throne," said Ysabell. "An eminence something."

"Eminence grease," said Mort absently. "Notice how he doesn't do any magic these days?"

"Shutupshereshecomes."

"Her Supreme Majesty, Queen Kelirehenna I, Lord of Sto Lat, Protector of the Eight Protectorates and Empress of the Long Thin Debated Piece Hubwards of Sto Kerrig."

Ysabell bobbed. Mort bowed. Keli beamed at both of them. They couldn't help noticing that she had come under some influence that inclined her towards clothes that at least roughly followed her shape, and away from hairstyles that looked like the offspring of a pineapple and a candyfloss.

She pecked Ysabell on the cheek and then stepped back and looked Mort up and down.

"How's Sto Helit?" she said.

"Fine, fine," said Mort. "We'll have to do something about the cellars, though. Your late uncle had some unusual—hobbies, and. . . ."

"She means you," whispered Ysabell. "That's your official name."

"I preferred Mort," said Mort.

"Such an interesting coat of arms, too," said the queen. "Crossed scythes on an hourglass rampant against a sable field. It gave the Royal College quite a headache."

"It's not that I mind being a duke," said Mort. "It's being married to a duchess that comes as a shock."

"You'll get used to it."

"I hope not."

"Good. And now, Ysabell," said Keli, setting her jaw, "if you are to move in royal circles there are some people you simply must meet. . . ."

Ysabell gave Mort a despairing look as she was swept away into the crowd, and was soon lost to view.

Mort ran a finger around the inside of his collar, looked both ways, and then darted into a fern-shaded corner near the end of the buffet where he could have a quiet moment to himself.

Behind him the Master of Ceremonies cleared his throat. His eyes took on a distant, glazed look.

"The Stealer of Souls," he said in the faraway voice of one whose ears aren't hearing what his mouth is saying, "Defeater of Empires, Swallower of Oceans, Thief of Years, The Ultimate Reality, Harvester of Mankind, the—"

ALL RIGHT, ALL RIGHT. I CAN SEE MYSELF IN.

Mort paused with a cold turkey leg halfway to his mouth.

He didn't turn around. He didn't need to. There was no mistaking that voice, felt rather than heard, or the way in which the air chilled and darkened. The chatter and music of the wedding reception slowed and faded.

"We didn't think you'd come," he said to a potted fern.

TO MY OWN DAUGHTER'S WEDDING? ANYWAY, IT WAS THE FIRST TIME I'VE EVER HAD AN INVITATION TO ANYTHING. IT HAD GOLD EDGES AND RSVP AND EVERYTHING.

"Yes, but when you weren't at the service—"

I THOUGHT PERHAPS IT WOULD NOT BE ENTIRELY APPROPRIATE.

"Well, yes, I suppose so—"

TO BE FRANK, I THOUGHT YOU WERE GOING TO MARRY THE PRINCESS.

Mort blushed. "We talked about it," he said. "Then we thought, just because you happen to rescue a princess, you shouldn't rush into things."

VERY WISE. TOO MANY YOUNG WOMEN LEAP INTO THE ARMS OF THE FIRST YOUNG MAN TO WAKE THEM AFTER A HUNDRED YEARS' SLEEP, FOR EXAMPLE.

"And, well, we thought that all in all, well, once I really got to know Ysabell, well. . . ."

YES, YES, I AM SURE. AN EXCELLENT DECISION. HOWEVER, I HAVE DECIDED NOT TO INTEREST MYSELF IN HUMAN AFFAIRS ANY FURTHER.

"Really?"

EXCEPT OFFICIALLY, OF COURSE. IT WAS CLOUDING MY JUDGEMENT.

A skeletal hand appeared on the edge of Mort's vision and skilfully speared a stuffed egg. Mort spun around.

"What happened?" he said. "I've got to know! One minute we were in the Long Room and the next we were in a field outside the city, and we were really us! I mean, reality had been altered to fit us in! Who did it?"

I HAD A WORD WITH THE GODS. Death looked uncomfortable.

"Oh. You did, did you?" said Mort. Death avoided his gaze.

YES.

"I shouldn't think they were very pleased."

THE GODS ARE JUST. THEY ARE ALSO SENTIMENTALISTS. I HAVE NEVER BEEN ABLE TO MASTER IT, MYSELF.

BUT YOU AREN'T FREE YET. YOU MUST SEE TO IT THAT HISTORY TAKES PLACE.

"I know," said Mort. "Uniting the kingdoms and everything."

YOU MIGHT END UP WISHING YOU'D STAYED WITH ME.

"I certainly learned a lot," Mort admitted. He put his hand up to his face and absent-mindedly stroked the four thin white scars across his cheek. "But I don't think I was cut out for that sort of work. Look, I'm really sorry—"

I HAVE A PRESENT FOR YOU.

Death put down his plate of hors d'oeuvres and fumbled in the mysterious recesses of his robe. When his skeletal hand emerged it was holding a little globe between thumb and forefinger.

It was about three inches across. It could have been the largest pearl in the world, except that the surface was a moving swirl of complicated silver shapes, forever on the point of resolving themselves into something recognizable but always managing to avoid it.

When Death dropped it into Mort's outstretched palm it felt surprisingly heavy and slightly warm.

FOR YOU AND YOUR LADY. A WEDDING PRESENT. A DOWRY.

"It's beautiful! We thought the silver toast rack was from you."

THAT WAS ALBERT. I'M AFRAID HE DOESN'T HAVE MUCH IMAGINATION.

Mort turned the globe over and over in his hands. The shapes boiling inside it seemed to respond to his touch, sending little streamers of light arching across the surface towards his fingers.

"Is it a pearl?" he said.

YES. WHEN SOMETHING IRRITATES AN OYSTER AND CAN'T BE REMOVED, THE POOR THING COATS IT WITH MUCUS AND TURNS IT INTO A PEARL. THIS IS A PEARL OF A DIFFERENT COLOR. A PEARL OF REALITY. ALL THAT SHINY STUFF IS CONGEALED ACTUALITY. YOU OUGHT TO RECOGNIZE IT—YOU CREATED IT, AFTER ALL.

Mort tossed it gently from hand to hand.

"We will put it with the castle jewels," he said. "We haven't got that many."

ONE DAY IT WILL BE THE SEED OF A NEW UNIVERSE.

Mort fumbled the catch, but reached down with lightning reflexes and caught it before it hit the flagstones.

"What?"

THE PRESSURE OF *THIS* REALITY KEEPS IT COMPRESSED. THERE MAY COME A TIME WHEN THE UNIVERSE ENDS AND REALITY DIES, AND THEN THIS ONE WILL EXPLODE AND . . . WHO KNOWS? KEEP IT SAFE. IT'S A FUTURE AS WELL AS A PRESENT.

Death put his skull on one side. IT'S A SMALL THING, he added. YOU *COULD* HAVE HAD ETERNITY.

"I know," said Mort. "I've been very lucky."

He put it very carefully on the buffet table, between the quails' eggs and the sausage rolls.

THERE WAS ANOTHER THING, said Death. He reached under his robe again and pulled out an oblong shape inexpertly wrapped and tied with string.

IT'S FOR YOU, he said, PERSONALLY. YOU NEVER SHOWED ANY INTEREST IN IT BEFORE. DID YOU THINK IT DIDN'T EXIST?

Mort unwrapped the packet and realized he was holding a small leather-bound book. On the spine was blocked, in shiny gold leaf, the one word: *Mort*.

He leafed backwards through the unfilled pages until he found the little trail of ink, winding patiently down the page, and read: *Mort shut the book with a little snap that sounded, in the silence, like the crack of creation, and smiled uneasily.*

"There's a lot of pages still to fill," he said. "How much sand have I got left? Only Ysabell said that since you turned the glass over that means I shall die when I'm—"

YOU HAVE SUFFICIENT, said Death coldly. MATHEMATICS ISN'T ALL IT'S CRACKED UP TO BE.

"How do you feel about being invited to christenings?"

I THINK NOT. I WASN'T CUT OUT TO BE A FATHER, AND CERTAINLY NOT A GRANDAD. I HAVEN'T GOT THE RIGHT KIND OF KNEES.

He put down his wine glass and nodded at Mort.

MY REGARDS TO YOUR GOOD LADY, he said. AND NOW I REALLY MUST BE OFF.

"Are you sure? You're welcome to stay."

IT'S NICE OF YOU TO SAY SO, BUT DUTY CALLS. He extended a bony hand. YOU KNOW HOW IT IS.

Mort gripped the hand and shook it, ignoring the chill.

"Look," he said. "If ever you want a few days off, you know, if you'd like a holiday—"

MANY THANKS FOR THE OFFER, said Death graciously. I SHALL THINK ABOUT IT MOST SERIOUSLY. AND NOW—

"Goodbye," Mort said, and was surprised to find a lump in his throat. "It's such an unpleasant word, isn't it?"

QUITE SO. Death grinned because, as has so often been remarked, he didn't have much option. But possibly he meant it, this time.

I PREFER AU REVOIR, he said.

### THE END

Lost? Confused?

Need some help navigating the morass?

Dip into this handy travel guide and discover

# THE WORLD OF

# TERRY PRATCHETT

## THRILLING ADVENTURE
(well sort of)

## WONDROUS MAGIC
(when it works properly)

## FLAT PLANET
(of course)

(It's a lot like our own...but different.)

# The world of
# TeRRY PraTChett

usually finds itself irresistibly represented by
Discworld—a flat, circular planet that rests on the
backs of four elephants, which in turn are standing on the
back of a giant turtle. Don't ask what the turtle stands on;
you may as well ask what sound yellow makes. This is the
backdrop for an intricate and delightful world that Booker
Prize–winning author A. S. Byatt hails as "more complicated and
satisfying than Oz," where every aspect of life—modern and
ancient, sacred and profane—is both celebrated and satirized,
from religion and Christmas to vampires, opera, war, and everything
in between.* Reading Terry Pratchett is the literary equivalent of
doing a cha-cha. It's exciting, it's invigorating, and those more
rhythmically inclined say it's got a good beat and you can
dance to it. Best of all, it's pure unadulterated, sidesplitting
fun. So isn't it high time you got away from it all by
visiting the Discworld? Don't bother to leave your
troubles behind. Bring them with you, because on
Discworld they'll look different and a whole
lot easier to cure.

* Opera and war often sound quite similar, of course...

# A Brief Musing on **DISCWORLD**
## (in theory and in practice)

**DISCWORLD** novels are, appropriately enough, about things on Discworld, but they have a tendency to reflect events or ideas from our world. In each case, subjects are covered in a distinctly "Discworld" way, but some of what's seen and heard seems to comment pointedly and very humorously on the lives lived in what we are pleased to call "the Real World." Discworld is definitely not our world but eerily resembles it, and the sheer contrary humanity of all the characters on this extremely flat planet is as challenging and hilarious as our own at its best and worst.

**TERRY PRATCHETT** himself sums it up best:

**"**The world rides through space on the back of a turtle. This is one of the great ancient world myths, found wherever men and turtles were gathered together; the four elephants were an Indo-European sophistication. The idea has been lying in the lumber rooms of legend for centuries. All I had to do was grab it and run away before the alarms went off.

There are no maps. You can't map a sense of humor. Anyway, what is a fantasy map but a space beyond which There Be Dragons? On the Discworld we know There Be Dragons Everywhere. They might not all have scales and forked tongues, but they Be Here all right, grinning and jostling and trying to sell you souvenirs.

Enjoy.**"** *

---

\* He's also been known to describe it in *The Discworld Companion* as "like a geological pizza but without the anchovies."

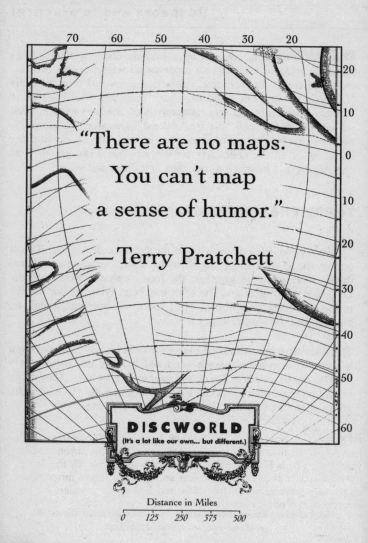

DISCWORLD "Map"

70 60 50 40 30 20

20 10 0 10 20 30 40 50 60

"There are no maps.
You can't map
a sense of humor."

— Terry Pratchett

DISCWORLD
(It's a lot like our own... but different.)

Distance in Miles

0 125 250 375 500

# The **GANG**'s all there!

Some characters show up all the time in the novels of Discworld; others you may be hard-pressed at times to find. Any way you slice it, Discworld would be much more akin to a drab, uninteresting sitting room without this cast of heroes, villains, and assorted none-of-the-aboves.

So without any further ado, here's a taste of some of Discworld's finest whom you may run into from time to time. . . .

**DEATH . . .** An obvious sort of fellow: tall, thin (skeletal, as a matter of fact), and ALWAYS SPEAKS IN CAPITAL LETTERS. Generally shows up when you're dead, or just when he thinks you ought to be. Not a bad chap when you get to know him (and sooner or later, everyone gets to know him).

**CARROT IRONFOUNDERSSON . . .** Captain of Ankh-Morpork's City Watch police force. Bulging with muscles, this six-foot-six-inch dwarf (he was adopted) remains honest, good-natured, and honorable despite the city's best efforts. Carrot may also be the true heir to Ankh-Morpork's throne (a subject filed under "I wouldn't ask if I were you").

**COMMANDER SAMUEL VIMES . . .** Head of Ankh-Morpork's City Watch, despite his best efforts to the contrary. A slightly tarnished walker along mean streets, and like all good cops knows exactly when it's time to be a bad cop.

**CORPORAL C. W. ST. J. NOBBS . . .** Call him "Nobby"—everyone else does. Looking sufficiently like a monkey to have to bear a written testimonial as to his actual species, this City Watch member has a known affinity for thievery—namely, anything that isn't nailed down is his (and anything that can be pried loose is not considered nailed down). But honest about the big things (i.e., the ones too heavy to lift).

**ANGUA . . .** Now a sergeant in Ankh-Morpork's City Watch (which has a very good affirmative-action policy; they'll take anyone except vampires). She is a werewolf at full moon, a vegetarian for the rest of the month. Her ability to smell colors and rip out a man's throat if she so chooses serve as useful job skills, and have done wonders for her arrest record if not for her social life. A definite K-9 cop.

# The **GANG**'s all there!

**ESMERELDA "GRANNY" WEATHERWAX . . .** The greatest witch on all of Discworld, at least in her opinion. Lives in the village of Bad Ass in the kingdom of Lancre (the village was named after a legendarily disobedient donkey, since you ask). A bad witch by inclination but a good witch by instinct, Granny prefers to achieve by psychology, trickery, and guile what others prefer to achieve by simple spells. She's someone to have on your side, because believe us, it's better than the alternative. Owner of a rather temperamental broom now made up entirely of spare parts. Any questions?

**GYTHA "NANNY" OGG . . .** The broad-minded, understanding, and grandmotherly matriarch of a somewhat extensive family, with fifteen children and countless grandchildren. She's had many husbands (and was married to three of them). Very knowledgeable on matters of the heart and associated organs. Likes a drink. Likes another drink. Likes a third drink. Make that a double, will you? She is the second member of the coven, which has included:

**MAGRAT GARLICK . . .** Once a witch, now the Queen of the kingdom of Lancre, this young witch doesn't adhere to the "old school" of witchcraft. She believes in crystals and candles and being nice to people—but she is a witch, so in a tight corner will fight like a cat...

**and AGNES NITT . . .** and while you're at it, why not meet Perdita as well? A witch with a split personality, the rather overweight Agnes Nitt walks the Discworld while Perdita (the "thin" person said to be within every fat one) whiles away her time daydreaming and offering unwanted advice and criticism. Gifted with an incredibly beautiful singing voice capable of any pitch or sound (comes in handy for belting out an aria in perfect harmony with herself).

**MUSTRUM RIDCULLY . . .** The Archchancellor of Unseen University. The longest-standing head of the University, Ridcully is notorious for his ironclad decision-making, the incredible lapse of time it takes to explain something to him, and his all-purpose wizarding hat (suitable for emergency shelter and the storage of alcohol). Is now ever more terrifying since he read a book on how to be a dynamic manager in one minute.

**RINCEWIND . . .** Simply put, the most inept wizard to ever exist in any universe. Rincewind possesses a survival instinct that far outweighs his spellcasting, and is such a coward that (if Einstein is right) he's coming back from the other direction as a hero. Guaranteed to solve every minor problem by turning it into a major disaster.

**THE LIBRARIAN . . .** It's the primary function of the Librarian of Unseen University to keep people from using the books, lest they wear out from all that reading. It also happens to be a primate function, given the fact that he's also a 300-lb. orangutan (transformed by a magic spell, but he prefers it so much he refuses to be re-transformed). Don't ever call him a monkey. *Ever.*

**LORD HAVELOCK VETINARI . . .** The supreme ruler of Ankh-Morpork. A keen believer in the principle of One Man, One Vote; he is the Man, so he's got the vote. Always in complete control of every situation he finds himself in, Lord Vetinari's sense of leadership and stability keep the city up and running…and you'd better believe that this is at the forefront of his mind at all times.

**CUT-ME-OWN-THROAT DIBBLER . . .** Not really a criminal, more of an entrepreneur who fits the needs of the times. Usually seen selling some kind of food in a bun (no matter how questionable its origins), C.M.O.T. Dibbler is always on the lookout for Discworld's latest business opportunity (again, no matter how questionable its origins). Not a man who asks questions, in fact, and he would prefer if you would also keep off ones like "what's in this sausage?"

**COHEN THE BARBARIAN . . .** The greatest hero in the history of Discworld. He's an old man now, but hasn't let that stop him. Don't laugh at him. In one of the most dangerous professions in the world, he has survived to be very, very old. Get the point?

**THE LUGGAGE . . .** Know it. Love it. Fear it. Constructed of magical sapient pearwood, the Luggage is a suitcase with lots of little legs, completely faithful to its owner, and completely homicidal to anyone it perceives as a threat to said owner. Baggage with a nasty overbite. Definitely *not* your standard carry-on.

**THE GREAT A'TUIN . . .** The gigantic space turtle upon which the entire Discworld rests (with four elephants sandwiched in between, of course). What is it really? How did it get there? Where is it going? (Actually, it is the only creature in the universe that knows *exactly* where it is going).

# DISCWORLD on $30 a Day

This is quite easy to do, provided you don't eat and like sleeping out of doors. There are about four continents on Discworld:*

## THE (UNNAMED) CONTINENT
Includes Ankh-Morpork, the Ramtops region, the witches' haven of Lancre, and the mysterious vampire-ridden domain of Überwald, whose fragmentation into smaller states after the breakup of the Evil Empire is occupying a lot of politicians' minds (anything strike you as familiar?).

## THE COUNTERWEIGHT CONTINENT
Home to the fruitful, multiplying, and extremely rich Agatean Empire. Has a certain "Far East" flavor, with a side order of Hot and Sour soup.

## KLATCH
Not loosely based on Africa at all. Honestly.

## XXXX
A mysterious place to be certain, but some of its secrets have since spilled forth in the novel *The Last Continent* (by the way, "XXXX" is the manner in which it's written on the maps, since no one knew what it was supposed to be called). A vast dry red continent, where water is so scarce everyone has to drink beer. Still, no worries, eh?

---

* According to Terry Pratchett in *The Discworld Companion*, "there have been other continents, which have sunk, blown up, or simply disappeared. This sort of thing happens all the time. even on the best-regulated planets."

## ANKH-MORPORK

> **"**There's a saying that all roads lead to Ankh-Morpork.
> And it's wrong. All roads lead away from Ankh-Morpork,
> but sometimes people just walk along them the wrong way.**"**
> —Terry Pratchett

Welcome to Ankh-Morpork, Discworld's most happening city and so carefully described it could be considered a character in its own right. Divided in two by the River Ankh—a waterway so thick with silt that it should really be considered a walkway instead,* Ankh-Morpork is one of those rather large cosmopolitan burgs that, like a lot of others with a similar claim to fame, always seems on the move but never really goes anywhere.

## TAVERNS
Some of the many watering holes you can frequent on Discworld, where revelers can go in as men, and come out still men but with fewer teeth:

### The Mended Drum
Originally known as The Broken Drum ("you can't beat it") before the fire, The Mended Drum ("you can get beaten") is hailed as the most reputable disreputable tavern on Discworld, where the beer is, well, supposedly beer (more colorful metaphors may apply). It's also here that you'll find some of the best in live entertainment that Ankh-Morpork has to offer . . . if getting slammed over the head with something heavy or a single serving of knuckle sandwich is your idea of fun.

**Other pubs of (dis)interest:** The Bucket; Bunch of Grapes; Crimson Leech; Stab in the Back; King's Head; Quene's Head; Duke's Head; Troll's Head (perfect for those with a death wish because it's still attached to the troll).

---

* "They say that it is hard to drown in the Ankh, but easy to suffocate."
  —Terry Pratchett, *The Discworld Companion*

# DISCWORLD on $30 a Day

## THE SHADES

Choose your path around Ankh-Morpork carefully, as you do *not* want to end up in the Shades. The oldest part of the city and about a ten-minute walk from Unseen University, the Shades is a yawning black pit with buildings and streets, an urban canker sore festering with criminal activity, immorality, and other similarly nasty habits. Every city has one. Need help? Don't expect any bleeding hearts around these parts, with the exception of your own. Multiple stab wounds can *hurt*.

## THE PATRICIAN'S PALACE

Lord Vetinari's pleasure dome, complete with dungeons, scorpion pits, and other various forms of entertainment. The Palace Grounds are a must-see. Besides the obligatory bird garden, zoo, and racehorse stable, the Gardens, designed by the blissfully incompetent landscaper Bergholt Stuttley ("Bloody Stupid") Johnson, highlight a garden maze so minuscule that visitors lose their way looking for it, a trout lake 150 yards long and 1 inch wide (perfect for the dieting fish), and a chiming sundial best avoided at noon (it tends to explode).

## UNSEEN UNIVERSITY

Welcome to Discworld's most prestigious (i.e. only) school of higher learning and the heart of Ankh-Morpork. Think of it as a wizard's college and chief learning center of the occult on Discworld, dedicated to serious drinking and really big dinners.

The wizards don't so much use magic as not use it, but in a dynamic way (a bit like the atomic bomb) and the time not spent eating is mostly taken up by interdepartmental squabbles (which of course never happen in *real* universities).

Be sure to visit the Library, if the Librarian allows you in, that is (hint: bananas will get you everywhere). Once inside, gaze in wild wonder at its violation of physics with seemingly endless rows and shelves of tomes magical and otherwise—theoretically all of the books in existence, as well as those that were never written. Remember: no talking, no reading, no kidding.

## School motto:

NVNC ID VIDES, NVNC NE VIDES

("Now you see it, now you don't.")

# CROSSWORD Puzzle

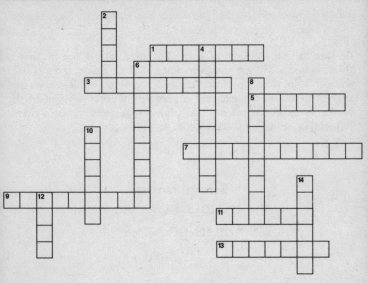

## ACROSS

1. Ankh-_____, Discworld's largest city

3. *Hogfather* spoofs this merry holiday

5. Terry Pratchett's Discworld novels cause these

7. Rodent equivalent of Death

9. An extremely flat planet

11. _____ University

13. Granny Weatherwax, Nanny Ogg, Magrat Garlick

## DOWN

2. The Reaper; the Surcease of Pain; SPEAKS IN CAPITAL LETTERS

4. Terry _____

6. Discworld's most incompetent wiz(z)ard

8. Discworld rests on four of these

10. Captain of the City Watch; possible sovereign of Ankh-Morpork

12. _____ *Music*

14. The _____ Drum

If you're stuck for answers (or would rather just cheat instead), turn to the last page.

# THE PRAISE! THE ACCOLADES! THE KUDOS!

Oh, why not just skip the formalities and hoist Terry Pratchett on our shoulders for a job well done?

"Superb popular entertainment."
—*Washington Post Book World*

"Consistently, inventively mad . . . wild and wonderful!"
—*Isaac Asimov's Science Fiction Magazine*

"Unadulterated fun. Pratchett parodies everything in sight."
—*San Francisco Chronicle*

"If I were making my list of Best Books of the Twentieth Century, Terry Pratchett's would be most of them."
—Elizabeth Peters

"Pratchett should be recognized as one of the more significant contemporary English-language satirists.
—*Publishers Weekly*

"Simply the best humorous writer of the twentieth century."
—*Oxford Times*

"Pratchett demonstrates just how great the distance is between one- or two-joke writers and the comic masters whose work will be read into the next century."
—*Locus*

**TEMPTED YET?** How about enticed? Maybe pleasantly coaxed? Go on—but remember, once you read one Discworld novel you'll want to read them all. Here they are, then, conveniently listed in chronological order of events—and you don't even have to start at the beginning to get in on all the fun...

### THE COLOR OF MAGIC
Introducing the wild and wonderful Discworld—witnessed through the four eyes of the tourist Twoflower and his inept wizard guide Rincewind.
ISBN 0-06-102071-0

### THE LIGHT FANTASTIC
Here's encouraging news: A red star finds itself in Discworld's way, and it would appear that one incompetent and forgetful wizard is all that stands between the world and Doomsday.
ISBN 0-06-102070-2

### EQUAL RITES
A dying wizard's powers were supposed to be bequeathed to the eighth son of an eighth son, but he never bothered to check the baby's sex. Now who says there can't be a female wizard?
ISBN 0-06-102069-9

### SMALL GODS
What do you do when your cup runneth over with little intelligence and a lot of faith, and your small but bossy god proclaims you the Chosen One?
ISBN 0-06-109217-7

### LORD AND LADIES
A group of not-so-cute elves invades the kingdom of Lancre—giving Granny Weatherwax the delightful task of taking out the Faerie Trash.
ISBN 0-06-105692-8

### MEN AT ARMS
Ankh-Morpork's City Watch are up against the Discworld's first gun. Guns don't kill people? This one *does*. Duck!
ISBN 0-06-109219-3

### SOUL MUSIC
Sure, there are skeletons in every family's closet. Just ask Susan Sto Helit, who is about to mind the family store a while for dear old Grandpa Death.
ISBN 0-06-105489-5

### INTERESTING TIMES

The Counterweight Continent is in urgent need of a Great Wizard. They get the incapable wizard Rincewind instead. See him run away from war, revolution, and fortune cookies.
ISBN 0-06-105690-1

### MASKERADE

Ankh-Morpork's newest diva (and wannabe witch) must flush out a Ghost in the Opera House who insists on terrorizing the entire company. Hint: that chandelier looks like an accident just *waiting* to happen...
ISBN 0-06-105691-X

### FEET OF CLAY

A killer with fiery eyes is stalking Ankh-Morpork, leaving behind lots of corpses and a major headache for City Watch Captain Sam Vimes.
ISBN 0-06-105764-9

### HOGFATHER

The jolly Hogfather vanishes on the eve of Hogswatchnight, and it's up to the grim specter of Death to act as a not-so-ideal stand-in to deliver goodies to all the children of Discworld.
ISBN 0-06-105905-6

### JINGO

A nasty little case of war breaks out when rival cities Ankh-Morpork and Al-Khali both stake a claim to the same island. Not like anything that happens on Earth at all.
ISBN 0-06-105906-4

### THE LAST CONTINENT

A professor is missing from Unseen University, and a bevy of senior wizards must follow the trail to the other side of Discworld, where the Last Continent is currently under construction. No worries, mate.
ISBN 0-06-105907-2

### CARPE JUGULUM (hardcover)

The vampires of Überwald have come out of the casket, and this time they don't plan to be back indoors by dawn. They *love* garlic.
ISBN 0-06-105158-6

# COLLECT THEM ALL and watch your bookshelf jump up and down with uninhibited glee. Well, not *exactly*, because it's a bookshelf. But *you* will.

# CROSSWORD Puzzle Answers

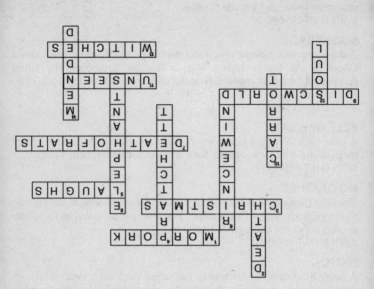